To Ashes

J.J. Rhodes

This novel is entirely a work of fiction. The names, characters and incidents portrayed in it are the work of the author's imagination. Any resemblance to actual persons, living or dead, events or localities is entirely coincidental.

First edition

DEDICATION

For everyone who relates to Rowan or Asher.

You are not alone.

CONTENT WARNING

This book contains scenes of: anxiety and panic attacks, verbal/emotional/physical abuse, anorexia, grief, survivor's guilt, trauma bonding, child abuse, murder, and suicidal thoughts.

PLAYLIST

Mind Over Matter by Young the Giant
Panic Room by Au/Ra
Elastic Heart by Sia
this is me trying by Taylor Swift
Somebody To You (feat. Demi Lovato) by The Vamps
War of Hearts by Ruelle
Daddy Issues (Remix) by The Neighbourhood & Syd
Swim by Chase Atlantic
Slow Down by Chase Atlantic
Birthday Cake by Dylan Conrique
Softcore by The Neighbourhood
Are You With Me by nilu
Mean It by Gracie Abrams
Haunted by Taylor Swift
Arcade (feat. FLETCHER) by Duncan Lawrence
Remember That Night? by Sara Kays
Afterglow by Taylor Swift
My Soul I by Anna Leone
The Archer by Taylor Swift
Daylight by Taylor Swift
World Gone Mad by Bastille

J.J. RHODES

PROLOGUE

August 15th, 2016

Hey Bent,

I know it's been a long time. I'm sorry. I'm so fucking sorry.

I've put off writing this letter to you because I don't know what to say. I promised to write you and then I stopped without a word.

I know I owe you an explanation, but there are just no words. I hate the person I've become. I feel like I'm living someone else's life, in a stranger's body. Writing to you helped for a while, until it didn't.

But still, you didn't deserve to be left behind. Does it help to know I didn't forget about you? I could never forget about you. Even if I don't write or talk to you much anymore, you occupy a part of my mind that will always be yours. I think about you every day, even if it's as

1

simple as I hope you're okay.

Well, anyways. Dwelling on the bad stuff only makes everyone feel like shit. You told me that, remember? I think I was eight or something. That stuck with me. Now, I'm taking your advice.

So. I bet you're wondering what finally made me pick up the pen and paper? You're going to make fun of me, I already know it.

It's a girl. Are we shocked? I've always come to you for girl advice, since I was like eleven and I didn't even know the first thing about girls or dating.

But this girl. Shit, man. She's easily the most beautiful girl in the world. No fucking contest. And she's nothing like any other girl—any other person—in the entire world. It sounds ridiculous to say, but she's just... wow.

I wish you could have seen her. It's not even her physical looks that hooked me—although, physically she is so perfect. Her wavy blonde hair, gorgeous green eyes, perfect little nose, flawless full pink cheeks.

Her looks initially caught my eyes, but it was her personality that pulled me all the way in.

Let me set the scene. I had just gotten off the bus, my new friend Maddox beside me. (Side note: he's pretty cool. You'd like him.) So, Maddox and I were walking into the school and I was pretty nervous for my first day. I'm sure you remember, I never liked first days.

Well, I walk into the hallway and the first person I make eye contact with is this girl. She literally took my breath away.

The second I caught her eyes, it was like something went off in my chest. Like a gunshot or something. I guess that's what people call butterflies or fireworks. Well it happened to me. Right there in the hallway.

I swear the whole world around me stopped. Until it started again. She turned back around, as quickly as when she looked at me, and she walked away.

I watched her walk away and screamed at myself to go talk to her. But, I'm a coward and I didn't (of course).

Now here's where things take an unfortunate turn: Maddox basically told me she was trouble. When he caught me staring at her—he said I was drooling, but he was definitely exaggerating—he told me not to get involved with her.

"Trust me, dude. She's mad drama. You don't want that," I think were his exact words.

The problem is: I'm not sure I can't not have her.

I swear, Bent, it's like she was made for me, or something. I felt it so deep in my bones, like when you finally find that one thing that could make your entire life a million times better.

So I don't know what to do. Maybe it's better if I just leave her alone. I'm not in a position to really be with a girl right now anyways. I'll just mess things up with her.

I just hope one day I can make her mine. Because I've never wanted to love someone more than her. Does that make me crazy? Maybe. I mean, I don't even really know her. But, one day I will. Just not yet.

Anyways, I guess that's it. Miss you. ~~More than you'll ever know~~.

-Asher

ONE
Rowan

Mom lies drunkenly on the couch with a bottle of tequila gripped between her chest and her hands.

"You know, Rowan. You are probably the most pathetic person I've ever met. Your sister was never pathetic." She sighs, taking a swig from the bottle.

I try not to cry at her words, but they don't ever get any easier, no matter how many times she tells me. "Five years since she died. And every day since, I wished it was you that died instead of her.

"On a scale of 1 to 10, how good was I in bed last night?" Maddox Cardiff's voice echoes through the classroom as he walks in, immediately pulling me out of my trance. Dread fills my body and I know what's coming.

"I give you a solid 4. Too shy and your body wasn't that exciting," he smirks. I flinch at his word and I can already feel the heat from my stomach creep up my neck, sending my already-rosy cheeks into full tomato-mode.

It's times like this when I wish I didn't have such a fair complexion that shows every bit of redness that appears on my face.

My best friend, Kennedy Benson, rolls her eyes to the back of her head and I'm afraid they might get stuck like that from the amount of force she put into it.

"I know you're a little slow, so let me put this in simple terms for you," Kennedy speaks up. "A girl like Rowan would never give a pig like you the time of day. But keep trying to stir shit up for a reaction. It's cute seeing how desperate you are," she mocks, giving me a look that says she's got my back. It's times like this when I thank the universe that I have her.

"Whatever," Maddox mumbles as he rolls his eyes. He walks over to his desk at the back of the classroom, brushing off Kennedy's comments.

Although, it takes him all of ten seconds to pick his balls up from the ground and he's already starting again. "Besides, you think I actually want Rowan? I got a line-up of bitches begging to hop on my dick. And I can guarantee they're way better than Rowan ever could be," he laughs with a stupid grin on his face. I would love nothing more than to wipe it off his face, but I don't have the nerve to actually ever do anything. So instead, I sit quietly and just take it.

"Maddox, shut the fuck up." Asher Madigan's voice filters in from the doorframe of the classroom. There's an edge in his tone, a warning to his best friend to stop. He walks to the back of the classroom and stares Maddox down as he takes his seat right behind Kennedy and I. "No one messes with Rowan, but me."

I nearly choke on my saliva at Asher's comment. His voice

is hard and he sounds unimpressed, but his words lay a whole other meaning below the surface that sends my head spinning. As if my face couldn't get more red, I'm starting to feel like a big fat stop sign.

Thankfully, Kennedy jumps in before anyone can pay enough attention to my reaction. "Careful, Asher. Keep talking like that and people will think you have a crush on her," Kennedy teases. She's trying to beat them at their own game and I appreciate her efforts, but I know this will only end one way.

"Aw, I know that would make you the happiest person in the world. But, don't worry, Kennedy. I don't want to fuck your friend." Asher teases, his expression hard.

A smirk plays on his lips and his next words nearly send me running out the door. "I just like to see her squirm."

Kennedy's eyebrows shoot up and she slowly turns back around in her seat to face the front, clearly as put off as me at that last sentence.

"All right, everyone. Quiet down," our first period teacher, Ms. Jacobs, announces to the class. She gets up from her desk chair and makes her way to the front of the room, glaring at Asher. I don't even have to look at him to know he has a stupid smirk on his face. Asher Madigan knows he can tease me all he wants and all Ms. Jacobs will do is glare at him.

It's the fifth week of our senior year and Asher and Maddox have been giving me a hard time nearly every single morning. Ms. Jacobs always hears it, but there's not really much she can do because they wouldn't listen to her anyways.

Asher basically runs the school because the students are afraid of what he will do to them if they crossed him and the faculty know there is absolutely nothing they could possibly do that would punish him. His parents don't seem all that involved and it's not like the school can really suspend him—he'll just serve his sentence and come back to do the exact same shit. And expulsion isn't an option since nothing he does warrants that serious of a consequence.

As long as he doesn't do anything illegal, Asher can do whatever he wants to whoever he wants. And that treatment is extended to Maddox because, as his best friend, the only person who could possibly put him in his place is Asher.

It wasn't always like that, though. Asher came to Fletcher High sophomore year and he wasn't nearly as bad as he is now. A lot of the girls had a crush on him. He had fluffy, shiny, almost-black hair and piercing blue eyes. He also stood tall at 6'2, with a sharp jawline, high cheekbones, and full lips.

But he was also very mysterious. He was quiet and kept to himself, barely had any friends. He was friends with Maddox, having met him during the summer before school started I assumed, but that was it. And they didn't run the school like they do now, not even close. In fact, no one has ever had as much power over the school as they do.

Back in freshman and sophomore year, there was a group of buff seniors with tattoos and piercings who appeared intimidating and scary on the outside, but they were harmless. Teachers put them in their place and they only minorly terrorized some of the students.

And then junior year, everything changed. Physically, Asher had completely changed. Sophomore year, he didn't have any tattoos, at least visible ones. But the first day of junior year, he was covered in them. All over his arms, on his hands, up his neck.

Before, when he would wear a t-shirt, he was pale and plain. Now, you could barely see any skin because there was so much ink. And then he got a nose ring and a lip ring. All black. His arms were also much more muscular and his shoulders were much wider. He looked like he could take on five tough guys at once and still win.

Not only did he look scarier, but he was meaner, too. He would shove guys into lockers just because he could and he would harass the girls, asking them when he could 'hit it' and if their dads knew the kind of clothes they wore. He was cocky, arrogant, and rude. Teachers tried to control him, but they quickly learned he didn't care and neither did his parents. So, they just let him tear up the school for his own amusement.

Junior year was also when I somehow got on his radar and he's never left me alone since. It was the first time we had classes together and I tried to be nice to him, but he wouldn't have any of it. So, I started to ignore him and I guess that's when he got pissed off. Because ever since then, he's continued to tease me and harass me from the start of class to the last bell nearly every day.

Once Maddox picked up on Asher's hatred of me, the two of them couldn't get enough. They would purposely pick me out of the crowd and say something rude, tease me about being a goody-two-shoes, or make me uncomfortable by teasing me with sexual jokes and innuendos.

Kennedy has tried to stick up for me several times, and she still continues to try once in a while, but it's no use. They're ruthless and they'll never stop. What baffles me the most is I have no idea what I did to them to deserve it. I've run it over a thousand times in my head, and I've only ever been nice to them. Or at least indifferent.

The conclusion I come to every time is that they're just sad little boys who like to pick on girls for fun. Black hearts and soulless, simple as that.

"And that's the bell. Enjoy your weekend everyone!" Ms. Jacobs calls out to the already-escaping students.

"See you at lunch!" Kennedy calls to me as she walks out of the classroom. I blink a few times to bring my mind back to the present and I realize I zoned out the whole class.

I suppose that's the kind of Friday I'm going to have today. Distracted and distant.

TWO
Rowan

After two more torturous classes, the lunch bell finally rings and I nearly jump out of my seat.

I slide my notebooks into my bag, zip it shut, and rush out the door with the other twenty tired teenagers. I walk across the school to the cafeteria and cross into the lunch line.

The cafeteria is busy, as it always is at lunch time, but there's something different about it today. There's an energy that sends a chill up my spine. It's a charged buzz, electricity circulating through the air as if the sky is about to open up and drop a bolt of lightning and clap of thunder. Maybe I'm reading too much into it, but it feels like the calm before the storm.

"Thank God, I'm starving." Kennedy appears at my side, diminishing the buzz in my head as she nudges my hip with hers. Her eyes ravenously scour the different stations until she finds her favorite: pizza. She grabs the tongs and pulls out three slices of pepperoni from the pie, placing them on her plate. "What are you having?" She turns to me after securing her food.

"You know what? I'm going to have some pizza, too." I decide, grabbing the tongs from her. My split second decision is definitely a result of the eerie chill still shivering in my spine. By getting pizza, I'm hoping it will distract me enough to relax the tiniest amount.

Kennedy's jaw falls open at my unusual request as complete shock takes over her face. "What?" I ask, dropping my slices onto my plate.

"You *never* eat pizza. You're all about salads and salmon and vegetables." She says, appearing genuinely shocked. "I'm serious, Row. I don't think I've ever seen you eat pizza in my life. And we've been best friends since we were 10."

"Oh, please, don't be dramatic. I eat pizza!" I defend myself, walking us over to an empty table. Her eyebrows move up in a disbelieving way and she looks unimpressed. It's a look that show me she's not buying my BS and I cave under her inquisitive stare. "Okay, I don't really. But I just can't be bothered right now to care about eating healthy." I state, rolling my eyes.

"Did something happen?" She asks, concern washing over her. Throughout our entire eight year friendship, I've only confided in her a handful of times, so this was, for the most part, untouched territory. One that would stay untouched.

"You mean, other than being teased and harassed every single day since the start of senior year?" I ask sarcastically, choosing to omit any other information. Kennedy sighs, remembering this morning's events. "He's driving me up the wall, Ken. I can't do this anymore!" I whisper-yell to my best friend.

The last thing I need is someone in the cafeteria to overhear our conversation, so I try to stay calm and quiet, but it's really hard. I want nothing more than to scream about how much I hate Asher Madigan. "I won't let him ruin my senior year."

"So, don't," she replies. I roll my eyes and take a bite of my pizza. I can feel the guilt staring to rise up my stomach, but I try to push it down and pretend to enjoy the slice. "Look, Rowan, you know I love you. But you've let this gone on for far too long. It was bad enough when they would pick on you a few times in junior year. But every day now? It's getting ridiculous and you need to stand up for yourself."

I laugh at how simple she makes it sound. "If only it was that easy."

"Maybe it is. Look, all you have to do is fight back. Taking the high road has proven not to work so now you need to get on their level. They go low, you go lower."

I think she can see the fear in my eyes because she grabs my hands and gives me a hard glare. "You know I will always have your back. So whatever you want to do, I'm on board. But you can't let two guys who share one collective brain cell tear you down and ruin your senior year."

She's right. I hate that she's right, but the point is that she is. I need to start fighting back. I need to let loose, bring out the claws, and take on Asher and Maddox.

"Okay." I reply simply. Kennedy gives me a questioning look, wondering if I actually mean it. "I'll fight back."

"That's my girl!" Kennedy yells, causing a few people around us to stare. She wraps her arms around my neck and gives me a quick hug. She pulls back and her smile is immediately wiped from her face. Her eyes dart to mine, warning me that the fight might come sooner rather than later.

"Well, well. What's got you two all excited?" Maddox asks, pulling out a chair two spots over from me on my right and swinging it around to sit on it backwards. He has a smug look on his face and I just know he's going to stir shit up.

Asher is right behind him and his face is hard as rock, looking almost pissed off that he even has to breathe the same air as me. He takes the empty seat beside me, between Maddox and I, but he sits on it normally and leans back, propping his right ankle on his left knee.

"Fuck off, Maddox. We're not in the mood." Kennedy says from my left side, picking up a slice of her pizza and taking a bite.

I immediately feel my heart beat begin to speed up and my palms are getting sweaty. I know I said I would fight back, but I thought I had a few hours at least to figure out exactly what that even means.

"Rowan, you're not going to eat that, are you?" Maddox points to my pizza, eyeing me. I push my plate towards him, losing my appetite with him and Asher sitting here now. He smirks and takes a big bite from the slice I had half eaten.

Asher eyes me silently. Probably plotting his next move. I begin to prepare myself for whatever he's about to say, but I never could have predicted what comes out his mouth next. "You never eat carbs. You always have a salad or vegetable mixture of some sort." Asher observes, flashing his gloomy eyes at me and holding my eye contact.

I clear my throat and look away, figuring out how to

respond to that. Before I can say anything though, Kennedy speaks up. "How do *you* know she never eats carbs?"

Maddox jumps in with his typical witty remarks. "Wait, that's actually weird as fuck. I mean, *everyone* loves carbs. It's the best food group. Who the fuck doesn't eat *any* carbs?" My cheeks immediately go red and I feel tears prick my eyes. I blow out a shaky breath and blink a few times to get control of myself. I will *not* cry in front of them.

After a few seconds, when I get myself together, I look back at Asher and lift an eyebrow. "So what? I like to eat healthy. At least I have the money to be able to eat healthy. You know, some people can't afford fresh vegetables." I challenge, fire coming to my eyes. "You would know a thing or two about living on a budget, right Asher? We all know what neighborhood you live in, after all. McDonalds for breakfast, booze for dinner." I sneer, trying to ignore the feeling in the pit of my stomach telling me I went too far. "Not exactly the kind of place that houses people who can afford vegetables and healthy food."

A red, hot anger crosses Asher's face and his soft blue eyes turn a fiery blue. His jaw clenches and tension fills his face, a vein in his neck popping out.

Then, as quick as the anger crossed, he recovers and his eyes turn icy cold, his demeanor returning to the normal intimidating, tough exterior. The chill in my spine from earlier returns as I watch a calmness wash over Asher's eerie expression. This can't be good.

My eyes flash to Maddox who has a look of complete shock on his face. His mouth is slightly agape and his eyes are wide. He knows I crossed a line and he's waiting for the explosive response.

Side-eyeing Asher, Maddox stays silent as he gauges Asher's reaction and I watch Kennedy do the same. We all know I went too far and I brace myself for the inevitable nasty retort.

Leaning forward in his chair, Asher purses his lips and comes close enough to my face that he can whisper and only him and I would be able to hear him. He pauses for a second and I watch something flash across his eyes, but I can't tell what it is. Without another word, Asher stands up, maintaining eye contact with me as he looks down on me.

"Good to know you're not the innocent good girl you make yourself out to be," he scoffs. He says it loud enough for the whole cafeteria to hear, even though he's still close enough that he didn't have to. He remains in his spot, towering over me, as he spits out his final blow. "No, you're just a cold-hearted fucking bitch." I wince at his comment, knowing I deserve it but hating it nonetheless.

Asher coolly walks out the doors of the cafeteria with an unreadable expression on his face. It's not anger, but he also doesn't look pleased with himself. He looks… almost disappointed. In what, I'm not sure.

As if on cue, Maddox rushes out of the cafeteria behind Asher just as I start to hear a cloud of whispers erupt from the other kids around us. I'm completely mortified. I can't even look at Kennedy because I'm afraid to see the look on her face.

Keeping my head down, I sling my backpack over my shoulder and grab my tray from the table. I walk over to the garbage, sliding everything on it into the trash and placing the tray on the stack on top.

I turn around to race out of the cafeteria doors, but I feel an arm slide across my shoulders. I turn my head and see Kennedy by my side. "I told you, no matter what I've got your back." She offers me a smile and guides me out the doors, just as the end-of-lunch bell rings.

I should've known from the moment I felt the chill in my spine when I walked into the cafeteria that something would happen. At least, I have Kennedy by my side. I'm going to need her, now more than ever.

THREE
Rowan

The rest of the day went by in a blur.

I had two more classes before I could go home and I felt like everyone was staring at me the entire time. But why wouldn't they? I had never acted like that before, especially not in front of the whole school. Even though Asher has picked on me and antagonized me for two years, I would usually brush it off and not give anyone a reaction. I would never stoop to his level. But, in a way, he had it coming this time.

I crossed a line, though. Sure, everyone knows Asher lives on the poor side of town, but I shouldn't have brought it up. And I shouldn't have insinuated that his parents were alcoholics. It was a shitty thing to do. Especially, coming from me—what a hypocrite.

"Are you excited for tomorrow?" Kennedy asks, pulling me from my thoughts. She's sitting on my bed, her textbook open in front of her even though I know she's not actually doing homework.

"Nah, it's just another day." I shrug, turning back to my laptop on my desk, trying to focus on the essay I'm writing. But now the spiraling thoughts are in my head and there's no way George Orwell is getting my attention anymore.

"You're kidding right?" Kennedy asks, coming up behind me and spinning my desk chair around to face her. "Your birthday is not *just another day.*" I sigh and drop my head to the back of my chair. "Don't give me that attitude. Do your parents have anything planned? A special dinner or something?"

I turn my back to Kennedy and try to hide my sadness. "No, they both have to work late, so we were just going to do something small, maybe on the weekend." I'm surprised how easily the lie rolls off my tongue. Kennedy doesn't know many details about my family issues or my personal ones—she just knows some vague stuff.

I can feel the sob rising in my throat, so I quickly look down to the floor. I wish I could say: *They haven't celebrated my birthday in five years. I'll be shocked if they even remember,* but I can't. The words don't come and I don't want her pity. It's always easier if people don't know the vulnerable parts of you, that way they'll never have the bullets to load the gun that will hurt you.

As if sensing the awkward silence, Kennedy speaks up. "Well, that's not acceptable. You're turning *eighteen.* We have to celebrate!" My eyes quickly go wide and I start to shake my head. "Oh don't give me that look. We can do something low-key." I've been best friends with Kennedy long enough to know that her version of a low-key celebration usually involves streamers, alcohol, and a hundred strangers.

"Absolutely not. I don't want a party and I don't really want to celebrate. I just want to stay in my sweats, put my hair up in a bun, and have a cozy night in." I reply, standing my ground. I hope I'm convincing Kennedy enough because I will not go to any party, let alone one meant to celebrate *me*.

Kennedy groans and sighs extra dramatically to signal that I'm 'killing her,' as she would put it. "Fine. What if we just go to the movies? You can't spend your birthday at home. We need to go out and do something, even if it's just watching a movie." I contemplate it, but the look on my face isn't convincing her. "You can wear your sweats and we'll watch any movie you want," she pleads.

"Fine." I give in, kind of liking the idea of a chill girls night out. "Maybe we can watch the new Sandra Bullock movie." I state, getting excited. Kennedy looks down at her phone to check the time and starts to pack up her untouched textbook.

"Sounds good. I have to go for dinner, but I'll look up show times and text you." She stands up from my bed and slings her backpack over her shoulder. "See you tomorrow, almost-birthday girl."

As Kennedy closes my bedroom door, I hear my mom say goodbye to her in the hallway. A few seconds go by and then my bedroom door bursts open without a knock. "I need lettuce for my salad." My mother demands, standing in my doorway.

"Okay?" I question, not really sure what she wants from me. Her eyes turn angry and she grips her hips with a huff.

"Do not give me attitude, young lady. Go get lettuce from the store. Now!" She yells, slamming my door shut. I jump at her sudden outburst, rubbing my hands over my face. No matter how often she yells at me and slams doors, it never scares me any less. It's been that way for five years.

Five years ago, my sister died. It was only her and I for a long time, and after she passed, it was only me. Since her death, the tension in my house has been high and I've been on the receiving end of all my parent's anger and grief.

When my sister died, a part of me died, too. Not only within myself, but within my family. My parents grieved as if they lost both their daughters, even though I'm still here. Now it feels like we're just three strangers living amongst each other.

Since I was twelve years old, all I wanted was my sister back. If my sister was still here, maybe the part of me I lost would be, too. If she was still here, everything would be better. My parents would be happier, I would be happier. Life would be better. But she's gone.

I sigh, trying to push these thoughts away. If I take too long, my mother will come back up here and yell at me again. That thought forces me up into my closet to change my shorts into jeans. I grab my wallet and keys off my desk and beeline it to my car before my parents have time to say anything else to me.

The drive to the grocery store takes less than five minutes and I'm silently thankful for that because it doesn't give me enough time to continue to wallow in the sadness that is my life. I pull into a parking spot and shift the gear into park, cutting the engine. I jiggle my keys out of the ignition and grab my wallet, then set out for the store.

Immediately as I walk into the store, I head straight to the produce section, wanting to get out as fast as I came in. I pick a head of lettuce that will satisfy my mother and I turn around to head to the check out, but I'm stopped in my heels.

The last person I want to see is standing two feet away from me, stocking the shelves. I watch him for a few seconds, frozen in my spot. I beg myself to move, to walk away, to do *something*, but my body betrays me.

Before I can spring myself into action, Asher turns around and catches me staring at him. A small grin plays on his face and I just want to wipe it right off. "You just gonna stare at me the rest of my shift?" He teases, turning back to the shelf. I watch as he grabs a few bottles of salad dressing and arranges it on the shelf.

I clear my throat, trying to come up with a witty remark, but I'm at a loss for words. "No," I spit out. It's all I can muster because my brain is flashing memories of all the horrible things I said to him earlier today. I shut my eyes and sigh, knowing I should apologize. It's the right thing to do and maybe this chance encounter is the universe's way of urging me to apologize.

I take a step towards Asher, tapping him on the shoulder so he'll turn towards me. "Asher, I'm really sorry for what I said earlier today. It was rude and I shouldn't have said it." I get the words out, feeling mortified and embarrassed at the whole situation.

"I don't give a fuck, Rowan." He spits out, turning back to his shelves. "Is that all?" There's anger in his voice and I don't know if it's because he's still mad about what I said or if he's just annoyed that I'm bothering him at work. Either way, I don't blame him. I just wish he would accept my apology and put us both out of our misery.

"I just want you to know I'm sorry." I say, hoping he'll

accept my apology and won't retaliate tomorrow. The last thing I want is for him to still be mad about this tomorrow and make my school day even more miserable than usual.

Asher turns back to look at me and stares hard into my eyes. "No you're not and don't pretend like you are. It just makes you look more pathetic than you already are," he spits out.

Tears prick my eyes and I have to look at the floor so he won't see the tears fall. I've never cried right in front of him before, even though his words have made me cry hundreds of times after-the-fact in the bathroom. But I've never given him the power to see me cry in front of him. Until right now.

My mother's words repeat in my head and I can't stop the thoughts now.

You know, Rowan. You are probably the most pathetic person I've ever met. Your sister was never pathetic.
Sometimes I wish it was you that died instead of her.

The tears are streaming down my face and I quickly try to wipe them away. But he sees them. His face falls a little and I see his eyes harden.

"Rowan." He says my name and there's a strain in his voice, confusion on his face. He's probably wondering why now, of all the times, I let his words get to me. And in front of him, no less. I need to leave. I can't be here with him anymore and I need to get home.

I turn around and rush to the self-checkout, wanting to buy my lettuce and get the hell out of here. Once I pay, I basically sprint to my car and get in the driver's seat. I sit in silence, but

I don't turn on my car because I don't want to go home. But I also don't want to stay here.

I have nowhere to go. No place where I belong. No place where I can relax. No place where I feel safe. Nowhere.

FOUR
Rowan

My arms hurt, my legs hurt, my head hurts, my heart hurts. Everything hurts, all I feel is pain.

There isn't a word to describe how much agony I am in right now. I want it to go away. All of it. I don't want to feel anymore and I don't want to live anymore. How can I go on without her? How can my parents go on without her? How could life possibly go on without her?

I watch as my six year old sister, my beautiful little Rory, takes her last breath. Her eyes are closed and her face is as white as a ghost. I'm holding her hand as I feel her body completely still. Her chest rises with the intake of her final breath and the air escapes her lips. Then she's gone. Just like that. The heart rate monitor goes flat and the only sound in the room is the dull tone from the machine. No one makes a sound, no one moves. We all just sit around her bed and watch her. Watch the life slip out of her. Our perfect Rory. Taken far, far too soon.

After a few seconds, a sob escapes my mother's throat. She can't stop herself anymore. She tried to stay strong for Rory in her final moments, we all did, but now that she's gone we can't hold it in anymore. My dad hugs my mother as they both cry and I fall into my sister's side.

It wasn't supposed to happen like this. She was supposed to live into her 80s. She was supposed to get married and have kids and be the best aunt to my kids. She was my best friend and we were supposed to grow old together. But life had other plans.

I wake up from my dream and I feel the wetness from my tears on my cheeks. I've been having this dream every year on my birthday since Rory died. Sometimes on other mornings too, but without a doubt, on my birthday every year since I was thirteen.

When Rory died, it was three weeks before my thirteenth birthday. She was only six years old, but she was my best friend. Most kids my age didn't get along with their younger siblings, especially the further apart in age they were. But not me. Rory and I were two peas in a pod, tied at the hip.

The day she got her cancer diagnosis, one year before she passed, was the second worst day of my life; the first obviously being the day she passed. Every day in the last year of her life, I prayed to God that she would be okay. Her prognosis was not hopeful, but I hoped and prayed she would beat the odds. I even bargained with whatever spirit would listen that I could take her place.

Take me, save her.

A week before she passed, she started to decline so severely that the doctors told us it was a matter of days. I prayed so hard that final week, begging whatever God that was out there to save her.

The morning she passed, we could all feel it. She was so weak and tired. When my parents went to get a coffee, Rory told me she would miss me the most. That was when I knew.

As we watched her pass away, I cursed any and all Gods. How could any higher power take such a hopeful, happy girl from the world at such a young age? She barely lived. She was only here for six short years. I got to live nearly thirteen, it should have been me.

Both my parents wish it was. I wish it was.

Guilt fills my body at that last thought. As much as I wish it was me that died instead of my sister, it's not an easy thought to have. It hurts because I know Rory wouldn't want me to think this way. She told me to be happy and live my life. I haven't done either of those things.

I look at the alarm clock and groan. My dream woke me up early, just like every year on my birthday. I still have over an hour before I have to be at school, but it only takes me half to get ready. Weighing my options, I decide to get up and just go to school early. Maybe I'll stop at Starbucks for my free birthday drink. That usually puts me in a better mood.

Usually my morning routine consists of curling or straightening my hair, putting on makeup, dressing in my pre-picked outfit, and grabbing an apple on my way out the door, but it takes more effort to do that this morning than normal. I just don't see the point of putting in all the effort today. My parents won't remember it's my birthday, no one besides Kennedy will say anything, and my heart is still heavy from my dream this morning.

Despite my dread, I still go through my whole routine though because I'm a creature of habit. I may despise the habit right now, but I still have to do it.

When I'm finished getting ready, I brace myself before I go

downstairs. I take a deep breath and rush out of my room. My parents are both making coffee and breakfast in the kitchen when I pass by. I decide to wait a minute to see if they'll notice me or acknowledge my birthday.

"Good morning," I say to my parents, waiting behind the kitchen counter in case I need to make a mad dash to my car. My mom looks up at me, stares at me for a second, and then goes back to making her breakfast.

"Morning, Ro." My dad mumbles, never taking his eyes off his coffee. I cringe at the nickname. After my sister died, he started calling me Ro, which sounds like the start of her name. Rory. I don't know why he started doing it, but I hate it. I'm not Rory and I never will be. They can't just use me as her replacement because she's gone.

"It's Rowan. Don't call me Ro." I snap, unable to bite my tongue like I usually do. This catches my dad's attention, *finally*. I think this is the first time he has actually looked at me in the last month. Maybe longer.

"Go to school, *Rowan*." He glares at me, giving me a silent warning with his eyes. I hate that he called me Ro, but I think I hate how he said my name just now even more. I can feel the tears prick the corners of my eyes and I try to stop them because I don't want to cry in front of them. But it hurts. It hurts that the day after my sister died, they forgot about me. It hurts that they don't acknowledge my birthday anymore.

It all just hurts.

I turn around and run to my car, locking myself inside. I grab two tissues and place them at the corners of my eyes, hoping to catch the tears before they fall down my face and ruin my makeup. The last thing I want is for people at school to see my messed up makeup and know I was crying.

Nothing has changed. Don't let it get to you, Rowan. Everything's the same as it was yesterday. Don't let it bother you today. I try to calm myself down and I succeed enough to drive to school.

As I pull into the school parking lot, I see that it's pretty much deserted. Makes sense, considering school doesn't start for another half hour.

There's only one other car in the lot and I immediately recognize it. It's Asher's. I wonder why he's here so early. What could Asher Madigan possibly be doing at school this early in the morning? All I know is I don't want to be here, especially now that I know it's just the two of us at school right now.

Dread fills my stomach as my mind recalls what happened at the grocery store yesterday. I haven't cried in front of anyone in five years and I've definitely never cried in front of Asher before, but yesterday I broke both of those records. I hope he doesn't say anything, in fact I hope I don't even come in contact with him until first period. At least then I'll have Kennedy to support me. But here, I'd be on my own and I don't think I can handle two one-on-one encounters in two days with Asher.

Grabbing my backpack from the passenger seat, I get out of my car and decide that I can go get a coffee from the cafeteria before I sit in our empty first period class. However, I only get a few feet from my car before my eyes go wide.

Asher is walking off the track field in gym shorts with a towel in one hand and a water bottle in the other. And he's shirtless. I knew he worked out more from the increased size of his biceps, but damn. His abs are incredible. And his shoulders are ripped.

I snap myself back to reality, remembering who he is, and I hope he didn't catch me staring. As good looking as he is, he's still an asshole. A huge, ego-maniac, asshole.

I decide to pick up my pace and rush to the front doors of the school so he doesn't catch sight of me. It's too late, though, and he's fast. He saw me and now he's coming towards me. Asher breaks out into a light jog and runs up to my side, catching my arm before I can slip into the school.

"Rowan," he says. It's different from how he said my name yesterday, more controlled now and less pained.

He lets go of my elbow and wipes some sweat from his forehead with his towel. I look up at him with anxious eyes, hoping he'll catch on to my severe discomfort and leave me alone for once. "I, uh... I wanted to know what happened yesterday." He gives me a sincere look and I'm taken aback.

It actually seems like he's genuinely... *concerned* about me. I'm hesitant to be having a conversation with him, let alone this kind of conversation. What changed between yesterday and today?

"It was nothing. You caught me at a bad time," I reply, hoping he'll accept that answer and leave me be.

"You came up to me?" He says, slightly upturning his voice at the end to make it sound like a question. He seems confused, which only makes me more confused. Who is this new Asher and what did he do with the old one? "You were... crying. I think," he adds.

"Why do you care? Did you want to apologize or something?" I ask, getting annoyed by his mood swings. One minute he's an ass and says all these disgusting things, and the next he's checking on me, or whatever this is.

"No. I'm not apologizing." He states, hardening his glare at me. He goes to say something else, but I've had enough.

"Right. Because that would be *pathetic* of you, to apologize." I say, spitting his words from yesterday back at him. I can't be bothered with this conversation, so I turn on my heels and head for the cafeteria.

I should've known better than to assume Asher Madigan had a heart. He's just a sad, heartless asshole who likes to push other people around. But he can't push me around anymore. I'm done putting up with his shit and feeling sorry for pushing back.

Fuck you, Asher Madigan.

FIVE
Asher

Rowan Lila Easton. Even thinking about that name gets my blood boiling.

I don't know why I even bothered talking to her today. After the grocery store yesterday, I saw the way she flinched when I called her pathetic and it made me feel kind of guilty. I nearly apologized right there. But she ran away before I could even talk myself out of it.

I stayed up all night thinking about her reaction, though. Why did those words hurt her so bad? God knows I've said worse things to her. She's never given me any kind of reaction like that before. It's usually either silence, a glare, or, more recently, a snarky comment back—never crying. I saw it in her eyes, she was trying to hold back tears.

All night I tried to fall asleep, but all I could see were her sad green eyes staring at me like I was monster. I guess my attempt to talk to her this morning was driven by guilt. But shit, what a fucking mistake that was. It's like yesterday didn't

32

even happen to her and she reverted back to her ultimate bitchy self.

"Did you want to apologize or something?" Her entitled response plays over in my ears.

"Right. Because that would be pathetic of you, to apologize." Fuck, she irritates me. Her and her better-than-everyone, holier-than-thou attitude.

Rowan pisses me off like no other, for what exact reason I don't even fucking know. All I do know is she gets under my skin and it drives me up the wall. I guess that's why I've been an asshole to her since junior year.

After my mother and I moved to Jacksonville right after freshman year, I tried to fly under the radar. I didn't want to meet anyone new or try to make any friends that whole summer. Maddox kind of forcefully became friends with me that summer, but other than him, I had no one. And I liked it that way. Then, when I started sophomore year, I kept my head down and ignored everyone. I just didn't want anyone to notice me.

My last few years at my junior high and first year of high school in Ohio were unbearable and I didn't want a repeat of that. I don't think I could've handled it. So the less everyone knew about me, the better. But then, Maddox had a plan to take over the school in junior year and we quickly rose to the top.

When I started junior year, I finally felt like I had some control and power in my life. People were afraid of me, instead of me being afraid of them. It felt good. What's that saying? If I can't have love, I want power? Shit, did that ever ring true for me. If I couldn't be happy anymore, at least I was powerful.

I first noticed Rowan the first day of sophomore year and she was a sight to be seen. Most girls that age are a bit awkward, trying to figure out who they are and all that. Rowan, though, she knew herself. She was confident and good at it.

Her long blonde, wavy hair and green eyes drew in all the guys. But it was her full, rosy cheeks and happy smile that drew *me* in. Either she was really happy or really good at pretending. For the first time in my life, I actually wanted to get to know someone. Until I learned more about her and what kind of person she was.

The summer before junior year, Maddox told me all about Rowan and her best friend Kennedy, how they were top of the class and thought they were better than everyone. Maddox told me everything, and the more I got to know about Rowan, the more she reminded me of the bitches from junior high. Goody little two shoes with their crisp clothes and polite, innocent persona, but underneath the guise, they were a living fucking nightmare to me.

In junior high, the whole school knew my family problems and these girls would use that to their advantage. They called me names, made fun of my family, and spit in my food after calling me white trash. That was the kind of girl I was told Rowan was.

Maybe that's why Rowan gets under my skin so much. It's one thing to be perceived a certain way, but she's actually like those girls. She proved it the other day with her comments in the cafeteria.

But whatever the reason is for my distaste for Rowan, I won't put up with that shit anymore. After her calling me poor at lunch and pathetic this morning, it's time for me to go on the offense.

I skipped first period this morning because I couldn't stand being in the same room as Rowan. Instead I planned today's spectacle. Twenty minutes after the start of lunch, I walk into the cafeteria and bee-line straight for Rowan's table. Maddox sees me heading there and he follows right behind me.

Once I reach her table, I step right beside Rowan and clear my throat to get her attention. She looks up at me and then her gaze falls to my hands. In my left hand is a greasy McDonalds bag with two burgers and fries meals, and in my right hand is an unmarked brown paper bag with a bottle of Jack Daniels hidden inside. I can see the fear in her eyes and it only feeds my adrenaline.

"What do you guys want?" Kennedy spits out from Rowan's side. I can't help the smirk that appears on my lips, knowing neither of them know what's coming.

"Hello to you too, Kennedy." I acknowledge her sweetly to get under her skin. "The other day, Rowan here seemed very interested in my lifestyle, so I thought I would indulge her." I place the two brown bags directly in front of Rowan just as Maddox clues in on my plan.

My best friend leans between the two girls and swipes their lunch trays before they can get to them. Maddox runs over to the garbage and throws out their lunches, so they're only left with what I'm offering them. "Go on, then. Try out the poor kid lifestyle, you might like it," I instigate.

Rowan's face goes red and she diverts her gaze to her lap. Her breathing intensifies and it sounds like she's desperate for air. The rhythm of her chest rising and falling speeds up rapidly and now she's nearly hyperventilating.

I watch as she plays with her fingers, touching each fingertip to her thumb on each hand as if she's counting.

What the fuck is she doing?

Kennedy looks up to me and follows my gaze to whatever is going on with Rowan. As if getting a secret signal from her best friend, Kennedy bursts out of her chair and pushes against my chest, forcing me to take a few steps back.

"Back the fuck up!" She yells, shoving me away. Maddox looks between us, unsure if he should intervene or leave it alone, since he can't exactly put his hands on a girl. "It's Rowan's birthday, can't you leave her alone for one fucking day?" She yells, clearly exasperated.

I flinch at Kennedy's words and close my eyes for a second. It's Rowan's birthday? I think back to her snappy attitude this morning and wonder if she was just in a bad mood because she's one of those people who doesn't like their birthday.

I open my eyes and look over Kennedy's shoulder. Rowan is still sitting with her back to me and her head down. Her shoulders are slouched and she seems visibly upset. She must really not like her birthday. Maybe that's why she's been more angry this whole week. And here I am antagonizing her even more.

Nah, fuck it. Hating your birthday isn't an excuse to be a bitch.

"What's wrong, Rowan? Too good to eat poor people food? What about the whiskey, too good for some alcohol, too?" I press, hoping to get a reaction out of her. One that isn't sad and makes me feel bad for her.

What I do get, though, surprises me. Rowan bursts out of

her chair and her chair falls over from the force of her getting up. She doesn't even wait for anyone to say anything before she sprints out of the cafeteria with more force than humanly possible.

My mouth falls open a little. I'm stunned at her outburst and confused why she's so upset. I didn't do anything that wasn't warranted. Nothing worse than her little poor person comment. Kennedy stands stunned in front of me, looking between Maddox and I.

"What the fuck is wrong with you two? You have no idea the kind of shit she deals with every day and your little stunt here is more harmful than you two fucktards even realize." Kennedy chastises us. I'm so confused by that statement. It was a stupid taunt, nothing serious.

"What kind of shit could good girl Rowan Easton possibly deal with?" I ask, sarcastically. I don't know what answer I expected Kennedy to say, but her next words were definitely not it.

"She's anorexic, assholes." Kennedy replies in a low voice for only Maddox and I to hear. "*Bastards*," Kennedy mumbles as she grabs both her and Rowan's backpacks and slams through the cafeteria doors.

My jaw is on the floor and my feet are frozen in place. I can't move or even think right now, I'm too consumed by guilt. An emotion that's popping up a lot more for me these days.

I had no idea. Rowan didn't look like she had an eating disorder, so how was I supposed to know? I guess that's the whole point of eating disorders, though. Anyone can have one and no one could know.

I guess I had Rowan all wrong. Maybe she isn't like those girls from junior high. And I've sort of just fucked things up for her.

I went *way* too far and I can't undo it. *Fuck.*

SIX
Rowan

That fucking piece of shit.

He thinks he's so tough, and funny, and untouchable. He thinks he can go around and do whatever he wants to people without consequences and that it's funny when his actions cause other people to have panic attacks.

I used to have panic attacks a lot. They would happen in public sometimes, but I was always able to control it. After a while, I learned new coping mechanisms and they would only start happening when I was at home. I haven't had one in public since right after my sister died, but today I couldn't control it anymore. Asher's antagonizing sent me over the edge.

I don't know why I let him get to me. But there was just something about him taunting me with McDonalds and whiskey in front of the whole school that I couldn't handle.

Anxiety isn't something you can explain. There's not always a concrete reason why someone starts to feel anxious or has a panic attack. But, today, I am almost certain it had to do with my eating disorder.

Recognizing you have a problem is always the first step, they say. Well, no shit, I have one. I've had one since I was eleven, according to my parents and my old therapist. The anxiety was why my parents put me in therapy when I was eight, but the anorexia was why I stayed for so long. Then, it was supposed to help with the grief I was experiencing because of Rory's death—but it didn't.

When I first started seeing my therapist, she diagnosed me with generalized anxiety disorder at the young age of eight. The anorexia came later. I stopped seeing her two weeks after Rory passed because I didn't want to talk to anyone and my parents were too caught up in their own grief and feelings to remember I was even there, let alone remember to drive me to therapy.

I admit, I should've kept going to see her, but how was I going to get there? Walk? I guess once I got my license I could've gone back, but by then it had been too long. And I was too stuck in my own ways to let some stranger come in and disrupt my self-help coping habits I'd adopted by then.

Living with untreated anxiety and anorexia has been debilitating, but I've been able to keep it under control for long enough that no one noticed. The only people that knew were my parents and Kennedy, but I think they all forgot or just thought I was handling it.

I *was* handling it. Until today.

Usually I could get through school without a panic attack. Sometimes, when I get home, the attack comes and I deal with it in the privacy of my room. There's no one around to witness it, so it makes it easier to pretend it just doesn't happen.

As far as eating goes, I try. I try so incredibly hard to eat like a normal person. But I've gotten so used to eating a certain way—*living* a certain way—that even I don't recognize the problem sometimes. I suppose over time it hasn't gotten *worse*, since I haven't looked physically ill to the point where people notice and are concerned. But it also hasn't gotten better.

My parents, of course, don't notice and I thought no one at school noticed my eating habits, until Asher pointed it out the other day. I guess that's why I was so mean to him when he and Maddox pointed it out. I didn't want anyone to know my issues.

I was panicking. Because that's all I ever do. Panic.

Now, I'm sitting outside the front doors of the school with my legs pulled to my chest and my head resting on my knees. I'm trying to do that thing my therapist told me before I stopped going to see her a few years ago. The five, four, three, two, one method.

Name five things I can see. I look up and I list off the things I see. An oddly shaped gravel rock, a big green palm tree, a really ugly orange car in the parking lot, a small yellow-ish leaf, and a discarded plastic water bottle beside the trash can.

Okay, four things I can touch. The ground, my jeans, my shoes, and the brick wall behind me. Now, three things I can hear. Bird chirping, kids inside yelling, and a siren far in the distance. Two things I can smell. My vanilla perfume and hand sanitizer. And one thing I can taste. The bile rising in my throat.

Don't worry, you're going to be okay. You'll get through it. This will pass.

I try to convince myself that I will be fine, just like I do every time I get an attack. I reach up to my face and wipe the tears from my cheeks. My hands are still shaking and my chest is tight, but the uprising in my stomach is starting to pass.

I keep repeating those words in my head: *you're going to be fine*. It's like my mantra. Everything will be okay. Because it will be.

I remind myself to practice my breathing techniques. Inhale for four seconds, hold my breath for seven seconds, exhale for eight seconds.

This helps. The shaking is subsiding and the constricting tightness in my chest is loosening its iron grip. I hug myself and rock slightly back and forth, cradling my body like a mother does for her child when the baby is crying.

Just as I'm starting to feel better, the doors beside me burst open. My head snaps to my right and I see Kennedy frantically look around until her eyes fall on me.

"Are you okay?" She asks and rushes to my side. She kneels down and drops my backpack beside her. I forgot I left that in the cafeteria in my mad dash out the door.

Kennedy brushes my hair back from my face, but I pull away. I don't feel like being comforted by someone right now. I would much rather be alone. Her face turns sad and she pulls her hands back. "I'm so sorry they did that to you."

"It's fine. I overreacted, I was being dramatic." I insist, hoping she'll drop it and we can stop talking. Wishful thinking.

"You were not dramatic, Rowan. You were pushed beyond your limits and that's not okay. Asher and Maddox have to recognize that they can't fuck around with people because they feel like it."

Before I have a chance to answer, the doors burst open again and Asher emerges. He looks around the parking lot and then snaps his head in our direction when he notices us. My back stiffens under his squinted eyes and I can feel the panic rising again.

Kennedy whips her head around after hearing the doors open and she immediately jumps up. "No. Absolutely not!" She yells, blocking me from Asher. He looks from Kennedy to me and back to Kennedy.

"I just want to talk to her, Kennedy." He says, a kind of sincerity in his voice. Asher's demeanor is drastically different from how he was in the cafeteria and the shock I'm feeling almost entirely blocks out the panic.

I'm stunned. How can he go from one extreme to other so quickly? And why does he look so… guilty? Kennedy must have told him something before she left. Something I did *not* want anybody, especially Asher, to know.

"You've done enough," she growls through clenched teeth. Part of me is intrigued about what Asher could want and the other part of me needs to know what he knows. I try to get up, but I'm still too shaken up to stand, so I sigh and relent to stretching my legs out in front of me.

"It's okay, Kennedy. Thanks for my backpack," I speak up. Kennedy spins around and gives me a glare that nonverbally says, *what the hell?* I raise my eyebrows at her and she gets the hint that I want to hear him out. She gives me a sympathetic look that tells me all I need to know.

Call me if you need me.

I silently thank her and she turns back towards Asher, giving him a challenging glare before she storms back into the school.

Asher watches as she disappears behind the doors and then turns back to me. He looks down at his hands and it looks like he's struggling to find the right words. "I know before I said it was pathetic to apologize when you didn't mean it," he starts and my interest is immediately peaked. "But I mean it this time. I'm sorry, Rowan." My mouth falls open a little because I never thought I would hear those words come from him.

I clear my throat, trying to figure out how to respond. Is he only apologizing because I had a panic attack? Does he know about my eating disorder? Is he apologizing for treating me like shit since junior year, or is it just for today? I don't know what to say so I look up at him and study him.

I see something in his eyes that I've never seen in them before. I think he means it; I think he's actually sorry.

"Why?" It's all I can ask and my voice is barely above a whisper. I almost think he didn't hear me until he tilts his head and considers my question.

"I guess because I didn't know about your eating disorder. I shouldn't have pushed you the way I did. Today and before."

I scoff at his reply, getting the answer I was afraid of.

He looks at me like I'm broken and *that's* why he's sorry. Not because he's acknowledging that he's an asshole and treated me like shit. No, he's sorry because he thinks I'm a fragile, weak girl who will snap at the tiniest inconvenience. He doesn't want any responsibility if I do snap, that's why he's apologizing.

"Oh, so now that you know about my *private* business,

you're suddenly sorry? I'm not some broken toy because I struggle with my mental health. I don't need your pity and I *definitely* don't need you to be nice to me. Or whatever you call this." I yell, finally finding the strength to stand up.

Yanking my backpack off the ground, I spin around and head out to the parking lot. When I make it to my car, I pause before getting in to look back at Asher. He's standing there, glaring at me. I watch as he clenches and unclenches his fists, and then storms back into the school.

He's pissed that I put him in his place. Good. He deserves it.

I stare back at the school for a second and decide I'm done with school today. I climb into my car and slam the door shut. The second I give myself a moment to breathe, the tears are back.

I sit in my car for twenty minutes and just cry. I cry because this is the shittiest birthday I've ever had.

I cry because I hate what my life has become. And I cry because I'm alone.

Happy fucking birthday to me.

SEVEN
Rowan

Kennedy and I didn't end up going out for my birthday last night. She called and asked if I was still up for it, but I wasn't, for obvious reasons. She offered to come over and hang out at my house, but I honestly just wanted to be alone. I needed space and time to breathe. That's all I needed—to breathe.

I know she was probably dying to know what happened with Asher and whether anything else went down, since I never returned to school. But truthfully, *I* don't even really know what happened. Or *why* any of it happened, rather.

All I know is he tried to apologize to me out of pity, I called him on his bullshit, I stormed off, and he got pissed. Like he had any reason to be pissed off. If anything, I was the one who should be pissed, what with the way he's treated me for two years and the way he mocks me by apologizing.

I'll probably pay for pissing him off—even though he had no right—eventually. Honestly, though, I can't be bothered. I have enough shit to worry about.

Right now, I'm staring up at my ceiling, waiting for my alarm clock to go off. I let myself cry all night to get it out of my system, but I won't let it affect me today. Yesterday was yesterday and it's in the past.

I'm back to regular Rowan again. Good student, always a smile on my face, and nice to everyone all the time. That's who I am, who I've always been, and I won't let Asher or anyone else take that away from me.

After what feels like an eternity of lying here in the darkness, my alarm finally sounds and I immediately turn it off. I rise out of bed and head to the bathroom, ready to start my day.

When I open the door, I take one look in the mirror and almost scream. I have no idea who that person staring back at me is, but it is *not* me. That cannot possibly be my face. It's all red and puffy and blotchy.

Shit. That is my face. This is why I never let myself cry for too long. I look like a goddamn train wreck.

I scrub my face with every skincare product I can get my hands on, hoping the swelling will go down and the redness in my face will slowly fade away. But I think I made it worse. I sigh and try to figure out what else I can do. An idea pops in my head and I cringe because I know it will not be pleasant, but it's all I can think of.

Turning on my heels, I run to the kitchen and grab a glass bowl big enough to fit my face. I fill the bowl half way with ice from the freezer and half way with water, and head back to my bathroom. Placing the bowl on my counter, I brace myself for the next minute of hell. This better work or I'll be pissed.

Before I can talk myself out of it, I inhale a deep breath and submerge my entire face in the bowl. I start counting up to sixty and—Jesus Christ, this water is *freezing*. This is by far the longest freaking minute of my goddamn life. Thirty more seconds. Shit, shit, shit! The things I do to look presentable is ridiculous.

Fifty-eight, fifty-nine, sixty! I yank my head from the bowl and immediately press a towel to my face. The towel isn't heated or warm by any means, but the contrast from the freezing water to this room temperature towel is heaven.

I sigh into the towel and then pry it away from my face to assess the situation in the mirror. I'm a little disappointed that there isn't more of a difference, but at least it looks a little better. My options now are to do the ice bath again or just apply a bit heavier makeup today than normal.

Yeah, makeup it is. I brush my teeth before I get started on fixing my face. Grabbing my makeup bag from beneath the sink, I lay out all my necessary tools. Moisturizer, foundation, concealer, bronzer, blush, highlighter, eye shadow, mascara, eye liner, beauty blender, brushes, and setting spray.

I was never really into makeup before, but when I got to high school, I realized it was kind of a necessity. So, I watched some YouTube videos and picked up the essentials from my local drug store. I learned how to do a full face of makeup and adapted a much simpler everyday routine for the days I don't want to sport a full beat face. It works for me and I'm content with my makeup skills. Of course, today I decide to do the full face routine in hopes that it will make me appear normal again.

The whole application process takes me nearly thirty minutes, but by the end, my face is almost back to normal. It still looks a little swollen, but as long as no one looks close enough, it isn't noticeable.

Satisfied with my makeup, I put all the products and tools back into my makeup bag and place it back in its place underneath the sink. Unfortunately my makeup took much longer today than normal, so I don't really have time to fix my hair. At least it looks okay and I just have to give it a brush through and a little fluff for some volume. Satisfied with how I look, I give myself a little nod in the mirror and head back to my bedroom.

The outfit I picked last night is pretty cute, so I decide to stick with it. I slide into my light wash blue jeans and throw on my slightly cropped pink collared t-shirt. There's a sliver of my stomach that's exposed, but I don't think it's enough that will get me dress-coded, so I'm content with it.

I give myself a once over in the mirror and slip into my white Adidas sneakers. Even though it's late September, the Florida sun is persistent and the heat stays in the low 80s, so I'm confident I won't get cold as long as I stay in the warmth. Unfortunately, though, our principal likes to keep the school's air conditioning ice cold well into November, so I grab a sweater just in case and throw my backpack over my shoulder as I make my way down the hall and out the front door to my car.

My drive to school is usually about ten minutes when I leave on time, but I'm running a bit later than usual this morning, so I'm caught in the morning rush traffic. It ends up taking me fifteen minutes to get to school, which isn't too bad considering I'm still technically on time, but I still feel late.

Quickly, I park my car at the back of the student parking lot and I nearly sprint out of my car. Just as I walk through the door to first period, I hear the first bell ring and I release a sigh of relief.

Kennedy is already sitting at her desk when I plop down into mine and she gives me a questioning look. I throw her a tight smile and start to pull out my notebook.

"You okay?" She whispers over to me. Right before I respond, Maddox and Asher prance into the room and I make eye contact with Asher. After a second, I quickly divert my gaze and open my notebook to a fresh page, writing the date at the top.

In my peripheral view, I can see Maddox and Asher walk down the middle row of desks until they disappear, which I assume is because they took their seats behind me. I debate saying something, but I talk myself out of it.

Last night, while I was contemplating my entire life, I decided I'm going back to normal Rowan. No more glances to the assholes and holding Asher's gaze and snarky comments. I'm going to ignore them like I did before and not give them the time of day.

I know Kennedy and I agreed that I should start giving them a taste of their own medicine and fight back, but all that's gotten me is a panic attack at school and Asher knowing my private information.

Alas, the feisty Rowan was short-lived and she won't be making another appearance if I can help it. I'm done playing these games and it's time Asher and Maddox grow the hell up. If they don't, I'm not sure I'll be able to take it anymore. And that will mean one of two things: either I'll breakdown completely or the bitchy Rowan might just make one final comeback.

And neither of those things are ones I want to happen. So, let's just hope Asher and Maddox are taking some lessons in maturity.

EIGHT
Asher

The second Rowan walked into first period this morning, I noticed.

Her face was swollen. Really swollen. And she was wearing twice as much makeup as normal.

Usually she wears some of that eye stuff and shiny stuff on her cheeks, but that's it. Today, though, she looks like one of those Instagram model influencers. It's like she took someone else's face and plastered it on hers. It's unnatural and it makes me wonder how red and puffy her face actually is under all that shit. Even under the dull cafeteria light right now, I can tell, so I know it must be pretty intense.

I wonder if it has anything to do with yesterday. I caused her to have a panic attack for fuck's sake. And then, when I went to apologize, she thought it was because I pitied her.

Maybe she's right, I guess it was partly because I felt bad after learning about her eating disorder. But still, it was an apology and it took a lot of effort to say it. The least she could've done was accept it. But, instead, she threw it back in my face and stormed off.

Her bitchy come-and-go attitude is really getting on my fucking nerves. Yeah, maybe she isn't *exactly* like those junior high girls, but she's not much better.

Maddox elbows me in the gut and it brings me back to the present in the cafeteria. I shoot him an angry look for elbowing me and he just chuckles to himself. Raising one of my eyebrows, I question what the hell is so funny.

"You're staring at her, dude. It's kind of creepy," he whispers to me. I appreciate that he didn't say it too loudly because I don't want the guys around us to hear.

I hope no one else noticed. Not that I really care. I mean, I was just looking at her. Pushing away the thought, I focus on my food and try not to look back up.

We're sitting in the cafeteria, eating lunch with a few of the other guys at our table. They're all guys I met through Maddox in sophomore year and they're nothing but a bunch of followers. They look for a badass dude who has tattoos, muscle, and doesn't give a shit about school, and they start to follow him.

It's like a silent agreement amongst them that the most alpha dude in the group is their leader. These guys aren't really friends in the traditional sense, they just hang in packs at school and get high or drunk after school until they get tired and go home to bed.

Before I met Maddox, he was one of the followers. Only because he had just finished freshman year and his alpha personality didn't really shine through yet. And he didn't know where to get illegal tattoos yet either.

He never cared about school all that much and his parents were too busy to really concern themselves with Maddox's life, so he found camaraderie in the group of misfits. But he wasn't close with any of the guys by any means, he just wanted people to hang with so he wasn't a loner.

I met Maddox my first day in Jacksonville. My mom and I had just pulled into our new driveway in my father's old pickup with the U-Haul trailer attached, when a kid around my age—with a smile way too big and an attitude far too eager for a neighborhood like this—walked up to my mom's window and knocked on it.

She was a little startled and intimidated, I think, by this random kid, so she only rolled her window down a crack. He introduced himself as Maddox, which I thought was a weird name, and said he lived a few doors down with his family. He saw us pull in and wanted to welcome us to the neighborhood. I thought it was the weirdest thing, and my mom did too I think, because she just said thank you and waited for him to leave.

Later that night, I went for a walk around the neighborhood to get out of the house since my mom was drinking. I ran into Maddox, who was returning from one of those group hangouts. We got to talking and he confessed that earlier on my driveway, he was actually stealing the whiskey our landlord always kept in the house. When we pulled in, he tried to make it seem like he was being neighborly, but he just didn't want to get caught.

That's when I knew this guy was going to be my best friend. I didn't click with many people, and I didn't want any friends when I moved here, but I liked Maddox. Meeting him was the first time in years that I woke up from my everyday hazy cloud and I actually saw the world around me. He was my first memory in years.

He's my best friend in the entire world and I never thought I'd have someone like him.

Over time, we went through a lot of shit together, Maddox and I. He was there for me whenever my mom got drunk and angry. I was there for him when his siblings all left him and his parents all-but forgot about him. He knows about my fucked up past and I know about his. We're the same in a lot of ways, and it makes me sad that he's gone through similar things as me. But, we've also gone through different things, things far worse than either of us could imagine for the other.

The other guys, though, we're not really friends. We're just acquaintances who have stuff in common. After Maddox and I became friends, he brought me to meet the group and they took me in. I became a follower, just like Maddox, and I watched how they acted throughout that summer, so I could pick up their mannerisms.

When I started sophomore year, I saw how they controlled the school. I admired their power, so I spent the summer before junior year getting more muscle, tattoos, and piercings. I wanted to be the alpha, the leader.

Junior year I took control, just like the previous leader, Ryker, before he graduated. All the other guys fell in line and Maddox became my right-hand man. The faculty knew they couldn't control me and the other students were terrified of me. The school became mine and, for the first time in my life, I was in control, I had all the power.

One of the guys at the table smacks his open-palmed hand

on the table and I am snapped back to reality. I look up to see what the commotion is about, but the guys are just screwing around and cracking jokes.

I try to fight it so hard, but the pull is too strong. I look over at Rowan, just to see what she's doing. But what I see makes me feel really sad, and really guilty. She's pushing her food around her plate with her fork to make it look like she's eaten some of it. But she's hasn't. She hasn't opened her mouth once to take a bite.

"Dude," is all Maddox says and it's all he needs to. I know what he's thinking. I need to let her go. I don't know what my obsession is with Rowan all of a sudden, but ever since senior year started, I couldn't leave her alone. At first, it was because she pissed me off and I wanted to piss her off for pissing me off.

But now, it's not because I don't like her. I still think she was a bitch yesterday when I tried to apologize. And that pissed me off. But now that I've had time to cool off, I realize it's more than that.

She intrigues me, ever since I found about her mental health issues. It's almost like, I realized that I'm not the only one with problems. Even the smartest girls with the biggest smiles and happiest attitudes can struggle. Everyone has demons, even if they don't show it. Rowan woke me up, in a way. Made me realize I'm not the only one fighting myself every day.

And it's because of that, I think, that my attitude toward her has done a complete 180. I see her differently and I feel guilty that it took learning about her personal struggles for that to happen. But she is so damn intriguing and I don't know how to get rid of this piqued curiosity and change in outlook.

But I need to get rid of it because she wants nothing to do with me. She made that abundantly clear yesterday when I apologized.

And I don't blame her, not really. *I* want nothing to do with me.

NINE
Rowan

It's been a long day. Actually, scratch that. It's been a long week.

And I was so hopeful, too, on Monday morning that it would be a good week. The sun was shining, it was still very warm outside, despite it being late September, and my parents had been surprisingly... content? My mom hadn't gotten drunk all weekend and my dad made me breakfast that morning.

But I should've known it was too good to be true. My mom made up for not drinking all weekend by getting absolutely plastered on Monday night. I haven't seen her that inebriated in a long time. She got drunker than she does on the anniversary of Rory's death every year. I don't know what caused her breakdown that particular night, but it was significant. And her words. Those words hurt more than anything she's ever said before. They were pure evil.

You know, Rowan. You are probably the most pathetic person I've ever met. Your sister was never pathetic.

Sometimes I wish it was you that died instead of her.

The worst part about her saying that is I know she meant it. Deep in her heart, she believes those words. *Drunk words are sober thoughts,* as they say. When she's sober, she would never say that, even though I know she thinks it. Even when she's somewhat drunk, but not yet plastered, I think she still has a small enough filter that would stop her from saying something *that* cruel. But when she's blackout drunk to the point that she was on Monday, any semblance of a filter is gone and her true feelings come out.

My whole life, my parents have preferred Rory over me. Rory was their golden child, their miracle after trying for a baby for so many years. I was planned, Rory wasn't, and that made her so much more special for them.

They wanted a big family, lots of kids. They even bought a house with five bedrooms, hoping to fill them all with blonde haired, green eyed babies. When I was born, they were happy because I was the beginning of their dream.

The first year of my life, I was loved and adored and spoiled. But as the years came and went, and they struggled to have more kids, they began to obsess over me in an unhealthy way. Doctors told them it would be a miracle if they had any other children, so I had to make up for it by being perfect.

For the first seven years of my life, I was under my parents' constant watch. Mom fussed over my hair and clothes, dad made sure I learned the alphabet, and as I got older, did my homework with me. Or rather, yelled at me while I cried at the kitchen table. Every aspect of my life was under the control and supervision of my parents because they wanted me to be perfect; they *needed* it.

I was smothered by them and I thought it was a normal thing for parents to do, until Rory came along. The best day of my life was the day she was born. Not only because I had a new best friend, but because I had a replacement.

I saw the way the spotlight had shifted the moment she came into our lives when I was nearly seven years old. I no longer had to be perfect, my parents no longer obsessed over me. They finally had another kid to focus on.

Part of me felt guilty, knowing what she would have to go through. All the expectations they would have for her. But I was relieved that I no longer had to take on the role of being their pride and joy, their dream come true, because it was too much for a little girl. Too much for me, anyway.

The first five years of Rory's life, she thrived. She was the happiest child and she was truly perfect in every way. She was everything my parents hoped I would become and she didn't even have to try. Not as hard as I did. Normally, that would cause a rift between siblings, maybe that should have made me envious or jealous. But I wasn't. I was insanely proud of Rory and honored to be her big sister. She amazed me every day, right up until her last.

When Rory passed away, my parents not only lost their daughter, but they lost their future dreams. She was their miracle and, when she died, so did all their hope. I was all my parents had left, and I think that made the grief worse. Normally, parents could find some comfort in their other children when one of them passes, but not mine. I wasn't enough for them, not before Rory was born and not while she alive. After she passed, my parents gave up completely.

I tried, I tried so incredibly hard to be enough for them. To ease their pain, their grief; to bring back some of their hope. I got perfect grades, never got into trouble. All my teachers told them what a joy it was to have me in their classes. Every adult I came into contact with praised my parents for what an amazing job they did. *You should be so proud to have a daughter like Rowan*, they said. But my parents didn't notice, they didn't care. Their perfect daughter was dead and they couldn't be bothered to celebrate, or even acknowledge, the daughter they still had.

Hearing my mother's words on Monday night broke me. I didn't think there was anything left to break after Rory's passing, and yet my heart shattered the moment those words came out of her mouth.

I tried so hard to be her perfect daughter for the past five years since Rory died. Harder than I did the first seven of my life. For these five years, I did everything I could to live up to her expectations for me. But, all the hope and pride I once held as their first born child crashed down on me all at once. Suddenly, everything felt pointless and my life became absolutely hopeless.

Starting my week losing all my faith in the universe should have been a hint at the kind of week that was ahead of me. I thought it couldn't get worse, and yet, it somehow did. Between my birthday being a disaster, Asher and Maddox's shit, and my breakdown at school, I'm exhausted. Beyond exhausted. I can't do this shit anymore. I need a break. A break from school, a break from my parents, a break from *life*.

So, yeah. This week has been absolutely terrible.

I walk into my house after school and pray that my parents are still at work. Usually they are, but with the way this week has been going, I expect anything now. Twisting my key in the lock and pushing the door open, I walk through the foyer and I'm halted in my steps. Even though I kind of expected this, I'm still shocked that she's actually here.

My mom is sitting in the armchair, facing away from me, and her left hand is bringing a mug to her lips. I don't have to look in the mug to know what's filled to the rim. I have two options: ignore her and try to sneak off to my room, or try to talk to her. Yeah, definitely the first option.

I quickly slip off my shoes at the front mat and I tip toe down the hallway towards the living room. Rounding the corner, I start making my way to my bedroom, but her voice stops me in my step.

"Hey," she slurs. I close my eyes and turn around, realizing she saw me and she's now talking to me.

"Hi, mom." I reply, walking over to her in the living room. I take a seat on the couch opposite of her and cross my legs underneath me.

Option two it is. "How was your day?" I ask, trying to make conversation and hoping she brushes me off so I can go back to my room.

"Oh, Rory, I'm so glad you're back. I've been waiting for you." Those words plummet my stomach to my feet and the air is lost in my throat.

She thinks I'm Rory. How drunk *is* she? Even though Rory and I shared similar features, like our blonde hair and green eyes, we looked very different, even at such a young age.

Where her features were more sharp and defined, mine were more soft and round.

"You look so pretty, sweetie." As soon as she says this, I realize why she thinks I'm Rory. I did a full face of makeup this morning and I purposely used the bronzer to make my features more angled and defined. I must look just like her.

"Thanks. I'm going to do homework," I reply. I'm trying to get out of there as fast as possible so she doesn't see the tears in my eyes. She says something to try and get me to stay, but I don't listen as I rush down the hall; I can't get out of there fast enough.

Instead of going to my bedroom, I head straight for the bathroom. Shutting the door, I desperately rummage through the cabinet below the sink for makeup wipes. I want this shit off my face *now*.

Finally, I find the wipes and I rip one out, scrubbing my face so hard that I just know I'm causing small tears in my skin. But, I don't care. I need my face to be clean. I need to look like *me* again.

I scrub for five minutes and then wash my face. Looking back up in the mirror, I'm flashed back to this morning when I was shocked at the reflection staring back at me. Only a few hours ago, I was horrified because my face was all puffy. Now, I'm horrified because my face is all red from the scrubbing and it's hollow from the nausea I feel building in stomach.

I'm never doing my makeup like this ever again. In fact, I'm never wearing any makeup again. I never again want to feel like I do right now. Like I'm so worthless that I unconsciously did my makeup this morning to make me look like my dead sister so that my mother would finally notice me.

In thirty seconds, I make a rash decision and collect all my makeup from under the sink. I load it all up in my arms and throw it in the trash can beside the toilet. Yesterday, I decided to go back to "normal Rowan," but I don't even know what that means anymore.

I give up. I'm done with trying so goddamn *hard*. No more makeup, no more pleated skirts, no more whatever I thought made me, *me*. I don't even know who I am anymore and I barely recognize myself in the mirror.

Who is Rowan Easton?

TEN
Asher

I'm exhausted. This week has been a fucking whirlwind.

In this week alone I've gone from not being able to stand Rowan, to really not liking her but being able to tolerate her a bit, to feeling kind of sorry for her, to feeling guilty about how I treated her, to kind of warming up to her. As a friend, obviously. But I doubt she would want to even be acquaintances with me, let alone tolerate me, after all the shit I've put her through.

Not that I want to be friendly with her, anyways.

I just want—I don't fucking know what I want. And that's what I mean when I say it's been a whirlwind of a week. At least it's Friday, I can be thankful for that.

This whole week has left me so confused, I don't even know what I want or why I'm even here. I'm sitting in my car in the school parking lot, fifteen minutes earlier than I need to be since I finished my run on the track early.

There's only a few other people here in the lot and I'm

65

feeling really stupid. I'm trying to remember why exactly I cut my workout short to sit here, early.

I guess I wanted to see Rowan before first period. I wanted to see her pull into the school parking lot and see if she's okay before she puts on her ready-for-school-all-chipper-and-happy face. The one that she always puts on the second she walks through the doors of our first period classroom.

I close my eyes and mentally slap myself when I realize what thought just passed through my mind. I can't believe I've paid such close attention to her that I know exactly what face she puts on for other people.

This is ridiculous, *I'm* getting ridiculous. I never hated her or anything, but I'm not supposed to *like* her. As a friend. I was just supposed to tease her and shake up her seemingly perfect life a little bit, that's all. But since I learned her perfect life isn't so perfect after all, everything's changed. *I've* changed.

The sound of three loud cars pulls my focus toward the entrance of the parking lot. I watch as three of my buddies pull into the school and park right beside me. I sigh, knowing I have to get out and entertain them so they don't get suspicious.

Pushing my door open, I get out and go around to the front of my car. Four of the guys get out of their own cars and walk over to me, creating a small cluster in front of my car. I lean back on the hood of my car and look at my watch to see how long I have to stay here. Only seven minutes until the bell, thank God.

After three minutes of stupid, thoughtless conversation with these morons, a small red Kia Forte pulls into the school. I know by the color and make of the car and the small 'Treat

People With Kindness' bumper sticker on the back window that it's Rowan.

I watch as she pulls into a spot a few cars down from me and gets out of her car. She's not wearing any makeup, which is very unusual for her, especially after her over-the-top look yesterday. Usually, she at least wears a little bit of makeup, but today she has nothing. Not even the black stuff that makes her typically-dark blonde lashes much darker and clumpier.

Jesus Christ. I need to get a fucking grip.

The fact that I know her eyelashes are usually a deep shade of blonde is fucking crazy. But I just can't stop watching her.

She slings her backpack over her shoulder and shuts her car door. That's when she notices me staring at her. She tilts her head to the side and looks at me, questioningly. She doesn't look mad, just confused. Hell, I'm confused, of course she would be confused.

Do I go up to her? Ask her why she decided to go for the natural look today? No. No, I can't do that. She'll get suspicious. The last thing I need is for Rowan to think we've made amends because I'm being friendly—no. That I can *tolerate* her now.

"…never do homework. What is she gonna do, give me detention?" I catch the tail end of the guys' conversation.

I can't listen to this right now. I need time to think, I need to be alone.

Frustrated with my torn state of mind, I grab my backpack and head toward the school, taking one more glance back at Rowan. She's still watching me, frozen in her spot beside her car. I debate one last time going over and talking to her, but I immediately push that thought out of my mind.

Keep walking Asher, I tell myself as I turn back around and make my way to the school.

As I walk up to the front doors, I can still feel Rowan's eyes on me. I need to stop thinking about her. Let. Her. Go. I remind myself: there is absolutely nothing special about Rowan Easton. She's just a girl with her own struggles and issues. No different than probably every other girl in this school, every other person on this planet.

As long as she stays out of my way and I keep some distance between us, I think I'll be fine. But if she continues to take up all the space in my mind, and in my physical surroundings, we might have a problem.

ELEVEN
Rowan

On Friday, I saw Asher staring at me in the school parking lot when I pulled in. He had those hawk eyes, watching my every move. It's Sunday now, so I've had a few days to process it.

It confused me because he looked genuinely interested in what I was doing, rather than his usual angry and judge-y stares. When he walked away, I was hoping he would say something in first period, but he just kept his mouth shut. So did Maddox. It was very out of character for the two of them.

This past weekend at least was better than last. My mom never said anything to me in her drunken state again, my dad continued to ignore me—which is sometimes better than when he actually talks to me—and everything at school on Friday was very tame. I'm hoping it continues this week at school.

I still think Kennedy telling Asher and Maddox about my personal business was invasive, but at least they have hearts because it stopped them from picking on me all the time. Now the issue is getting everyone else at school to see that I'm not

69

some lame girl who they don't want to associate with. I was never very close with anyone else at school, but when Asher and Maddox started their witch-hunt for me, I basically was isolated from everyone else at school.

Walking into first period, my eyes drift to the two jerks sitting behind my desk. They're engrossed in a conversation about whatever it is they're talking about—I don't understand a word of it since they're using a bunch of niche lingo.

They don't notice me, or if they do, they don't show any sign of it at all. I don't dwell on it, and I simply walk over to my desk beside Kennedy. She gives me a glare, which is a good morning smile in Kennedy-land.

One of the first things she told me when we first became friends, back when we were kids, was that she hates mornings and to never expect her to be cheery until at least 10a.m. We were eight years old and Kennedy already knew herself better than I know myself at eighteen. That was the moment I knew she was going to be my best friend and it's been us against the world ever since.

This morning is unusually calm and quiet, between Kennedy's moodiness and Maddox's and Asher's silence. I think it's too good to be true and I start waiting for the other shoe to drop, but it doesn't come. Ms. Jacobs gets on with her lesson and no one says a word.

In fact, not a single person in the entire class even mumbles or whispers to their friends. The eerie quietness starts to edge at my nerves and an uneasy pit is growing in my stomach. I feel like something bad is about to happen and I can't quite put my finger on it.

"So, does anyone have any questions?" Ms. Jacobs asks the

class as she finishes up the first part of her lesson. She always breaks up her lectures into parts and, after each part, she pauses to answer questions about the previous section.

Sometimes it gets annoying and tedious, but it's not necessarily a bad thing. She just wants to make sure everyone understands, and she's a good teacher for that.

I keep my head down, finishing off the last of my notes when the shoe I've been anticipating and dreading finally drops. Asher opens his mouth behind me and my heart plummets to my toes.

"Yeah, I do. Rowan, what's it like being hated by everyone in this school?" Asher asks, chuckling. Immediately, whispers explode from every corner of the classroom. A red, hot fire burns my skin and crawls up my chest, spreading to my neck and my cheeks.

"Oh... shit. She didn't know no one can stand her," Maddox teases. His fake concern and mocking tone only further embarrasses me and the humiliation starts to physically form in my stomach. A deep pressure pushes on the lining of my stomach and my fingers start to tremble, shaking my hands uncontrollably.

Kennedy snaps her head to the two jerks behind us and she immediately jumps in to defend me. "Will you two fuckwads find a new hobby? Your teasing is getting boring and predictable."

I start counting up to sixteen—my favorite number—on my right hand, pressing my thumb on the ball of my four fingers. Repeating the same on my left hand, I start to drown out the war of words going on around me.

As I feel the pressure in my stomach start to subside and

the heat begin to cool on my skin, I refocus my eyes on the events involving me. I take a deep breath and, while still slightly shaky, I prepare myself for battle.

Remember when I said it was back to normal Rowan? No more fighting back? Yeah, I don't think so. There's only so much shit and confusing signals a girl can take. And this is my limit. I don't give it a second thought before I turn around in my chair and carefully choose my words.

"It's okay, guys. You don't have to project your own conflicting emotions onto me. You see, your life perspective is so skewed and vain that you don't realize it's not *me* who people hate. It's you two. You guys are just so obsessed with me that your own hatred for me clouds reality. Don't be embarrassed though, they have therapy for that."

I inhale a deep breath, running out of air during my demeaning speech. While a part of me feels bad for how hurtful I was just now, I remember all the horrible things they've done to me and my guilt immediately melts away into oblivion.

Kennedy gives me a triumphant smirk because she knows how hard that was for me. And she can probably tell that I'm slightly second-guessing myself, so she wants me to know she's proud of me. She squeezes my hand and raises an eyebrow at Maddox and Asher, challenging them to say something back.

Conceding, Asher sinks further into his chair and gives a warning glance to Maddox that he shouldn't retaliate. Maddox is quite annoyed that he has to shut up and take my insults, but the look on Asher's face scares me more. He's not visibly mad at all. But there's an icy coldness in his eyes and his blue sapphire irises look nearly black.

He's livid.

A small voice in my head tells me to be afraid of that look, to fear that he's about to do the worst. But the louder voice, the one that pushed me to fight back and that's screaming at me now, tells me to relax and take the win. I'm sure I'll get some kind of punishment later, but for right now I've won. That thought comforts me, even if it's only for a fleeting moment.

Ms. Jacobs takes the lack of talk back from Asher and Maddox as the signal that she can continue on with her lesson. The rest of the class returns to their earlier silence and no one says a word as we all silently listen to Ms. Jacobs.

Or rather, like me, we all ignore her and let our minds disappear into our heads.

TWELVE
Asher

I tried. I really fucking tried.

Okay, well, I didn't try *that* hard. But still. I gave myself the weekend to think about it. To think about how I should probably try to be nicer to her, or whatever. But after seeing Rowan bright and cheery on a Monday morning at school, after I spent the entire weekend with constant thoughts about her in my head, everything just became too much. She was getting too comfortable and I was becoming too *un*comfortable. I had do something.

And you know what, so fucking what? It's not like she's innocent either. Somehow, she's managed to weasel her way into my thoughts and take over my entire brain, clouding it so much I can't tell up from down or right from left. It's fucking crazy the shit she's doing to me. Maybe she deserves a little teasing here and there. And seeing how she fought back yesterday, I definitely can't let up now.

I can't believe on Friday, when I saw her in the school

parking lot, I actually thought I was starting to *like* Rowan. Jesus, was I fucking wrong. She's an entitled bitch and she proved it yesterday morning in Ms. Jacobs' class.

I thought maybe I could let it go, but after she showed her true colors with her attitude, I gave myself time to mull it over and I decided she was going to pay. I mean, she had to, right? I can't just let it go.

She may have won the battle yesterday, but this is war now and it's only the fucking beginning. Rowan is in for a rude awakening this week when she realizes my silence after her talkback yesterday was only because I was preparing my battle plans.

Game on, Rowan. I'm about to become your worst fucking nightmare.

I gave her a break this morning in first period because I wanted her to get comfortable, feel secure and safe. That way, she would be even more caught off guard when I came at her.

Now, I'm watching Rowan eat her lunch. Or rather, push her salad around in her bowl to make it look like she's eating. A pang of concern hits me in my chest, but I immediately push it down, far enough away that it's not even a tangible thought in my mind anymore.

Those are the kind of things that could distract me, and I need all the focus I can get right now. Maddox already knows the plan, but he didn't seem as eager to carry it out as I thought he would be. I figured after Rowan's verbal assault yesterday, he would want revenge. But when I shared with him my plans, he seemed hesitant.

Oh, well. This plan is happening whether Maddox is on board or not. And he wouldn't dare go against me or not back me up. Especially when it comes to Rowan.

Just as I see Rowan burst out in laughter, I know it's my time to strike. When she's most comfortable, she's also the most *vulnerable*, and then my actions will have maximum effect. I give Maddox a nod and he knows it's go time. He gets up and disappears into the back of the cafeteria where the lunch ladies prepare the food.

A couple of my guys—Aaron and Michael—see the signal and they walk over to the cafeteria doors. It's the only way in or out of the room, so they block it to make sure no one can leave. More specifically, so Rowan can't leave.

No one notices what's happening until I blare my blow horn right behind Rowan's head. She jumps out of her seat and turns to find the source of the noise, making eye contact with me.

The look of horror on her face is priceless and it's almost sweet enough of a reward that I'm not even sure I need the rest of my plan to happen.

But the anticipation and adrenaline are flowing through my veins, willing me on and confirming that I need to see it through.

Maddox comes up to my side and he gives me a firm nod, letting me know everything is in place. I can see the reservations on his face, but he doesn't verbalize any. Smart guy.

Rowan releases a strong huff and grabs her backpack, storming to the door to get away from me. Exactly as I predicted. Perfect.

Aaron and Michael hold their post and I watch with amusement as Rowan tries to get them to move out of the way. She tries everything—from asking them politely to move, to physically trying to shove them out the way.

Unfortunately for her, these are two of the biggest guys at our school, in both weight and height, and they are absolute units. There's no way her thin, 5'8, muscle-less frame will be able to even slightly budge these guys.

She stomps her foot and her arms fall by her sides, her hands balled up in tight fists. She's at the end of her rope. Good.

"Oh, Rowan. Haven't you learned by now?" I yell over to her across the cafeteria, everyone around us falling completely quiet to watch the event. "I *own* this school. Everything you do, from sitting at a certain desk in your classes to walking down the halls, is approved by *me*. If you try to do something I don't like, guess what? It's not going to happen because *everyone* here listens to me. All the kids, the staff, the teachers. Everyone."

I let my words sink into her head as I stand back, watching her triumphantly. From all the way over here, I can see the heated humiliation on Rowan's skin and the silent anger in the way her body tenses.

As I walk closer to her, I notice her angry emerald eyes turn to a shade darker than forest green. I've never seen so much fury in her eyes, nor have I felt such a boiling hot gaze on my skin come from her before.

This doesn't discourage me, though. I'm only just getting started.

"You have absolutely no power here, Rowan." I say to her and only her. "And I'm going to show you just how little you matter here," I add, ready for the next phase to begin.

But as I take a step closer, I see something in Rowan that I've never seen before. It's out-right, pure, unrealized terror. She's defeated, and even that's too passive of a word. She is beyond the point of defeat; she's physically trembling in fear.

When I realize the impact my actions are having on her, panic begins to set into my stomach. My hands start to tremble uncontrollably and I feel my lungs starting to constrict in my chest. Everything is turning blurry and dizziness is manifesting in my head. I've never felt this kind of alarm before, but there's a powerful voice in my head that's screaming at me to stop what I'm doing.

I have so much more planned, and the reality that I won't get to do half of it makes me angry. There were so many parts to this plan, so many props and tools. I was ready to completely humiliate her and push her off her self-righteous pedestal.

But the nausea in my stomach is quickly rising up my throat and I know if I continue, I'll puke all over this fucking cafeteria.

My eyes start to glaze over and I search desperately for Maddox as my view goes completely cloudy. I'm able to briefly make out Maddox's body—mostly from his ridiculous bright red sleeveless Ron John's shirt—and I know he gets the message.

I hear loud footsteps slamming into metal and I can only imagine Maddox, in his traditional fashion, is climbing on top of a table. "Alright, everyone. That's all for today's show! Back to your regular scheduled programming," he announces.

I can't bear to look at Rowan right now, and part of me thinks I won't even be able to see her from my blurring vision.

It feels like death is squeezing my heart, gripping my throat, and ready to pull me under to the dark side.

The rest of the day is a blur and, before I know it, I'm back home in my bed, trying to process everything.

What the *fuck* just happened?

THIRTEEN
Asher

So, I had a fucking panic attack yesterday in the cafeteria.

I was tripping so hard, I was sure someone slipped something in my fucking lunch because that was the only explanation I had for why my body was reacting that way right before everything went black.

Immediately after Maddox's announcement, I burst out of the cafeteria doors and bee-lined it for the restroom. Usually, I would check to make sure I was the only one in there, but that thought didn't even cross my mind. I just needed time to catch my fucking breath. Everything happened in flashes and I don't remember everything that happened. All I remember is it felt like I was in there for hours while I tried to calm down.

The next thing I remember is Maddox driving me home, but I was in such a daze that I didn't even realize until he was walking me into my house. My arm was slung over his shoulders and his arm was steadying my body on my stomach as he dropped me on my bed.

At some point last night, my car made it back on my driveway and I can only assume Maddox drove me home in my car, then walked back to school after he dropped me off to retrieve his own. We don't exactly live all that close to the school—in fact, it's pretty fucking far, especially to walk.

And even though it's a fucking hike and a half, he still did it for me of his own volition. And he didn't ask me a single question about what happened at lunch, or after. I've never been more grateful to him, that's for fucking sure.

After Maddox left and I fell asleep for a few hours, I woke up and immediately started looking up what the fuck happened to me. I swear to God, I thought I was having a heart attack.

It felt like there was an iron-grip hold on my heart, squeezing all the blood out and wringing it dry. My mouth was dryer than the Sahara desert and my head was pounding so hard I thought my brain was trying to escape. There was a ringing in my ears and I couldn't see for shit. I genuinely thought I would pass out.

But, after consulting a very reliable source—WebMD, of course—it appears it was a panic attack. The main reason is because I'm the picture of perfect health, so heart attack doesn't make sense, and there was an obvious trigger: Rowan's reaction while I was terrorizing her.

What a twisted way for the universe to fuck with me. I give Rowan a panic attack, so it gives me one when I continue to mess with her.

Although, I guess the universe did a good job because now I feel even worse about everything I've done to Rowan. It was like a wake-up call—although, more along the lines of the cops busting down my door at 3a.m. and dragging me out of my house naked.

Everything I've done to Rowan has probably, in one form or another, manifested into a panic attack for her. Which means, nearly every day, I induce this type of panic-anxiety in her. And she just has to breathe through it, wait for it pass, and then go on as if everything is normal.

I couldn't even handle the pressure and shaking and panic for five seconds before Maddox had to intervene. What kind of guy does that make me?

At the very least, it makes me a piece of fucking shit.

Guilt—a *very* familiar feeling to me these days—resurfaces and I'm left having to figure out what to do. I've been playing this ping pong, back-and-forth game in my mind for the past few weeks, trying to figure out how to go about this.

Part of me hates that I care enough about Rowan to feel sorry for her and want to stop the teasing. That's the part that tells me to continue the teasing like nothing's changed because I shouldn't be feeling this way about Rowan. It's also the part of me that hates that somehow I've gotten kind of attached to her.

But the other part of me is screaming at myself to get my head out of ass and make amends. This part, that's the one that reminds me most of the boy from sophomore year. The boy I once was. He's still inside me somewhere, albeit very deep down and nearly completely hidden in my psyche. But he's there, and he's been screaming at me for a year and half to end this bullshit.

The constant battle in my head is leaving me in a permanent state of whiplash and I just don't know what to do. I don't know where to go from here, and the idea of falling further down, below the rock bottom I'm already at, is horrifying.

I never thought it could get worse than it was before, and yet here I am.

It's one thing to own the asshole that you are and not give a second thought to other people's feelings as you terrorize them. It's another to realize that you don't have to act this way—you *shouldn't* act this way—and to start struggling with your own moral compass.

I don't know which is worse. Acknowledging your asshole-ness and accepting it, or continuing to act like an asshole but hate yourself for it.

Goddamn it, I hate my life. And the absolute worst part of this whole fucking thing is I'm the reason I'm in this position. Maybe the circumstances that got me here were out of my hands, but it's my fault I've fallen so far from grace and continued to stay down here in hell instead of digging my way out. I can't use my family issues and past trauma as an excuse, not when I've let them affect me this much. I'm not the only person who has issues, so I shouldn't use it to justify my actions. And yet, that's exactly what I've been doing the past two years.

All these thoughts have circulated on a loop in my mind for a while now, and it's starting to feel like a tornado in my head. After yesterday, it's only gotten worse and I decide that I need the day off today.

I'm still going to school, mainly because I need to see Rowan and make sure she's okay after everything I put her through. But I'm taking the day off from reigning terror. It's the least I can do, after all.

I just need to make sure I hold myself back long enough so I can figure out what the fuck I'm going to do. How the hell I'm going to fix this, if that's even what I want to do.

If I can even fix it at this point, honestly.

FOURTEEN
Rowan

This whole week has been absolutely brutal with Asher's teasing. He's humiliated me, insulted me, and ripped me to shreds. I thought it was bad before, but this week was even worse.

When he trapped me in the cafeteria, I was so petrified that I genuinely thought I would die right there in front of everyone's eyes.

It was more likely than not my insulting and humiliating speech I dished to him and Maddox on Monday that sent him over the edge. But it's like something switched in him and he upped the ante tenfold on everything he was doing.

Like when he trapped me in the cafeteria earlier this week. I was so petrified that I genuinely thought I would die right there in front of everyone's eyes. I think he could see the terror in my eyes because he got Maddox to stop the taunt. But still, it was humiliating. Especially when he went around flexing his power over people and no one stood up to him.

They just let him say that he basically owned them, or whatever.

Another example of Asher's ridiculous power is last night. It was a Thursday, but there was a huge football game so one of the jocks threw a party afterwards at his parent's house. Kennedy and I were hoping to go because we have yet to go to a party this year.

Okay, Kennedy was hoping to go, which meant I was getting dragged there. But when Ken texted a cheerleader, Sydney, about where the party was, Sydney said we weren't invited because Asher put a blacklist ban on us from parties.

That, along with everything else, including the cafeteria incident, enraged me beyond belief. How is it that some alpha leader of a bunch of outcasts has so much power over every single person at this school? It's bad enough he messes with me at school, but now he's telling people at school to not be friends with me and they're listening to him. They're actually letting some guy tell them what to do and how to act.

Kennedy was pissed because we were being singled out for God knows what reason and it was ruining our senior year experience. We didn't end up crashing the party last night, even though it would have made Kennedy really happy. We decided instead to go catch a movie, like we were supposed to do on my birthday.

But I was still pissed. Even now, sitting in first period at the end of the week, everything's piling up and I'm so beyond angry right now. And I know Kennedy is, too. We're fed up and we've had enough.

"Party starts at eight, my house." Maddox instructs a couple of guys at the back of our first period class. I turn to see Kennedy's reaction and I immediately know I'm not going to like what she's about to do.

She turns in her seat and interrupts the conversation behind us. "Can't wait, Maddox. Thanks for the invite!" She says, sarcastically. She's trying to rile him up and I just know this isn't going to end well.

Maddox gives a condescending pout and I can see him biting back a smirk. "Oh, I'm sorry, did you want to come?" He turns to Asher and flashes him a smile. He's purposely messing with us and he's telling the boss man to *'just wait'* for what's coming.

Kennedy gives him a challenging glare back and says, "Oh well, I assumed since you were talking about it so loudly in the open that the invitation was welcome to everyone. Including all those on your little blacklist." Kennedy bites back. "Or are Rowan and I the only ones banned from parties?"

Maddox's smile falters a little bit and I see Asher's head snap over to Kennedy. They didn't know we knew. Or maybe they forgot about it and are just remembering it now. Either way, it's about time someone called them out.

"Blacklist is a bit harsh, don't you think?" Maddox asks, trying to remain cocky and in control, but he's faltering. "Besides, Kennedy, you're welcome to come to any party you want. It's Rowan who's not," he adds. My eyes go wide and my heart sinks.

I always knew Asher and Maddox just held some ridiculous grudge against me, for what reason I still don't know, but this goes beyond a simple grudge and some teasing. What the fuck did I ever do to them? Why do they ban *me* from parties and no one else? And why did everyone just go along with it? I always knew I was never the most social person, but I guess a lot of people really don't fucking like me for them to simply accept not inviting me to anything.

I can feel the tears in my eyes start to burn, but I try to hold them back. I will *not* cry in front of people again. I look up and see Asher studying me. He shifts awkwardly in his seat and I can tell he's uncomfortable. The only thing I can do right now is take some power back. Show them that I couldn't care less about their stupid parties.

"Like I would want to go to any of your lame parties anyways. I've been to that side of town once before and I don't necessarily want to go back. No offense, Maddox. It's just not the kind of place I would choose to spend my time in, if you know what I mean," I seethe. I'm being mean, but I don't care. Everyone in this fucking school is mean, so why do I have to be the bigger person? I watch Kennedy's reaction and I can see she's stunned that I'm standing up for myself again.

"Well, you're missing out. Everyone's going to be there. It's going to be epic," Maddox continues. He's trying to make me feel envious that the whole school will be there and I won't.

"It doesn't really matter, anyways. I'm busy. Contrary to popular belief, not everyone wants to go to one of your stupid parties. But who knows, maybe I'll make a surprise appearance. We'll see," I taunt. I don't actually have any plans, but I'm not backing down this time. Kennedy shoots me a questioning look, knowing I never have plans on Fridays, or ever, so I just give her a subtle glance to trust me.

Maddox opens his mouth to retort, but Ms. Jacobs interrupts him. She starts her lesson and I turn back in my seat to face the front. After a few seconds, Kennedy leans over to me and whispers, "Do your plans happen to involve crashing a party tonight?" Normally I wouldn't want to be anywhere I'm not welcome, but for the first time in my life, I actually want to go to a party.

I give Kennedy a daring look and I try to push down the panic that's slowly rising in my stomach. She breaks into a wide smile and bumps my shoulder with her own.

This is me finally fighting back. This is me taking some power back. This is me, living my fucking life the way *I* want to.

No person, not Asher and not Maddox, will tell me what to do anymore. I'm in control, no one else. The world is in for quite the ride.

FIFTEEN
Asher

I don't know what has gotten into Rowan, but the girl I saw this morning in first period was not her. I feel like I've been thinking that a lot lately, but this was way different. *She* was way different. She was less apologetic and more daring—even more so than the past few weeks.

Truthfully, everything that made Rowan, Rowan has changed recently.

Last week, she completely changed her face makeup, today she completely changed her personality. What's next? Next week she'll change her hair? I feel like she's changing a bunch of different things to try and see what parts of herself she doesn't like and what parts she wants to keep the same to create a new, different version of herself.

Obviously, she didn't like the different face since this whole week she has had no makeup at all. But the attitude I got from her today? I think that will be staying for a while. The first time she ever showed me that kind of bite, she was immediately remorseful. I could see it on her face, and it became even more clear when she apologized after. She couldn't handle getting down and dirty with the devil. But today, she insulted our neighborhood again and showed absolutely no regret. In fact, she got even more confident; she was even pleased with her attitude.

Rowan's getting bolder and stronger, while I'm over here getting weaker. I can barely even be in the same room as her without my mind wandering to a thousand different places it doesn't belong. Like the smell of her new perfume this morning. Or the way she styled her silky blonde hair this morning. Or her long tan legs—Stop! Stop, I need to stop.

This is what I mean. This morning she was talking about that stupid party ban I put on her and all I could think about was her green eyes looking at me with an intense, serious glare. I wanted so badly to take the anger out of her eyes.

But as I listened to her words, I realized she had good reason to be angry. That blacklist, or whatever she called it, was really fucking childish. I just didn't want to risk running into her at a party and take away any fun I could possibly have had. But who the fuck was I to stop her from going to parties?

Although, considering she only found out about it now, when I did it a few weeks ago already, means she probably didn't even entertain the idea of going to one anyway until now. But still, what a petty thing for me to do. I can recognize that.

I just hope and pray she doesn't decide to come to Maddox's party tonight. Her comment earlier that she might check it out seemed like a pretty empty threat to me, but you never know. This new Rowan is becoming very unpredictable and she might just show up out of spite. I just don't think I can handle being at the same party as her tonight.

I seriously need to distance myself and get my head out of my ass so I can shake this… well whatever this is. Obsession? Intrigue? Curiosity. Yeah, we'll go with that.

"Dude, don't spill on the couch!" Maddox yells at some guy from school. Tim, I think his name is? Brady? Mark? Whatever-his-name-is has a red solo cup filled to the rim with beer from the keg, but he's already so far gone that he can't even stand in one place without swaying back and forth. Every time his body goes one way, his drink follows and beer spills over the edge. Maddox is trying to get him outside so he at least spills in the backyard, but he's not succeeding.

Someone behind what's-his-name explodes in triumph as he wins a game of beer pong, shoving what's-his-name a little. Normally, a sober person would easily recover, but what's-his-name is so drunk that he completely topples over the back of the couch and lands on the cushion, spilling all the contents of his cup along the way. I'm sitting on a two-person love seat across the living room, but I feel a very light, faint sprinkle of liquid shoot out on my arm. The couch gets hit the hardest and the normally-light brown color of the cushion is instantly turned a very dark brown, almost black.

"Chad!" Oh, that's his name. "What the fuck, man?" Maddox yells so loud everyone turns and watches the commotion. "Get the fuck out before I kick your ass!" Maddox threatens, grabbing Chad by his collar and ripping him off the couch. Maddox hands him off to another guy, who throws Chad out the door.

"Un-fucking-believable," Maddox sighs, taking a seat

beside me. "I have one fucking rule: don't spill on the furniture. What does that fucker do? Gets so plastered that he spills his entire goddamn drink all over my mom's favorite couch!" He seethes, growing even more pissed than he already is. "How would I even clean that? Fuck, I'm getting murdered." He continues, clearly exasperated.

"Just let it dry up and leave it. I'm sure she won't notice," I offer.

Maddox has had this couch since I met him and it always had stains on it. He told me it was a second-hand couch because that was all they could afford at the time, but that his mom loved it anyways because it was the first piece of furniture she ever bought herself. Both his parents are almost never here anyways, and when they are they're in their bed, so I doubt they'll even notice during the few minutes they're actually in the living room. "If she notices, just convince her it's been there for a while and you don't know how it got there. She'll be none the wiser."

"Yeah, you're right. She probably won't even say anything 'cuz she won't even notice. That would involve her actually spending time in this house." Maddox concludes, relaxing back into the couch.

"Where are your parents tonight, anyways? How did you get the place to yourself all night?" I ask, realizing we've never had a night to ourselves in his house because his parents are always home after work, even though they're usually in their room.

Maddox chuckles to himself silently, trying to bite back the smirk on his face. "She's visiting my aunt in Georgia for the weekend while my dad's on a 'business trip.'" He says, using quotation marks around business trip. He's unable to hold back his laughter and I don't really see how this is so funny.

"Little does my mom know," he continues, "I know she hasn't spoken to my aunt since I was eight and they had a blow-out fight over my mom's state of her life. You know, considering she's an absentee parent, has a side piece, and is a workaholic. My mom's probably staying the night with her secret boyfriend, that she also doesn't know I know about, while my dad is with his mistress." I'm not sure why Maddox is laughing as hard as he is, but it must be an ironic situation for him that I'm just not understanding.

Just as I'm about to respond, my eyes are immediately pulled to the front door. Two girls walk in, one with shoulder-length straight hair and wearing a sparkling loose blue dress. But it's not her that gets my attention. It's the other girl. She has long blonde wavy hair that falls down her back and she's wearing a short, tight red dress that cups her ass perfectly.

I close my mouth, so as not to physically drool, but it's all I can do to stop the sensation I'm feeling deep in my stomach. This girl is hot and she fucking knows it. Her face is turned away from me the whole time since she walked in, so I can't get a good look at her face, but I don't have to see it to know I'm going after her tonight.

"You see it too, huh?" Maddox asks me, staring over at the two girls. Their backs are to us right now, but I'm sure they know every guy at this party is staring at them, trying to figure out ways to pursue them tonight.

Just as I'm about to get to my feet and go talk to the girl in red, my eyes nearly bug out of my head and my heart stops beating. The girl turns her head toward me, looking at someone in my direction, and I see who she is.

I need to breathe. Figure out how to breathe. Inhale, exhale. One breath, two, three. I think I'm having a heart attack.

I'm trying to remember how to fucking breathe, unable to take my eyes off her, as her eyes slowly find mine and hold my gaze. We're looking in each other's eyes, neither of us willing to look away. Or, in my case, physically unable to look away.

"Holy shit," Maddox mumbles under his breath. He's watching me, trying to make sense of my reaction. He sees me staring at Rowan, and her staring back. His eyes are going back and forth between Rowan and I.

"Who knew Rowan had that kind of body underneath all those proper school girl clothes?" It takes all I possibly have to not punch Maddox's teeth in right now.

After what feels like eternity, Rowan snaps her head back and continues back to her conversation with a few other guys and the other girl, who I assume now is Kennedy. My heart rate is still beating sporadically and I can't seem to catch my breath. If I don't figure out how to breathe properly, I'm pretty sure my heart is going to pound so hard it'll fall out of my chest and roll over to Rowan.

One thing. I needed *one thing* from Rowan. To stay the fucking hell *away* from me. And not only did she come to this party when Maddox all-but told her not to, but she came dressed like *that*. Unbelievable.

Maddox snaps his fingers in front of my face and I realize I'm still staring at Rowan. I snap my head over to Maddox and I glare at him, pissed beyond belief. I'm not really mad at him, more so at the situation. There's no way I can stay here while she's here.

"You okay?" He asks, a very confused and almost concerned look on his face.

I clear my throat and try to get some of my composure back. "I'm fine. I just don't know why she thought she could waltz into your house and join the party." I say, spitting out a complete lie to try and cover my true feelings right now.

"We both know that's not what you're thinking right now," Maddox mumbles under his breath. He leans back in the chair and a small smirk plays on his lips. I raise my eyebrow at him, warning him to stop whatever it is he's thinking. I just hope he didn't see and understand what just happened to me when I realized Rowan was the girl in red.

"Look, man. You're my best friend and I'll always be honest with you. I've never seen you have *that* kind of reaction over a girl, ever. That's all I'm saying," he shrugs.

"Whatever you're fucking insinuating, stop thinking it. Rowan pisses me off and I'm just annoyed she had the balls to show up here. Someone needs to put her in her damn place, that's all *I'm* saying." I spit out. Maddox studies me for a minute and then stands up, shaking his head. He disappears into the party and I'm left here, watching Rowan's every move.

She's still with the same group of people, but they're all dancing to the music now. As I watch her dance and shake her ass in that way-too-tight, way-too-short red dress, I can't help but wonder more about her. Seeing her tonight has, once again, completely changed the way I once saw her. She seems happier, more carefree right now than I've ever seen her before. She actually seems like she's having a good time.

I thought she was changing herself to become a different

Rowan, but maybe she's not actually changing herself. Maybe she's finally becoming who she always was, deep down. I never bothered getting to know the real Rowan, so maybe this is her finally letting her true self shine through.

A small smile plays on my lips at that thought, but it immediately vanishes when I see a guy push himself up against her backside and grab her hips. She whips her head around, hesitating a little at the contact. I watch as she tries to pull away a little, but the guy just pulls her back to him. I look at her face and an anger boils inside my chest.

She's uncomfortable, but she's too nice to tell that guy to fuck off. She only gets feisty with me, it seems.

My fists tighten so hard my knuckles turn white and I want nothing more than to knock that guy out. But my brain tells me not to. I would cause a scene and Rowan and I aren't even friends. People would get suspicious. I'm supposed to make her life hell, not save her. Besides, she's a big girl, she can take of herself.

Just as I decide to leave it alone, the guy spins her around to face him and slings his hands to completely grab her ass behind her.

That's it, that's the fucking line. I storm out of my seat and dart over to the interaction. A gasp escapes Rowan's lips when I suddenly appear right beside her.

"Little close, aren't you?" I glare at the guy, shoving myself between Rowan and him. Rowan stumbles behind me and gets out of the way, so she can see the interaction. I'm a little taller than the guy, so I try to use my height to my advantage and tower over him as much as I can. Instead of intimidating the guy though, his face breaks into a big smile.

"Asher! What's up, man?" He asks, and I realize he knows me. I have no fucking clue who this guy is, but somehow he knows me. I use this as my out, so no one thinks my actions are suspicious. I back up a little bit and give him a nod of acknowledgment.

"Hey man," I brush him off. I grab Rowan's elbow and pull her down the hallway to a little corner near the door. There's a few people around, but they're not paying attention to us in the least.

"*What* are you doing?" She demands, ripping her arm away from me. There's an anger in her face and her emerald green eyes turn a slightly darker shade. Either because she's pissed at me or because she's had a little bit too much to drink. Probably both.

"What happened to your big plans?" I ask in a teasing voice. I want to make her think I'm teasing her and not at all freaking out internally, even though that's exactly what's happening. I don't need her to know whatever the fuck is going on inside my body and mind right now.

"I told you I might make an appearance. You can't ban me from parties, Asher. Don't be childish," she huffs, crossing her arms over her chest. When she does this, her boobs push together and I get a perfect view of her cleavage. I have to physically restrain myself from looking down at her chest, hoping she doesn't see the conflict on my face.

"Why don't you go home? No one wants you here," I spit out at her through clenched teeth. I'm being incredibly rude to her again, but I don't think I can stay much longer at this party if she's going to stay here, especially dressed like that.

"Get over yourself Asher. For the love of God, leave me

alone and let me enjoy one night without your disgusting treatment of me." That sentence sends my heart plummeting to my feet. I do treat her disgustingly and she has every right to be pissed. She doesn't deserve the way I tease her all the time. I just *need* her to leave this party.

Before I can spit something back at her, she turns around and stomps away. I consider going after her, but the guilt I feel for treating her like shit overpowers. Instead, I cower back to my seat on the couch and sip my beer.

I try to focus on something else, anything else. But my eyes keep getting pulled back to Rowan. Her, in all her glory, dancing, talking, laughing, enjoying herself. I've never seen her have fun and it's a nice sight to see.

A small smile breaks on my face as I watch her laugh at something Kennedy said. My heart in my chest finally slows down and my breathing returns to its usual rhythm. I finally breathe a sigh of relief, but the feeling doesn't last long.

"Swim" by Chase Atlantic erupts in the speakers and I watch as Kennedy pulls Rowan to an open space so they can dance to the song. Rowan's had much more to drink now and I can tell she's gotten way more relaxed. The guy from earlier returns to her backside, but this time she doesn't flinch away from his presence or his touch.

I watch Rowan flip her hair over her shoulder and grind her ass against that guy, biting her lip and getting more comfortable in her movements. Earlier, anger was boiling in my chest at that guy for getting close to Rowan when she didn't want his touch. But now, I can feel the fury rising in my throat at the fact that he thinks he can come back and get some, even if Rowan doesn't seem to mind his presence this time.

I've honestly never wanted to punch a guy so hard in my life. He better get the fuck away from her before I permanently destroy his face. He doesn't deserve to be dancing with her or have her ass grinding on him. The only guy she should be grinding on is me.

Wait. No, I didn't mean that. I don't want her grinding on me. I don't like her like that. In fact, even the thought of that repulses me.

But, as I watch Rowan turn around and rub her ass up and down his legs, jealousy brews inside me. I've never wanted to be another guy so badly in my life.

Oh, *shit*. Shit, shit, shit! No, I can't like her. She's Rowan. No way. But the more I watch her, the more I realize. I do. I like her. I *like* her. And not just as a friend.

Fuck.

SIXTEEN
Asher

"Fuck," I mumble.

I storm off the couch and through the back door into the backyard. There are quite a few people lingering around and they all stare at me as I heavily breathe in and out, trying to get control of myself.

Everything feels wrong, up is down, left is right, and I like Rowan. I'm attracted to her. And the more I think about it, the more I remember I always was. From the first time I saw her. I just tried to suppress it.

I always thought Rowan's ability to make me so mad was because she was so much like the junior high girls. But I realize now that she's absolutely nothing like them. When she would react back to the shitty things I was doing to her, she was just in fight or flight mode. She wasn't doing it unprompted and out of spite; she was doing to me what I was doing to her.

And as much as I hate to admit it, I think she got under my skin because I liked her and I couldn't have her, I was just not in a place where I would ever be good for her. That first day I saw Rowan, I was pulled to her and I wanted to have her. But back then, I was going through so much and just trying to process what the fuck my life had become. I couldn't be with her.

Besides, I didn't want to be attracted to anyone or come to be dependent on them. I wanted to be the lone wolf, so I looked for any excuse to dislike her. I took Maddox's word about her stuck-up attitude and saw what I wanted to see: that she was a bitch.

But deep down, I knew I couldn't have her. Not back then, or ever. I wanted to be with her so bad and I knew I wasn't good for her. So, I began to resent her. But tonight, I finally got some clarity. Or rather, I got my head out of my ass. Just watching Rowan with another guy snapped me back to reality, a reality where I like Rowan Lila Easton and I'll do whatever it takes to have her.

The slap in the face that I needed for two years finally came and, with that, it opened the floodgates of overwhelming, confusing, and twisted feelings. I can't believe I've been the biggest fucking asshole on the planet to Rowan, all because I didn't want to feel those feelings and I preferred to ignore them. What kind of dick acts like that? Me, that's who. And now I have to figure out what the fuck I'm going to do.

I look around and realize I'm still standing in the backyard outside, but luckily most of the people here have stopped paying attention to me. I need to think. How do I even begin to fix things? Do I tell her how I feel? No, there's no way in hell she feels the same. In fact, she probably hates me, and I wouldn't blame her. I guess I should start with apologizing.

That's probably step number one in a long list of fixing my shit.

Deciding I should at least try to talk to Rowan, I turn back toward the house. I get to the back door and look through the screen door to find her. My eyes scan the crowd of people and finally settle on Kennedy in the back of the kitchen. I guess I could start there.

I walk up to Kennedy and tap her on the shoulder. She turns to face me and, within a matter of seconds, her face goes from a big smile to an angry look. "What do *you* want?" She asks, disgust evident in her voice. I put my hand on her upper arm and guide her to a quiet corner away from people.

Clearing my throat, I try to find the words. "I want to apologize. For what I put you and Rowan through." I say, simply. "Especially, Rowan." I add, hoping she sees I'm being sincere. She looks at me very skeptically and squints her eyes at me.

"Why?" She asks, confused, but I just stare at her. I don't want her to know how I feel, but I need her to accept my apology.

"Look, tonight, I just realized how much of a dick I've been. I'm sorry," I offer again. I stand there, waiting for her to say something. I shove my hands in the pockets of my jeans and quietly rock back and forth on my heels.

I know it's strange for me to apologize. After all, I've always been a stupid dick. But, this realization tonight hit me harder than I'll ever care to admit. Rowan has never deserved the way I treated her. And, knowing my brother would be disappointed in the guy I've become, it's just too much. The urgency I feel right now to fix everything hits me hard and I need to do this.

After what feels like forever, Kennedy finally speaks again. "You have a crush on Rowan, don't you?" She whispers, eyeing me carefully. My face immediately goes beet red and I choke on my words. How the hell could she tell by me just apologizing? I swear to God, girls know everything.

"Look—I don't—I haven't—" I stammer, trying to find the words. Frustrated, I look down at my feet and bring my voice to a low tone. "I'm not sure. I just know I don't *not* like her. I have a lot of shit to figure out, but I thought I should start with apologizing."

Kennedy considers my words for several long seconds, before releasing a small sigh. "Look, Asher. I won't say what you did was okay because it wasn't. It was wrong and *so* mean. I get you probably have a lot of issues, just like anyone, but it doesn't mean you can go around picking on girls just because you like them and don't want to admit it to yourself."

Kennedy purses her lips, as if deciding if she wants to continue or not. I can see she's torn, which is rare considering she always speaks her mind, even when most people would hold their tongues.

She's absolutely right, though. And I feel like shit about it. "You're right. I know that. But I can't go back and change it. All I can do is apologize and try to change," I reply. I watch her reaction closely and it seems like she's coming to terms with it. She nods her head just the slightest amount and I know we've come to a common ground.

"But if you ever hurt Rowan again, even just a little bit, I *will* kill you. Don't think I won't." She threatens and I completely believe her. Kennedy is one badass girl and I don't doubt for a minute that she would kill someone for her best friend. I offer Kennedy a tight smile and turn around to go find Rowan.

My eyes scan the party once more, but all I see is a bunch of tall guys. Rowan's tall enough, standing at 5'8, but all the guys in here are six feet or taller and they would easily be able to hide her. I decide to take a seat back in my spot on the couch and continue looking for her. You would think she'd be easy to spot in her little red dress, but no such luck.

I start to get exasperated because I want to get this conversation over with. I'm not expecting her to like me back or anything, and I'm not even sure I'll tell her that I have these feelings, but I at least want to apologize. I want things to change, even if we only become civil with each other. I can ignore my feelings for her if I need to, hell I've done it for long enough, but I can't go on knowing she can't stand me for what I did to her.

Well, ignoring my feelings for her just got a hell of a lot harder. My eyes finally find Rowan and I immediately hate what I see. She has her arms around that guy's neck and they're swaying together to the music. I can't help but feel jealousy and anger in my chest. Knowing he gets to touch her like that, while I have to sit here and watch, it's agonizing.

As I continue to watch them, her eyes look over the guy's shoulder and they catch mine. As we continue to hold eye contact, her smile quickly fades and it's replaced by a confused, angry look. There's a small frown on her lips and her eyebrows crease together. She can tell I'm not happy and she probably think it's because I don't want her at this party, dancing and enjoying herself. She's partially right. I don't want her dancing with that guy, but I do want her here so I can talk to her.

Right when I think Rowan's going to look away and go back to dancing, I see something snap in her. She rips her arms away from the guy and she marches over to me. My breath catches in my throat and my heart starts beating rapidly out of control.

She wants to confront me. She thinks I'm being a dick again. She wants to talk right now, right *here*, in front of all these people. This is the worst possible thing that could be happening right now.

"What the hell is your problem?" She yells, coming up right in front of me on the couch. She's standing between my legs and I have to shift my body to hide my evident hard-on. She lets out an exasperated sigh and crosses her arms in front of her chest. Thankfully, I don't think she notices how turned on I am right now. But, she's clearly pissed.

Trying to play it cool, I crack my face into a relaxed smile. "I don't have a problem." I let out, hoping she can't hear the tension in my voice and the way my heart is demanding to be let out of my chest. I'm so nervous right now, if I had a heart monitor connected to my body, it would break.

Rowan scoffs and steps an inch closer to me. She's so close, she could practically be sitting in my lap, not that I would mind. My heart probably would, though, because it would send me into full blown cardiac arrest. I try to swallow the nerves as I look up at her, hoping she'll just walk away.

Before I even realize what's happening, she's leaning forward and hauling me off the couch by grabbing both my arms. I start to panic when I realize I'm being dragged up the stairs and shoved into Maddox's room.

Rowan slams the door behind us and pushes me further into the room and farther away from her. She stands all tough and mighty with her arms crossed and looking scarily angry. I've never seen her this mad before. It's kind of hot. And also absolutely terrifying.

To ease the tension and nerves I'm feeling in my stomach, and the burning sensation in my pants, I do the first thing that comes to mind. I tease her. "Woah, careful now. People will think we're fucking in here. Wouldn't want people to talk about you behind your back now." It's probably not the best way to go about this, especially if I want her to forgive me, but she caught me off guard and honestly I'm nearly shitting my pants right now.

"Cut the bullshit, Asher. I brought you here so you can finally be honest and let go of your fake alpha tough guy facade, now that we're away from curious eavesdropping ears. So, explain." She demands, an icy expression taking over her face.

"Explain what?" I croak out, aware at how weak I sound.

"What I ever did to make you hate me!" She yells and sadness immediately washes over me and replaces some of the nerves. I know I teased her and messed with her, but I never hated her. Not once. And yet, all this time she thought I did. She thought *she* did something to make me hate her.

"I never hated you," I whisper, unable to bring my voice any higher. I can feel the thickness growing in my throat and the guilt settling in my chest. Guilt is a feeling I am extremely familiar with these days and I hate that I'm feeling it now. But it's because of my own actions that I am, so I can't really blame Rowan for that.

That's the funny thing with guilt and blame. People blame others for their situations, causing those other people to feel guilty. So they then blame other people for their guilt. However, in this circumstance, I'm not blaming anyone other than myself for my guilt. It's my own fault. No one else's. Mine.

Rowan hesitates, looking at her feet and wringing her hands. She finally looks up and makes eye contact with me. "Then why do you treat me like this? Like I'm the trash beneath your shoe?" She asks, her voice barely above a whisper. I watch as tears prick the corners of her eyes. She doesn't let them fall though. That's my girl. Tough and standing her ground.

"I'm sorry, Rowan. I really am. I shouldn't have been so mean to you." I apologize, hoping she'll see the sincerity in my expression. She looks shocked, but her eyes stay on mine for a minute and she studies me. Then, as if she decided I'm lying, she shakes her head.

"You're not sorry. If you were, you wouldn't have been throwing daggers at me with your eyes earlier tonight. And then again, five minutes ago."

"What?" I say, taken aback. I didn't realize she noticed I was watching her all night. Shit, she's more perceptive than I thought. Although, she's wrong. I wasn't throwing eye daggers at her, I was fighting with myself about my feelings for her. If anything, I was trying to figure out whatever the hell is going on with me.

"Oh my God, what is *wrong* with you?" She asks, completely exasperated. "All I ever did was try to be nice to you. But you've held a grudge against me and made it your mission to hurt me." She confesses, wiping away the tears on her cheeks that have slipped. "God, I hate you," she mumbles.

That last sentence completely sends me over the edge. I can't hold myself back anymore. Just knowing she hates me completely shatters whatever piece of a soul I have left.

"Don't say that," I plead. I take a step toward her and her eyes shoot up to meet mine. "Please don't say you hate me."

"Why? It's not like you don't deserve it. You've made my life a living hell, Asher!" She yells, standing her ground.

"I know I have, I know. And you didn't—you *don't* deserve it." I whisper, stepping even closer to her. Our bodies are so close now that our chests are nearly touching. She's so close to me, I could reach out and pull her to me.

"That boy from sophomore year, what happened to him? He looked so sad, but he was at least nice. He never would have treated me like this. What happened to him?" I'm stunned at her words. She noticed me back then? I nearly punch myself for letting myself get to this point. I miss that boy, too.

I take a deep breath and try to stop myself from doing what I've wanted to do since I first laid my eyes on her. But there's no more control anymore. I reach forward and grab her cheeks, pulling her face to me and crashing my lips on hers.

I kiss her like I've never kissed anyone before. I kiss her to apologize for every shitty, fucked up thing I've done to her. I kiss her to show her that I'm still that boy deep down. And I kiss her for that boy, who just needed someone to be there for him, but couldn't handle depending on someone again.

And she kisses me back.

I pry my mouth from hers for one second to look in her

eyes and make sure she wants this. And all I see reflecting in those beautiful eyes is a small shimmer that wasn't there before. That's all I need to see to know she feels it too.

I pull her back to me and back us up to the wall. My hands travel down her body in her skin-tight dress and feel every curve of her. She frantically grabs my shirt and pulls it over my head, using her fingers to slide down and feel every curve of my abs. I smile against her mouth and grab the back of her thighs to hoist her up in the air. She immediately wraps her legs tightly around my waist and I carry us to the bed, never separating our lips.

Placing her on her back on the bed, I feel her squirming underneath me to get her arms out of her dress and take off her bra. I help her free her arms and my hands continue down her body to pull her dress up. Once her dress is off, I work on her bra and toss it somewhere in the room, beside her discarded dress. I take a peak down and I groan, seeing her perfect boobs right in front of my face. I move my face to suck on her nipple and she moans at the contact.

I return my mouth to hers and I use one hand to massage one of her boobs, while my other hand travels back down to her lace thong. I grab the string on her hip and rip the underwear clean off of her as I hear her gasp in my mouth. Tossing it to the side, I bring my hand down to her center and start massaging her clit. I feel her whimper at my sudden contact and I swallow her moan in my mouth.

This is everything I've ever needed and more. I can't get enough. Separating our mouths, I start heading south, kissing and nibbling my way down her chest, boobs, stomach, and right above her sweet spot. Preparing myself, I line up my mouth with her clit and look up to her. Her head is settled back into the bed, but her hands find my head and she tangles her fingers in my hair.

Taking that as all the confirmation I need, I connect my mouth with her clit and slip one of my fingers in her entrance. She gasps and squeezes her thighs with my head buried between, showing me she's enjoying this just as much as I am.

She squirms a little bit and then starts to slowly grind her hips against my face as her pleasure starts to take over, and I have to place my other hand on her stomach to settle her. I continue sucking on her clit and I slip in another finger. I continue pumping my fingers into her, taking pleasure in every second of this. I never thought I would be in this position with her and it's easily the best sex I've ever had. And I'm technically not even having sex with her.

I feel her thighs start to tighten around me just as she starts to reach her climax and I revel in every moment of this. "Asher," she moans and I can't help the feeling that comes over me. Watching her come and hearing her moan my name almost sends *me* over the edge. Fuck, she's so hot.

I briefly pull my mouth away from her center to watch her come undone while I continue pumping my fingers into her. "Quiet, baby. This isn't the place you want to be screaming my name," I warn. I watch a small smile play on her face and her eyes squeeze shut as she throws her head back and her legs start to shake. Knowing she's coming, I put my mouth back on her clit and help her ride this high for as long as possible.

Once she finishes, I crawl my way back up to her mouth, kissing her skin on my way up, and I connect my lips to hers again. This kiss is more slow; we're both taking it in. I pull away the slightest bit so I can look at her, and I smile. "Did you think your night would turn out like this when you decided to come to the party?" I ask, partly astonished and partly euphoric. But something changes in her expression.

Rowan's eyes harden and she starts to crawl out from underneath me. She stands up and grabs her dress from the door, putting it back on. I turn my body and swing my legs over the edge into a sitting position at the side of the bed. "What?" I ask, confused at her sudden change in demeanor.

She stops and places her hands on her hips. "I can't find my, um… my underwear." I nearly burst out laughing because I guess she doesn't remember I completely ripped it off. I hold in my laughter though, as I spot the ruined material and pick it up with my pointer finger.

"Here. Doubt you'll want to wear it though. It's a little… damaged." I smirk, seeing the humor in the situation. Rowan doesn't think it's funny, though. She snatches her thong from my finger and scowls at me. She stomps over to the door and picks up her clutch that fell off her shoulder at some point. Probably when I crashed my mouth to hers.

Rowan opens her clutch and throws the underwear in there as she turns to the door. She stops for a minute and turns back to face me. "Forget this ever happened." She demands, and I'm a bit struck. Shame and confusion start to mix in my mind because I thought she wanted this just as much as I did.

This is why I pushed her away so long ago. So I wouldn't have to feel this. Rejection and regret.

I contemplate what to say and decide to be the better version of myself, the one I told Kennedy I would try to be. So, instead of saying something mean, I decide to go for sarcastic. "No can do, darling. This memory will be replaying in my head for a *long* time. The way my tongue—"

But before I can continue, Rowan freaks out. "No! I don't want to hear this," she yells and storms out of the room.

I guess she didn't find it funny. Oops. Shit, now I have to fix this, too.

Well, at least I know I definitely like her. There's no way I can forget this night or let her go now. Not a chance.

And that new personality of hers that she debuted tonight? It better be staying because it fits her so well.

SEVENTEEN
Rowan

Holy shit. FUCK.

Asher fucking Madigan just went down on me.

We almost had sex.

He doesn't hate me.

Jesus Christ.

My mind is going a million miles a minute, I can't keep up. Not that I want to right now. There's too many thoughts flying through my head, including ones I don't want to think about. Ever.

I just stormed out of the party because there's too much going on in my head right now and I need some air. The cool breeze hits my cheeks the second I step outside and it's like a shock against my hot skin. Taking a deep breath, I inhale the sharp air and let it fill my lungs completely, only exhaling when the haze in my mind starts to clear and the alcohol loses its grip on my thoughts.

Because my mind being clouded and me being intoxicated

is the only explanation I have for why I would ever let what just happened, happen.

I start walking home because Kennedy's mom dropped us off and I'm freaking out way too much to talk to Kennedy and have her ask all these questions. Plus, there are no buses in this area and an Uber is too sketchy late at night as a young woman. So walking home it is.

I'm still quite tipsy, but surprisingly much more sober than I thought I was and I'm not stumbling over my feet like I should be. Still, I need to focus on putting one foot in front of the other and not falling off the sidewalk.

What the hell was I thinking? Asher has made my life hell for the past two years. He never gave me a moment of peace at school, even when I needed it most. Instead, he continued to taunt me and break me down. And now, here I am, nearly losing my virginity to him.

The furthest I've ever gone with a boy was kissing, and it was only once in junior year. Josh Connors asked me out, we went to see a movie, and then he kissed me in his car before I got out. I was so repulsed by the kiss that I thought I was a lesbian.

When I told Kennedy, she suggested I kiss her to see, since she's a lesbian and it could've been a good test. I loved Kennedy, but I was definitely not a lesbian. Or maybe I just wasn't into her that way. Then, I thought I was asexual because I've never craved any sexual experience and I hated when people touched me.

But the moment Asher kissed me tonight, my entire body exploded, every nerve felt ignited, and I knew I was definitely *not* asexual. And most definitely into guys. It was like his touch awoke something in my body. I felt alive and I craved it the longer he kept his lips on mine. I needed his mouth everywhere, his hands all over me. I wanted my hands to touch every inch of his skin. It was more than just wanting him, I *needed* him. In every way. If we had gone further, I wouldn't have stopped him. And that thought terrifies me.

At least I know now what my sexuality is. That's somewhat of a relief—it was actually something I spent a lot of time thinking about. But I can't believe Asher, of all people, was the person who helped me realize that.

In sophomore year, I let the thought of having a crush on him cross my mind a few times because I always thought he was really cute and he seemed nice, albeit a bit shy. But when I saw his real personality later on and he started to be an asshole to me, I became completely turned off by him. And kind of turned off by anyone, both in a romantic and a sexual way.

The more I go over the events of tonight in my head, the more I realize how crazy I am. I knew what I was doing when I realized he was watching me on the couch with his hawk eyes and I started dancing with that guy. I wanted to make him mad, show him that I can enjoy myself at a party without giving a damn what he thought. And maybe a very, *very* small part of me wanted to see how he would react to it. Would he be angry? Vengeful? Jealous? I wanted to know if he had the same feelings I had, no matter how much I buried them. Obviously, he did.

Now I don't know what to do. I can't ignore this—this feeling in the pit of my stomach that's telling me this is a bad idea. But I also can't ignore my heart telling me I'm attracted to this guy.

Although, it's one thing to be attracted to someone and to *like* them. Asher is a dick and it will take a lot for me to even *think* about liking him.

He did seem sincere when he apologized, though, even if I told him I thought the opposite. I was just trying to protect myself—my heart—from him. Too late now, I guess. Tonight, I saw a different side of him and it's making me question everything.

None of this changes anything, though, because I can't let it. I need to protect myself. I have enough shit going on in my life, I don't need Asher and his confusing behavior and constant changing attitudes to make my life even more complicated.

Sure, Asher is the only person I've ever had a real crush on and he's the first person to make me feel anything even remotely arousing, but that means nothing. I've gone on this long in my life without romantic or sexual experiences, I don't need Asher to change that. That's why I need to forget this happened, and I need him to forget it, too. The last thing I want is for him to have expectations, and then when I turn him down, for him to get mad and retaliate. I've known Asher long enough to know how he works.

A loud roaring engine pulls me from my thoughts and I turn my head behind me, my gaze falling to the road. I watch as an all-black car slows down behind me and pulls up right beside where I am on the sidewalk. A chill runs down my spine and fear boils in my stomach. This is how girls get kidnapped, I've seen the stories in the news.

I look back ahead of me and consider my options. I could run, but chances are whoever is in the car could outrun me.

Would anyone even hear me if I screamed? Would they care? It's a pretty residential neighborhood, but it's not exactly in the best part of town, so people here probably hear girls screaming all the time and just ignore it.

Looking back to the car, I watch as the door opens and my brain immediately goes into fight or flight mode. I turn back ahead of me and start sprinting as fast as my legs can go. I'm not exactly a runner, but I am athletic enough. I know I'm at least ten miles from my house, though, and I know I definitely can't run this fast for that long. But that's my only option right now, so I continue pounding the pavement and pushing my body forward.

Just as I am about to turn a corner, I hear heavy breathing in my ears and I feel two long arms wrap around my waist. My body goes rigid and I start panicking. I'm being kidnapped. The arms pull me up off the ground and spin me, throwing me over a set of wide shoulders.

My face is met with the person's back and I get a whiff of their body scent. Smokey wood, fresh shampoo, and sweat. I know this smell. It was filling my nostrils, completely encompassing my body half an hour ago. As I make this realization, I hear the voice mumble, "I run on the track every morning and you thought you could outrun me?" A low laugh erupts from his chest and my anger grows.

Yeah, it's definitely him.

I start screaming and hitting my arms against his back, kicking my legs at his chest. I want him to let go of me right now. "Put me down!" I yell, continuing to kick and scream as much as I can.

Finally, he drops me to my feet and shoves me into his

passenger seat. "Sit," he orders me, pointing his index finger at me like he's berating a child. "And don't you dare move," he adds before he shuts the door and walks to his side.

I could run back out of the car, but chances are he would catch me again. After all, he runs every morning, he's definitely much faster than me. Instead of getting him more upset, I decide to stay put and take the ride home. I'm actually really tired, I probably wouldn't even be able to make it home by walking.

Asher flings himself into the driver's seat and cranks the car. He looks over at me and I give him a weary look. "What?" He barks, staying parked on the side of the road with his hand on the gear shift.

"Aren't you drunk?" I question, figuring there's no way he would've done what he did with me earlier if he wasn't at least a little drunk.

"No. I only had half a beer. You think I could run that fast if I were drunk?" He asks rhetorically, irritation clear as day on his face. "That all?" I nod my head in a daze as the realization hits me that he was completely sober the whole night. Everything he said, everything he *did*, was with a completely clear mind. He knew exactly what he was doing the whole time, and he did it anyway.

"Where do you live?" He asks, interrupting my thoughts. When I look at him with a blank stare he repeats himself. "Your address. I'm driving you home, where am I going?"

Oh yeah, he doesn't know where I live. Do I want him to know where I live? Asher watches me with a close eye and there's an expression on his face that I can't quite place.

"Uh, I live one street over from the movie theater." I

choke out, feeling so many different things, I can barely focus on the words coming out of my mouth. A million thoughts are racing through my mind and the last place I want to be is here with Asher as he drives me home. This car is way too small, I don't think I can stay in this tiny car with him for much longer.

I feel the beginning buzz of a panic attack coursing through my veins, causing my fingers to shake and my chest to squeeze tight. The only thing I can do is start counting my fingers to try and distract myself. *One finger, two fingers, three, four, five—*

"So, you're anorexic?" Asher blurts out, keeping his eyes on the road. My entire body halts and I whip my head to the side, staring at him in horror.

"*What?*" I ask, completely caught off guard. Where the *hell* did that come from? And how the hell did he know? I had a feeling Kennedy told him and Maddox something personal about me to get them off my back, but not *that* personal. "Why the fuck would you ask me that?"

I think I'm going to throw up.

He stops at a red light and turns his head to me, a sincere and almost sad look on his face. "Kennedy told me," he says in a low voice. He hesitates a moment and then raises a cautious hand and tucks a piece of hair behind my ear. I watch as he pulls his hand back and looks down at it. "I know that shouldn't change the way I see you, but it does. It made me realize I never should have treated you like shit in the first place because I had no idea what you could have been going through."

I consider his words, but it all seems like too much right now. I can't handle it. "I don't want to talk about it, Asher." I whisper, looking down at my own hands in my lap as I turn away from him. From the corner of my eye, I see him nod slightly and turn back to the just-turned green light.

"Okay. But if you ever change your mind..." He doesn't finish his sentence and he doesn't have to. I know what he means. And I think it's the nicest thing he's ever done for me up until this point. He's really showing that he's trying to change and my heart swells a little bit, thinking about that.

Maybe that shy, innocent boy from sophomore year is finding his way back. I hope so, at least.

We stay silent the rest of the drive to my house and I can feel the panic slowly start to subside. I thought being stuck in a tiny car with Asher was my worst nightmare, but now it doesn't seem so bad. He was able to settle my nerves and distract me with one awkward conversation. I can appreciate that.

The streets are quiet, even though it's a Friday night. I watch as Asher zips down the road and turns this way or that way. It's a much quicker drive than I thought it would be, considering it's like we live in two different worlds. But, it's only fifteen minutes. So, I guess our worlds aren't all *that* different.

Although we've been silent, it's not necessarily an uncomfortable silence. Neither of us said a word because we didn't have to. We knew our place, our relationship—if you could even call it that. Talking would only make things awkward and there's not really much to say. It's better if we just think to ourselves and keep quiet, so that's what we do.

Nonetheless, I've been burning with questions the entire ride. Or rather, one question in particular. When Asher pulls onto my street, I direct him to my house and let him pull into the driveway. I pause for a second, deciding now is the time to ask what I've been dying to know. "Can I ask you a question?"

Asher turns his head toward me and nods once.

"What changed tonight?" I ask, pausing and deciding to clarify my question. "At school today, you were your typical asshole-self. Even earlier at the party, you were teasing me as usual. But then, all of sudden, you're staring at me the whole time I'm dancing, like you're jealous or something, and then... in the bedroom... And now, you insist on driving me home." I ramble, losing my breath completely. I pause and take a deep breath, deciding to wait for his response now.

Asher considers my question, or question*s*, and looks at me for the longest minute of my life. Finally, he opens his mouth and looks me directly in the eye. "I thought you were different before. Stuck up and entitled and rude. But tonight, I saw a different side of you. A side I liked." He pauses and looks down at his hands. "You're not who I thought you were."

I nearly scoff, flabbergasted at his admission. I can't believe I thought he was actually a decent guy. No, he's still an asshole. He terrorized me every day because he *assumed* I was someone I'm not? And then, when he decides he just wants to get with me, he thinks we can have sex without a second thought and everything will be fine? What a dick!

"So instead of getting to know me, you decided to terrorize me, embarrass me in front of the whole school, ruin my birthday, and make my life hell? All because of who you *thought* I was?" I yell, my anger growing and rising to the surface. "And then, you think you can seduce me and everything will be fine?" I watch his eyes go wide and his mouth fall open slightly, regret evident on his face, but I don't care anymore.

He really is just an asshole.

"Fuck you, Asher." I seethe, shoving open the car door and slamming it behind me.

I stomp into my house, not looking back at the car because I know it will only make me start crying. I can't believe I actually started to think he was changing, that he was actually sorry. I'm obviously the biggest idiot on this planet.

God, I hate myself. And I really, really cannot stand Asher Madigan.

EIGHTEEN
Asher

I really fucked up. I mean, I knew that already before tonight. But tonight, I think I made everything ten times worse.

What should've been me apologizing and hopefully showing Rowan I can be a better guy, turned into making her feel like a cheap hooker. Now, she thinks I thought I could fuck her and all would be forgotten when that's the *last* thing I thought.

Honestly, never in a million years did I think what happened tonight would've happened. I didn't even acknowledge before now that I had feelings for Rowan. *Romantic* feelings. No way did I think things would escalate to that level.

I definitely don't regret what we did, but I'm mad at myself that I didn't use my fucking brain and realize it would make her feel like a slut. She's not a slut, not even close, but I made her feel like one. If anything, I'm the slut.

I have no idea how I'm going to fix this. I'm not even sure

I should fix it. Maybe Rowan is better off without me. But I don't know if I can let her go. She's the first person to make me feel alive. I feel like I finally woke up from a six year slumber, like I'm fucking sleeping beauty or some shit.

But seriously, the past six years of my life I've been living in a haze, every day blurring with the last and mixing in with the next. It wasn't until tonight that I finally got clarity, not only with Rowan, but with my life as a whole. It's crazy that one person can do that for me, but she has and she doesn't even know it. I need to figure out how to show her. How to win back her trust, or at least her respect.

"Hypothetically, if a guy really fucked things up with a girl, how would he go about fixing it and showing her he's not a bad guy?" I ask Maddox, who's sitting beside me on his couch.

After I dropped off Rowan, I mentally kicked myself the whole way back to Maddox's. I could've gone home, but I didn't want to be there right now. I needed my best friend, for no other reason than to help me fix this shit.

Maddox eyes me for a minute, then shakes his head, chuckling to himself under his breath. "I fucking knew it," is all he says.

"Knew what?" I play dumb, not wanting to admit it just yet. Admitting it to myself and showing it to Rowan is enough emotional whiplash for one night.

"I'm not an idiot, dude. You've had a crush on Rowan since you first laid eyes on her two years ago." He replies and I suddenly feel like an idiot. After I saw Rowan for the first time sophomore year, I wouldn't shut up about her to Maddox. It wasn't until he told me what she was actually like that I let the fascination go. Except, she was never the way he described her. Which means…

"Wait, you knew this whole time? Is that why you fed me all that bullshit about her being an entitled bitch and a goody-two-shoes?" I demand, getting agitated.

He fucking knew I liked her and told me a bunch of lies about her! For what reason, I don't know but I'm going to find out.

Maddox sighs and chugs the rest of his beer. He turns to me, a little bit of fear in his eyes. He knows I'm stronger than him and I could easily beat the shit out of him, so he's probably hoping I'm not as pissed as I sound. Unfortunately for him, I'm holding back most of my anger right now.

"It wasn't that serious. Honestly. What I told you was what most people thought of Rowan at the time. I mean, was it actually true? Probably not. But we had just become best friends and I didn't feel like watching you get lost in some girl. Girls *always* come with a lot of baggage and they need attention." He pauses, looking at me with caution. "You were already so broken, for what happened back in Ohio. I just thought I would spare you the drama."

I'm fuming. I'm so mad, I could kill him. All this time, I treated Rowan like shit because I thought she was just another stuck up bitch and I refused to let her tear me down. But all I was doing was trying to protect myself from a version of her that didn't even exist. A version of her Maddox let me believe was the real her.

But also, it was a version of her I willingly believed, instead of taking the time to get to know her. I close my eyes and rest my head in my hands. I feel like I'm having a brain aneurism.

"If it makes you feel any better, I think she really likes

you." He adds and I almost punch him. I have to physically clench my fists and take several deep breaths to stop myself from losing my shit.

"Not anymore," I mumble.

"That's not what I saw tonight." I lift my head and see Maddox giving me a small smirk. If only he knew what happened after we left the party.

I sigh, not wanting to explain everything and hash it all out. "Let's just say, when I drove her home, I really fucked up." He nods his head, as if he knows exactly what happened now from my vague response.

Am I that much of an asshole? I tell him I fucked up and he doesn't need to know anything else because he thinks he knows the whole story now? Damn, I really need to change.

"So, how do I fix this?" I ask him. Maddox doesn't have the best track record with girls, but if there's one thing he's good at, it's getting them to forgive him. Usually he just gives them one of his infamous looks and they drop their panties right there. That's not what I want at all with Rowan, but hey, maybe he's a secret romantic who can help me out. It's worth a shot.

Maddox thinks carefully and then his eyes go wide and a devilish grin breaks out onto his face. "No. No, no, no." I say, knowing exactly what he's thinking before he even says it.

"Oh, come on. She'll see that and jump right into your bed!" He pleads and I give him one of *my* infamous looks.

Where his infamous look is a smirk and I-want-to-fuck-you eyes, my look is an I'm-going-to-kill-you glare.

"Maybe a strip tease might be enjoyable for you, but I am *not* doing one." I shake my head. I can't believe Maddox is my best friend, a guy who does strip teases for girls to apologize when they're mad at him. I swear to God, he finds a way to make everything sexual, even apologies. "Especially not for Rowan," I add.

"It works every time," he singsongs and it takes all my effort not to wipe that stupid grin off his face. I ignore him and think about some reasonable ways I can make it up to Rowan. Before I can stop it, a memory pops into my mind.

"Bent, be serious! I really want to impress her," I whine to my older brother. "I want her to think I'm nice so she'll be my girlfriend." Bentley laughs and ruffles my hair.

"First of all, Ash, you're eleven. You don't need a girlfriend yet." He chuckles and then crouches down to me. "But, since I'm fourteen and I'm your wise older brother, I'll tell you my secret. If you want a girl to like you back, all you have to do is be a gentleman."

"What does that mean?" I ask, confused.

"That means, you bring her flowers, tell her you think she is beautiful, and always be nice to her. Never, ever, be mean to any girl. Especially if it's the girl you like. Got it?" Bentley informs me and pats my back.

"Yeah, I got it." I tell him, beaming a big smile. He gives me a smile and shakes his head a little bit. That's how he shows me he's proud of me.

I love it when he's proud of me.

Turning around, Bentley grabs our backpacks off the kitchen chair and gestures for me to follow him. "Now let's go to school."

The memory sends an electric jolt through my body, causing my heart to ache and my chest to cave into itself a little bit. My brother was always giving me advice, and I would always listen. But somehow, in the last few years, I ignored everything he ever told me and did the complete opposite.

It's time I finally start listening to my brother again. After all, he was the perfect example of a gentleman and the best person I've ever known.

NINETEEN
Rowan

I slept like absolute shit last night.

When Asher dropped me off at home, I was fuming. I was so mad. He made me so angry, it was all I could think about for hours. By the time three a.m. rolled around, I pretty much kissed sleep goodbye.

And honestly, I'm still *so* mad. Just when he started changing my mind on the kind of guy he is, he reminds me he's nothing but a piece of shit.

Like I need any of this shit. I have enough heartbreak and problems in my life, I don't need some guy stirring more shit up. Asher's always been a dick, and I knew it the moment he started picking on me. No decent human being would do some of the shit he's done.

And yet, I almost lost my virginity to him. What the hell was I thinking? That was the first time I've done more than kiss anyone and I let it happen with Asher. I mean, he was really good. *Really* good.

No, God, no, I can't be thinking these things! Have I learned nothing? That's how he gets me. He does shitty things, does something good to make up for it, and then I'm left looking like the idiot when he goes back to being his real self. His piece-of-shit self.

As I close my laptop, not accomplishing any school work, I hear the doorbell ring. Confusion clouds my mind because no one ever rings our doorbell. The only person who ever comes here is Kennedy and she always walks in with me.

Plus, it's a Saturday night. And an unusually warm one. Almost everybody is out, holding onto the last nice night of the fall.

Remembering that the door won't answer itself, I rush out of my room. "Who the hell rings the doorbell at this hour of the night?" My mom bitches from her spot on the couch as I walk down the hall. She doesn't make a single move to answer the door, though. Why am I not surprised?

I roll my eyes at my mother's comment because, of course she would think it's the middle of the night. She's already half in the can and it's 7:30p.m. My dad doesn't even look in my direction when I walk to the door, keeping his eyes on his book, and something tells me he didn't even hear the doorbell ring. Either that or he just doesn't give a shit. Both are likely scenarios.

I open the door, fully expecting it to be one of our neighbors. My breath catches in my throat when my eyes meet the piercing blue ones in front of me.

Before I can even think, I'm pushing against his chest to back him onto the other side of the porch and quickly closing the door behind me. I hope my parents didn't catch a glimpse of him. The last thing I need is them questioning who this boy is on our front porch.

"What the *hell* are you doing here?" I whisper-demand, keeping my voice low so my parents don't hear. I look over my shoulder, praying they don't grow curious and come out here to make a scene.

Asher is holding a bouquet of light pink peony tulips. I only know what kind they are because I see them all the time at Trader Joe's. But, these one are absolutely beautiful. "I would've gotten roses, but these were the only flowers that were pink. And pink's your favorite color, so…" his voice trails off.

"How do you know pink is my favorite color?" The question comes out before I can tell myself not to ask it, since it doesn't really matter. But, my mouth moves faster than my brain apparently.

The corner of Asher's mouth turns up into a small smile and he looks down at his feet, seeming part nervous, part giddy.

"Almost everything of yours is pink," is all he says. I can't believe he noticed that almost everything I wear and own is pink. I watch as he uncomfortably shifts on his feet and puts his free hand into the front pocket of his jeans. His eyes find their way back to mine and he gives me a small smile.

What the *hell* is going on?

Standing here under the harsh light of my porch, I finally notice the stark contrast between Asher's blue eyes and dark, almost black, hair. The darkness of his hair clashes with the brightness of his eyes. It's jarring, to say the least.

Something small changes in his expression—almost like

he's unsure of what to say—and I realize I'm staring. My heart nearly jumps into my throat as his eyes bore into mine. Those sad, icy blue eyes. Always crawling deep under my skin and finding their way into the warmth of my body. His gaze is hard to read. He looks torn up inside, and really remorseful.

I reach out and quietly grab the bouquet, bringing them just under my nose so I can smell them without making it obvious. I don't know why he's here, but I'm not about to let my guard down. And I really need him to leave before my parents find him here.

"They're beautiful," I say, a little breathless. That's the effect his presence has on me, especially when he shows me this side of himself. The nice side.

Taking another glance over my shoulder, his voice pulls my eyes back to him. "Is everything okay? Are you okay?" He asks, concern overtaking the sadness on his face. The remorse remains, though, and almost deepens in the tight crevices of his face.

"I'm fine, Asher. Everything's fine. Did you need something?" My impatience is evident in the way I hurriedly ask him this. The concern doesn't leave his face, though, and I'm worried he'll see that everything's definitely *not* fine right now.

He looks at me for a long moment and then he takes a deep breath. "I'm here to apologize. For everything. For how I've treated you this whole time, for how I treated you last night, and for letting you think I hated you. You never deserved any of it. Everything I did was so fucked up and I'm sorry. And I'm especially sorry for what happened last night when I was supposed to be apologizing. There was never a moment where I thought I could sleep with you and everything would be fine. I would never think that."

He finishes his little speech and the agitation is growing in my chest. Not because of him, though, but because of the looming threat of my parents on the other side of this very thin door.

I can see the sincerity in his eyes though, just like I saw it last night. But his actions so far have contradicted his words, so I don't really know what to believe. I think he sees the hesitation on my face because he starts speaking again.

"Look, I'm not perfect and I never claimed to be. But I'm trying," he adds, watching my face for an indication to continue. "I would really like it if you could give me another chance. I know you've given me so many and I don't deserve it, but I want to prove to you that I'm not the person I've been acting like the past two years." Anticipation and hope is written all over his face and I feel my heart reach for him slightly. But my head knows better.

He can't expect me to forgive him for everything he's done right now because he brought me flowers and gave me a speech. I need to see him act on his words. He needs to prove it.

I'm still undecided on what to do because I don't know what's the right thing or the wrong thing in this situation. All I know is it's only a matter of minutes before my mom's curiosity outweighs her drunken disregard and she comes out here.

"Let me take you out tomorrow. We can hang out and I can show you I'm being honest. I want to prove to you that I can be a better guy, Rowan." He pleads to me and his eyes look so sad, and so honest. It's really confusing me right now. "I don't want to be the guy I've been for two years. I want to be better. For y—to you," he corrects himself.

"Okay, okay. Fine. Tomorrow. Pick me up at noon." I agree just to get rid of him. I'm still not sure how I feel, but I just need him to go. "Please go now," I whisper to him and look back over my shoulder.

Asher eyes me for another minute and the panic is starting to set in, deep in my stomach. I guess he decides it's not his problem right now because he nods and gives me a small smile as he walks backwards to his car.

When he finally turns around to get in his car, I quickly push through the front door and see my mom in the hallway making her way to the door. Five more seconds and she would've been outside, seeing Asher and causing a scene.

Without making eye contact with her, I walk around her to the kitchen, grab a vase from under the sink, and walk down the hallway to my bathroom. I fill the vase with water and place the flowers in. Then, I take them to my room and put them on the back corner of my desk.

They really are gorgeous. I've never gotten flowers before and I truthfully don't know much about the different kinds of flowers, but I think it's safe to say these are now my favorite. Not because he got them for me or anything. They're just really pretty. And pink, I love pink.

As I lay back on my bed, my mind drifts to what I agreed to. I will not be excited for this hang-out—date—whatever you want to call it. I will not let myself get excited. Asher has proven to be an asshole one too many times and I need to stop being naïve enough to believe he's changed just yet.

As Maya Angelou said, *when people show you who they are, believe them the first time*. I need to start listening to her and living by that quote.

Asher has shown me who he is a million times. Still, I find myself questioning if that's his real self, or just the facade he plays up for the world, to protect himself from the pain and cruelty and heartache.

And sometimes, when it's late at night and I'm staring up at my ceiling, thinking about all the things that have happened in the last two years, I let myself wonder. What kind of things happened to Asher to make him this way? What kind of horrible things has he experienced that made him such an asshole sometimes?

Maybe it's not his fault that he is the way he is. Maybe life threw him battle after battle and now he's just broken down. Maybe the Asher I saw today was the real him, deciding to fight back and expose himself to the potential pain.

I'm not saying I want to fix him, I think he needs to do that himself. But part of me wants to know the real Asher Madigan because there's a small whisper in my ear, a feeling in my gut, that's telling me the real him is the one I saw today. He reminded me of that boy from sophomore year again. Nice, polite, with sad eyes but a big heart.

I'm so screwed.

TWENTY
Asher

"Dude, I can't believe she said yes." Maddox exclaims from where he sits on my bed as I throw a simple white t-shirt over my head.

My hands are shaking slightly and I try to steady them, so Maddox doesn't catch on. "I mean, no offense, but I thought for sure she would slam the door in your face."

I chuckle, agreeing with him. I'm really grateful he's here right now to take my mind off my nerves before my date with Rowan. "Yeah, I am too." I mumble, trying to steady my voice.

Maddox shakes his head and leaps off my bed. "Well, man. I've gotten you this far. Unfortunately, I won't be tagging along on your first date, so this is where I leave you." He theatrically declares. I love the guy but he is such a melodramatic pain in the ass sometimes.

"Yeah, yeah. Later," I say to him as I look back in my mirror and smooth out my black jeans. I'm hoping once I get in my car, the nerves will wear off and my self-confidence will return again.

Maddox continues standing in my bedroom doorframe with a smirk on his face. I shoot him a questioning look and he chuckles to himself. "You are *so* lame," he laughs and walks out the door. "If you see any hot chicks, give them my number!" He yells from my front door and then lets himself out. Sometimes I really question my choice of best friend. And he thinks *I'm* lame?

Shaking my head, I grab my wallet and keys from my bedside table, and I head out the door. My eyes catch a glimpse of the clock on my car dash and I realize it's still only 11:30a.m. It takes me about fifteen minutes to get to Rowan's house, which means I'm pretty early, but I'm honestly too nervous to just sit around at home and wait any longer. I've already been up since eight this morning and been anxiously waiting for a reasonable time to start getting ready.

Deciding I'm not really all that early, I crank my car and pull out of my driveway, turning right out of my street and down the main road.

I spend my drive thinking about my life and I realize this is actually the first date I've ever been on. I've hung out with girls before, and then later hooked up with them, but I've never actually taken one out on a date.

In fact, I've only ever had a crush on one other girl and that was when I was eleven, so it wasn't even a real crush. Rowan is the first girl I've actually liked and wanted to take out on a date before. She's the first girl I've ever put in effort for.

The girls I've hooked up with have all been because I was horny and they were coming on to me. Simple as that. Not that there have even been all that many, though. I only started caring about that sort of thing last year. And even though a bunch of girls have tried to get with me, I've only had sex with three. So many people think I'm a man-whore, but it's not really true.

I still hope Rowan doesn't know my reputation with girls though, considering people think I've been with way more girls than I actually have. But, she probably does. Actually, she definitely does. I'm just hopeful that she doesn't care about it. If she did, I don't think we would've gone as far as we did the other night, and I don't think she would've agreed to go out with me. Although, I think she only agreed because she wanted to get rid of me. For what reason, I don't know yet. But I'm going to find out.

Seventeen minutes early, I pull into Rowan's driveway and I start contemplating whether or not to get out. After how nervous she was yesterday when I showed up out of the blue, I think I'm going to play it safe and wait in my car until right at noon. That way she'll be expecting me and hopefully won't be as guarded.

As I sit here killing time, my eyes take in Rowan's house. It's a decent sized red-brick two-story house, fit for a middle-class family. It's at least double the size of me and my mom's tiny two-bedroom house, if not bigger.

If I had to guess, her house probably has five or six bedrooms. There's a window on the far right side of the ground level and, from the outside, it looks to probably be a bedroom. On the top story, there are three windows facing the street with dark curtains blocking the view in and out of the rooms. Either no one is currently in those rooms, they're sleeping, or no one ever uses them. I can only imagine there are identical rooms facing the back of the house, but I'm not about to go wandering out of my car to check.

Although, sitting here, I can't help but wonder why her family has such a big house. From what I know, Rowan doesn't have any siblings. Who knows, maybe she has a younger one that doesn't go to our school. But I'm pretty sure she doesn't or I would've heard about it by now. So, why would her family need a house so big if it's just the three of them?

As I'm deep in thought, a curtain from the far left window on the top floor is pulled to the side and a woman's face peaks into view. She eyes where I am on the driveway for a quick second before she slips away from the window and the curtain falls back into place.

The encounter leaves me with a chill in my spine and I'm slightly disturbed. Something tells me I shouldn't have seen that woman in that room, and she shouldn't have seen me on her driveway.

Deciding I should get ahead of this, rather than continue to sit on the driveway like a creep, I get out of my car and head for the front door. I lift my hand to knock, but before I can make contact, the door swings open.

"Who are you?" The woman before me demands. She's the same one from the window. Now that she is up close, I can see her bone structure is much more sharp and defined, very different from Rowan's, but the green eyes and blonde hair are unmistakable. This is Rowan's mother. Her eyes are sunken in, she has quite a few wrinkles for someone who I assume is so young, and yet her face is eerily pale. I can smell the strong odor of alcohol on her breath, and I assume from her slightly slurred words that she's drunk. She's also likely an alcoholic from the way her skin has aged so much for someone so young. I've seen enough alcoholics in my life to recognize one when I see them.

Extending my hand forward, I introduce myself. "I'm Asher Madigan. I go to school with Rowan," I say to explain my presence. When I say Rowan's name, I watch as a moment of confusion flashes across the woman's face before it disappears and her scowl returns. It's as if she forgot who Rowan was for a minute. Weird.

"The girl is busy. What do you want?" She spits out, not easing up one bit. My nerves start to come back with more force than before because this is not how I wanted to meet any of Rowan's family.

Opening my mouth to respond, I'm saved by Rowan running to the door. She yanks the door open and squeezes herself between me and her mother. "I'm going out, mom. Bye." She says, completely out of breath. Rowan pulls the door closed, forcing her mother back into the house.

Quickly, she rushes down the steps to my car and she has an iron grip on my arm to drag me with her. By the look of her frazzled state, I think she heard her mom interrogating me and ran to my rescue.

"Come on," she urges me to my car. I feel like I just got whiplash with everything that happened in the last two minutes. Taking a second, I stand back and look at Rowan, feeling a heat coming to my cheeks. She looks beautiful, even if she did have to rush to the door.

Her thick blonde hair is tucked behind her ear and hangs in

natural, loose waves down her back. She's not wearing any makeup, and I think this is how I like her the most. All natural. She's wearing a pink short-sleeved shirt that sits slightly low on her chest and hangs loosely down her stomach, exposing the smallest amount of her skin.

Her blue jeans hug her hips perfectly and widen as they go down her body, hanging loosely off her legs. There are rips at her knees and one on her upper thigh. I want to touch the small area of exposed skin on her thigh so badly.

"Are you going to keep staring or unlock your car?" She asks me, irritation and a slight anxiety clear in her voice. I don't think she's irritated with me, though. She wants to get away from her house as fast as possible. And I don't blame her. From the thirty seconds I spoke to her mom, I want to get the hell out of here as quickly as possible, too.

I don't verbally respond, because I'm not sure my voice won't crack. Her presence shocks my nerves with an overwhelming force and my heart is pounding in my chest. Instead, I reach and open the door for her. She gives me a tight smile and slides into her seat.

Closing her door, I rush over to my side and take a deep breath before I open my door and climb in. As I settle in, I blurt out the first thing I can think of to break the awkward silence.

"Which bedroom is yours?" I ask and she shoots me a confused look. "I got here early, so I was looking at your house. From what I can tell, there's at least four bedrooms. I was just curious," I clarify. Fuck, could I be any more embarrassing?

"It's the one on the main floor, far right." She says, turning to grab her seat belt and click it into place.

"Why?" The word escapes my lips before I can stop myself from prying. I mentally kick myself for that.

She gives me a long sideways glance before looking back at the house. "They wanted to keep the upstairs bedrooms for their younger kids," is all she says and confusion clouds my brain.

'The younger kids,' but I was pretty sure she was an only child.

"You don't have any siblings." I reply, more as a statement than a question. She responds with a quick "yup," and just like that, the conversation is done. My confusion and curiosity only grow, but I don't want to push the subject. She is much more complex than I ever thought and I'll make it my mission to figure her out.

The rest of our drive is in complete silence. It's not really awkward, but I wouldn't go so far as to say it's comfortable. I think we're both just thinking and trying to find our new dynamic, now that we've reached a kind of common ground.

I pull up to the local arcade, where I'm taking her, and I turn to watch her reaction. Her eyes go wide and her lips curve into a small smile, but she quickly tries to hide it by biting her bottom lip.

As I've been doing quite a bit lately, I mentally kick myself for ever treating her horribly in the past because now she's guarded and doesn't want to show her happiness in front of me.

"You ever been?" I ask hoping she'll warm up a little bit. She shakes her head and I can see a small sparkle in her emerald eyes. "I've only come a few times, but it's always so fun. I thought you might like it."

She looks into my eyes for the first time today and releases her bottom lip from her teeth to let her smile loose. It's not a big smile, but it's definitely a start. "I've always wanted to go. Never had a reason, though."

That makes me sad. She probably had a hard time making friends when I started harassing her at school. I don't know why she didn't have many friends before I came, but maybe she's always been on the shy side.

"Well now you do. Come on," I get out of the car and jog over to her side to open her door for her. I debate grabbing her hand as we walk into the building, but I decide not to. I'm already pushing my luck with getting her here, I'm not going to mess it up by being too forward just yet.

We walk up to the front counter and buy a bunch of tickets. Rowan tries to pay for her own portion, but I intercept and add them to mine. Giving me a look of disapproval, she crosses her arms over her chest, but I ignore her. No way in hell am I letting her pay for anything on our first date, especially one that I asked *her* out on. I may not have been the nicest to her in the past, but I'm going to be a gentleman from now on.

Walking into the arcade room, Rowan immediately goes for the virtual race cars and I follow behind her. We play three rounds, and she beats me on every one.

"I thought you said you've never been to an arcade before," I say, flabbergasted.

"I haven't. Doesn't mean I've never played video games before," she teased back.

After the first twenty minutes, we finally find our rhythm

and we've been getting along really well. She's actually really fun to be around and she's hilarious. I never knew she had such a good sense of humor. I guess I didn't really know anything about her. My own fault, obviously.

We continue playing a bunch of different games, from the dancing squares to the basketball hoops. After about an hour, my stomach starts to growl and I ask if she wants to check out the food stand.

"Uh, you go ahead." She responds wearily and I nearly punch myself in the face. What kind of brainless idiot asks a girl to go eat when he knows she's struggling with an eating disorder?

"I'm sorry, I wasn't thinking," I apologize. She quickly shakes her head and her eyes go wide.

"No, no. That's not—I didn't—I'm in recovery." She stammers and trips over her words. "I'm just not hungry. Honestly. I ate before I came." I'm not sure if she's telling the truth, but who I am to question her?

"Okay," I respond, smiling at her to show I'm not pushing the topic. "Do you want to come with and watch me eat?" I ask and she laughs. Okay, good, she's laughing, which means the mood isn't ruined. She agrees and we walk over to the stand, where I order a hot dog, fries, and a drink.

We find a small table and I sit down with my food, placing my fries in the middle between us in case she wants to steal a few. The first few minutes are silent as I inhale my hot dog. After I finish it, I take a few gulps of my drink and start asking her questions to finally start getting to know her.

"So. I don't really know anything about you except your name and where you live," I state the obvious. An embarrassed smile plays on her lips and I can tell she's interested to see where I'm going with this. "What's your family like?" I think I hit a sensitive spot because she flinches at my question and then tries to hide her reaction.

"Uh, well, there's my mom, who you met. Sorry about that, by the way. She's... got her issues." Yeah, no shit. "There's also my dad. And then me. Just the three of us. That's it." She says it with a finality that indicates she doesn't want to talk about it anymore. "What about you?"

"Just me and my mom," I respond, also not really wanting to talk about my family. It's way too much and I'm not even sure I'll ever really tell her much. It's too personal and makes my fucking heart bleed any time I think about it.

Rowan nods her head in understanding, but doesn't say anything more. I can tell she's not sure how to have an actual conversation with me. The whole day we've been good at dancing around our history, especially the more recent events between us.

We've been having a pretty good time and I don't want to ruin it, but it feels like I need to get this off my chest sooner rather than later so we can move on.

"Look, I want you to know how sorry I am. Honestly. I want to change and treat you better. Please forgive me," I say. Usually I wouldn't want to come off as desperate, but sometimes the best way to show you are being sincere is by showing your true emotions.

She sighs, like she's mentally arguing with herself. Finally she opens her mouth and says, "That's the problem, Asher. Last time I almost forgave you, you thought everything would be fine and things went way too far. I mean, we almost had sex."

She's not wrong. Well, I didn't think everything was fine and could be glazed over at the party, but I did take things too far.

"I know. I wasn't thinking and I let my body control my actions, instead of my head. I want you to know I won't let it happen again." I really hope she accepts it and we can move on because I don't think I can figure out many other ways to say I'm sorry. "The next time I touch you, it will be on your terms," I add, a flirtatious smirk on my face.

"Woah, who said there will be a next time?" She questions, but I can tell by the slight amusement in her voice that she's teasing. This is good. Really good. "So, you run?" She asks, changing the subject.

"Yeah, every weekday morning at the school, and around my neighborhood on weekends. Been doing it since I moved here." I respond, remembering our encounter last week before school right after my morning run.

She asks me why I run so much and I hesitate, not sure I really want to get into the specifics. "Let's just say I need a distraction and a way to get out my frustration. Better than hitting someone," I laugh and I see her face tense. Maybe joking about hitting people isn't the best conversation to have on a date.

She recovers from her tight smile and I change the subject. We talk about a bunch of things, like our favorite seasons—hers spring, mine fall, perfect match—our favorite foods—hers is popcorn, mine is pizza—and if we could spend a week anywhere in the world, where it would be—Paris for her, Tokyo for me.

The more I learn about Rowan, the more I realize I really had no idea who she was. I thought I had her all figured out, but she continues to surprise me every time she opens her mouth. It's refreshing, and honestly a little bit sad that I could've had this kind of relationship with her all along if I just got my head out of my ass. Oh well, I can't change the past, but I can damn sure control the future.

We keep talking for another half an hour, and just as I'm about to suggest we go back into the arcade, the mood is ruined. Her mom texts her, asking her to come home. Although, something tells me it was more of a demand, now that I've met her mom once and seen the kind of person she is.

I drive Rowan home and the drive back is nothing like the drive here. She's much more lively and willing to talk to me. She's definitely opened up more and let her guard down. I hope so, at least.

Pulling into Rowan's driveway, I stop the car and turn it off. I'm not really sure what to do now, but I guess I should walk her to her door. I get out of the car and go to open her door, but she flashes me a worried look. I don't think she wants me to bring her to her door, in case her mother comes out again.

After a second, she reluctantly gets out of the car and walks to her door without saying anything to me, so I just follow her. When she reaches her door, she turns her body to face me with her hand still on the doorknob behind her, and she gives me a tight smile. "Thanks for today," is all she says.

I take the final step up onto her porch and stop right in front of her. Brushing a loose strand of hair behind her ear, I give her the most sincere smile I can and I watch her worried green eyes melt just the tiniest bit.

"Thank you for agreeing to come. Even though it was the first date I've ever been on, it was definitely the best." I say and I watch her laugh a little, the tight smile replaced with a real one.

"It was my first date, too." She quietly replies, looking down at her feet. I grab her chin and raise it to make her look at me. Her eyes flash with shock that I touched her face, so I quickly pull my hand away.

"Can I give you my number? I would really like to go out with you again," I ask. Slowly, my nerves disappear when the small smile on her face doesn't disappear and she nods her head. I give her my phone and she makes herself a contact.

Giving me a small wave, she turns toward her door and slips through. As I walk back to my car, I can't help but break out in the biggest smile I've had in the last five years. Maybe even in my whole life.

I knew Bentley was right. I should've listened to him sooner and maybe this whole situation could've been avoided. But, it is what it is and I'm not really all that mad about it anymore because it got me here. I'm just grateful I got to have a second chance—or rather, a twentieth chance—with Rowan.

Today was everything I could've hoped it to be. I hope Rowan feels the same.

TWENTY-ONE
Rowan

Two hours after my date with Asher, my skin is still buzzing and the giddiness remains, flowing from my stomach to my chest and up to my head.

I don't know what got into me, but my smile hasn't been able to leave my face. I can't remember the last time I felt this... happy. This free from my normal life. This *excited* for something new.

Today felt like an escape, one I didn't know just how desperately I needed. I needed the escape from my parents, from school, and from my everyday life. Asher gave me that. Other than his apology—which was sweet and seemed sincere—he didn't push any conversation about forgiveness or talking through any complicated issues. He just genuinely wanted to get to know me—he wanted to understand what makes me, me. Simple things, like what I like and don't like, how I would spend an ideal afternoon, and what I want my future to look like. Things that didn't require any thought or a meticulous answer.

I couldn't have asked for a better way to spend my Sunday and I'm still slightly amazed that it was with Asher. This guy has given me more whiplash in the last two weeks than anyone or anything ever has in my entire life.

He goes from being the biggest asshole and the cause of one of the worst panic attacks I've had in a long time to being so sweet and kind. This afternoon, he was a perfect gentleman.

Not only did my opinion of who he is change, but also his physical attractiveness. I always could objectively acknowledge his attractive face and body, but I never let myself think about it for too long because his personality was so ugly it clouded any physical attraction to him. But today, I finally got the first glimpse at who Asher is apart from the front he puts up. I got to see who Asher is deep down. And it definitely changed my opinion of him.

Asher Madigan is gentle and puts other people first. He always let me win, if I showed him how badly I wanted it. His heart is bigger than mine. He cares so deeply, more than most. I saw this when he talked about Maddox and their friendship.

But there's a coldness in his eyes, an icy layer that protects himself from others. It's the cold exterior that I noticed when we would get into it in the past two years. Today, though, I didn't see it. Instead, his blue eyes were warm, like the sun reflecting on the ocean on a warm, sunny day. Honestly, Asher's the definition of an anomaly, but part of me is thankful for it. Because it gave me today.

It wasn't until I got home that I realized how much I was missing out on as a teenager. Dating, going out, having a fun Sunday afternoon at the arcade just because. My entire life has revolved around taking care of my sister, and then my parents, getting good grades, and pretending to be this "perfect" person. I can't remember the last time I did something because *I* wanted to and just because I could. Asher let me have that today and he probably didn't even know how much I needed it.

It's kind of overwhelming. And this giddiness isn't helping me as I try to settle my thoughts long enough to figure out what any of this means.

Deciding I need to get out of my house, I drive over to Kennedy's house. She's always here for me when I need her and, right now, I need her more than ever.

Not only do I want to tell her about my amazing day, but I want to know what she thinks. There's still a small part of me that is very suspicious and cautious of Asher because of all he's put me through. I'm sure Kennedy will have opinions—ones that are objective and accurate—and I need to hear them, even if I don't like it or want to hear exactly what she has to say.

I reach Kennedy's driveway and I pull in, cutting the engine. I decide to text her that I'm here, so she's not surprised when I ring the doorbell. A few seconds after I send the message, Kennedy appears at the door and I walk into her house, going straight to her room.

"So, what's the emergency?" She asks me inquisitively the second she closes her door. I take a seat on her bed and cross my legs underneath me.

"It's not really an *emergency*. I just need to talk to you," I try to play down the severity of the issue right now.

She studies me for a second and then replies. "It's about Asher, isn't it?" Her words catch me completely off guard. Am

I that transparent? I swear she must be psychic. We haven't even talked about him in so long, it's so weird that she was able to guess it immediately.

Sensing my confusion, Kennedy pipes up again. "He apologized to me at the party. For treating both of us like shit."

"What? When?" I ask, my mind going a million miles a minute. If he apologized to both Kennedy and I, maybe that's a sign that he actually means it? This new information changes a lot.

She laughs a little to herself and mumbles, "before you guys had sex." My jaw drops and I can't hide my shock from her.

"We did *not* have sex!" I yell after finding my voice again. She gives me a *'yeah right'* look and I realize she, along with almost everyone else at that party, saw me drag Asher to a bedroom upstairs. I was obviously a little tipsy, since I couldn't foresee how that would look to all the party-goers.

"I swear we didn't have sex. I just brought him to a quiet room to confront him in private. He was being such an asshole, glaring me down from across the room the whole night. I swear, I didn't know it would lead to—" I start and quickly shut my mouth. I *was* going to keep that detail to myself, but my rambling had other plans.

"Oh, hell no. You're going to finish that sentence," she threatens me. I mentally slap myself in the face and release a frustrated breath.

Trying to find the words, I decide it's best to probably just come right out and say it. "He went down on me. We stopped before anything else could happen."

"Did you orgasm?" She spits out and I don't know what I

expected her to say, but it definitely wasn't that. There's no way the words will leave my mouth, so I just nod my head. When I do, she screams and jumps off the bed, falling onto the floor.

"Asher fucking Madigan gave you an orgasm!" She yells, rolling around on the ground and kicking out her legs like crazy person. I shush her, afraid her parents will hear her and grow curious. They're super cool and they actually taught her about orgasms and everything when she was a kid, but I don't need them to know *my* business.

"Will you relax?!" I whisper to her while she has her hands over her mouth and starts to calm down. "God, that isn't even what I wanted to talk about."

She immediately shoots up from the ground and resumes her position on her bed. "You mean there's more?" There's a glimmer in her eyes and I know she's getting a hell of a kick out of this.

"He was kind of an asshole after the party. As per usual. But then, he demanded to drive me home afterwards. And then, on Saturday, he showed up at my house with flowers and apologized. And…" I pause, watching Kennedy hang on to my every word. "He asked me out," I finish and she starts screaming again.

"Did you say yes?" She demands and my acute, anxious awareness slowly starts to relax when I see how excited she is. I guess, even though it *is* Asher, it's still really exciting. It's the first time I've ever been asked out and brought flowers and taken out on a date. They're all really big milestones for any teenage girl.

I nod my head at her question and I let her scream it out.

After she seems to settle down and want details, I tell her all about our date today. How perfect it was, how kind and caring and amazing he was. How much fun I had.

Kennedy blushes and holds her hands close to her chest as she listens to me. I can see the happiness in her face and I know she's holding on to every word I'm telling her. In a way, I think she's living vicariously through me.

Kennedy's gay and, unfortunately for her, there aren't any other lesbians at our school, so she's never been asked out or gone on dates or anything. She went on one date back in middle school with a boy, but it was a group date at the movies where they watched Pirates of the Caribbean: On Stranger Tides.

After, she told me she realized she was gay when she wanted to kiss Penelope Cruz in the movie rather than her actual date. She ended up coming out freshman year and, since no other girls that we knew of were out, she never really had any romantic experiences.

After I tell her everything, including my reservations, she sits and processes everything. I feel like I'm on the edge of my seat waiting for her to say something, *anything*.

"First of all, I am so happy for you. It sounds like you had such an amazing time. And, as much as it pains me to say it, the Asher you got to know today seems very sweet. He sounds nothing like the guy we've gone to school with the past two years." She closes her mouth and thinks again for a few minutes.

"Come on, tell me what you really think." I prompt her, wanting to know if I'm being really naïve and gullible right now. If I'm being honest, as great as today was, there's been a small voice in the back of my head every minute telling me how ridiculous I'm being and that I shouldn't trust Asher as far as I can throw him.

She looks me in the eyes and contemplates saying what's really on her mind. I can tell because she opens her mouth and then closes it and then opens it again, three times. Finally, as if deciding on what she wants to say, she progresses slowly. "You know, I want to tell you to be careful and keep your guard up for a little longer. But, if I'm being completely honest, I'm relieved. And a little bit shocked."

My eyebrows shoot up and I give Kennedy a surprised look. Kennedy is always the most guarded person I know and she's always ready for anything. Her life moto is literally 'expect the unexpected,' so I'm not sure what she means when she says she's shocked. And also that she's *relieved*? What in the world is there possibly to be relieved about?

Seeing my speechless shock, Kennedy continues. "When Asher talked to me at the party, he told me he would change. I guess I didn't believe he actually would put in the effort that that requires, until now. Hearing how he apologized more than once the last few days, and how we was with you today, and that he literally brought you *flowers*. It all just seems… genuine. And that wasn't something I expected from him, is all. But I'm glad he's doing it." She clarifies and my heart warms a little bit.

I didn't know how much I wanted—needed—her approval before now. But it feels so good to have it. To know she supports me 100%, even if it might end with my own humiliation—or even heartbreak—is all I could've ever asked for in a best friend.

"So you believe him, then? You actually think he's

changed—that he's going to be better?" I ask and I hope she does, or else I'm not sure *what* I'm going to feel when I leave here tonight.

She considers my question with so much thought, I would think the question is life or death. Although, in this situation, it very well could be. You never know with vulnerability in relationships, and all.

"Yes," she finally says. "I do believe him. I'm not saying it won't be hard, this whole thing between you two. But I see a hopefulness in your eyes that I haven't seen since we were kids. You've had such a hard time for so long and you deserve this. So, because of that, I think you owe it to yourself to at least give it a shot with him."

Those words hit me like a ton of bricks. My heart squeezes in my chest and tears burn the back of my eyes. It feels like there's a hand tightening on my lungs, restricting my breathing and preventing me from focusing on anything else.

For the longest time, the one word I would use to describe myself, my life, was hopeless. And to be told by my best friend that she not only noticed my lack of hope, but that she also sees a newfound optimism in me? It's overwhelming and terrifying, but also uplifting.

Sensing I need comfort, Kennedy crawls across her bed and envelops me in a hug. We stay like that, our bodies and arms intertwined, for a long time. When I finally pull away, I realize the tears didn't fall. I didn't let them. Because as scary as this whole situation is, it's also opened my eyes.

I realize now, with Kennedy by my side, I can take on anything. Before now, I thought I was alone. Even though Kennedy never gave me any reason to think she wouldn't be there for me, I let myself believe that I had to go through everything on my own—that I only had myself to rely on.

But, I realized just now, that couldn't be further from the truth. Even when I didn't know it, Kennedy was always here for me. Even if she didn't know exactly what was going on—since I always kept everything very private and close to my heart—she was there when I needed her. Through my eating disorder, my anxiety, my family problems. She's always been there. And in this moment, she reminded me of that.

Being forced to recognize that she's always been there for me, and knowing now that she always will be, I know she's absolutely right. I should try with Asher. Because, if it works out, the reward is more worthwhile than if I take a scary risk and things don't work out.

So, there's one of two ways this can go: Asher will really change and make me the happiest I've ever been, or he won't change, I'll get played, and my heart will be broken. That possibility alone should scare me, but in this moment, I realize it doesn't. Because I will be okay, no matter what happens.

Five years ago, I thought I would never be okay again. And, yet, here I am. One good day and I'm already feeling optimistic. Thanks to my best friend, who helped me realize it. Which means, even if things don't go the way I want them to with Asher, I will find other things that will bring back a little hope in my life, with Kennedy by my side. It is possible. And I will be okay, no matter what.

"Thank you, Ken," I whisper to her. She has no idea the kind of epiphany I just had, thanks to her. She'll never know just how much she means to me, and everything she's done for me. But when she pulls me in for another hug and squeezes me a little tighter, I know I'll spend the rest of my life by her side. Supporting her, just like she supports me, every day.

TWENTY-TWO
Asher

"I'm giving you the silent treatment," Maddox announces to me when he opens his door.

I decided to come over after my date with Rowan because I could use someone to talk to about it and I could really use his expert advice. Mainly, though, I just want to play on his PlayStation with him. Although, with his sudden attitude, maybe this wasn't a good idea.

I laugh at his wonderful hosting skills and hospitality as I walk through the door. Following him straight to his room, I ask why he's ignoring me. When he doesn't answer, I realize he actually is following through with his declaration.

"You know, it's not a real silent treatment if you have to announce it to me before you start." I point out to my best friend who's a five-year-old-stuck-in-an-eighteen-year-old's-body. He gives me a pout and I nearly die laughing right there. He really is like a child.

He doesn't say anything as he leads us to his PlayStation

setup, gesturing for us to start playing. The guy knows me too well.

Maddox has one of the best video game setups I've ever seen. Not that I've seen many, I've never had one, for obvious reasons, and I don't really have any other friends. None whose house I would go to and spend time with on an hourly basis, at least.

Every time I come over to Maddox's house, it amazes me the amount of cool shit he has. Even though he's my neighbor and lives on my street—which is in a not-so-great neighborhood that's full of all kinds of people who can't really afford to live in a house but do anyway—his house is still one of the nicest ones. It's a pretty good size, has four nice-sized bedrooms, and a pretty nice backyard. His parents definitely take care of their house and it shows.

Maddox told me once that his parents used to be middle class, and they lived in a much better neighborhood in Fort Lauderdale and a way bigger house when he was younger. But when the financial crisis hit in 2008, they were hit hard and had to move here. Although, he says it's not all that bad. He was only eight when they moved, so he pretty much grew up living like this. It was much harder for his older siblings—two older sisters and three older brothers—when it happened.

Now that all his siblings are moved out, Maddox has his own room and it is pretty great, if I do say so myself. Queen sized bed, a long desk beside his bed with a monitor, his PlayStation, a really cool gaming chair, and his TV on a bookshelf across from his bed. I'm pretty sure everything in this room was either bought by Maddox himself, since he works at the local grocery store with me, or was a gift from his parents for birthdays and what not.

Even though most parents would prefer a larger, nicer house in a better neighborhood, Maddox told me how his family has gotten used to their lives, with their valuables and saving their money. Maddox always told me, after they financially recovered, they probably could've moved. Especially since his parents became workaholics and are almost never home—out making money, or whatever. But then he wouldn't be able to have half of his stuff, so he's fine with staying here. And I'm fine with it too, because it means I can use his stuff, since I could never afford even a controller, let alone a PlayStation or a monitor. Plus, I like having him live down the street from me. He is my best friend, after all.

I grab the green controller that I always use from Maddox's desk and ignore him ignoring me as I take a seat on his bed. Maddox takes a seat in his chair and sets up the game. We play Madden15 for about twenty minutes until I finally beat him.

It's not as exciting as it usually is because Maddox refuses to talk to me. I've tried several times to get him to say something, but he just mumbles under his breath if he makes a wrong move or if I make a better play than him.

"Will you just spit it out? What the hell did I do?" I ask, fed up with this ridiculous silent treatment. He's acting like he's my girlfriend and had a dream that I cheated on him.

"You missed our weekly Sunday dunch." Maddox pouts and, after a second of shock, I burst out laughing. He really *is* acting like my fucking girlfriend.

Dunch was something we started to do on Sundays because we slept in too late for it to be brunch or lunch and it was too early for dinner, so we settled on dunch. It was Maddox's idea, something about spending time together and bonding or whatever. I think it was just an excuse to get me to buy him food.

I hold my stomach as the laughter rolls around in my body and tumbles out my mouth. "You're mad because I skipped *dunch*? You are such a girl," I say between bouts of laugher. Maddox just glares at me throughout my five-minute laughing fit.

"I'm being serious! We always said we would never choose a girl over each other and on your first date *ever*, you do exactly that!" He yells at me and it only makes me laugh harder. "You promised you would be back in time, and of course you weren't, and I was left sitting here waiting," he adds.

I've never loved Maddox more than right now, I think. Only he would do a weekly tradition on Sundays and then get mad at me for missing *one*. Quite a unique guy.

"We got carried away, I'm sorry. I promise I'll make it up to you," I respond. Knowing it will appease him, I stifle my laughter and shake my head.

His mouth curves into a small smirk that he tries to hide and I know he's over it now. "So, was the date at least good enough to miss dunch?" He still tries to hide his smile and keep his pout to seem moody, but I know he's actually interested.

I let a small smile appear on my face because I just can't keep it in. "It was… amazing. *She* was amazing," is all I say. At first, I thought I would want to tell Maddox every detail and talk about it for hours like we're a couple of girls, but the more I reflect on the date and think about Rowan, the more I want to keep it all to myself. I want it to be special and I'm afraid if he knows everything about the date and about Rowan, it'll no longer be just mine.

I also don't want to hear any crap from him about how I was a dick to her for so long. It's a constant reminder in my head whenever I think about Rowan, which is often. I feel so guilty every time that thought comes up and I don't need another person reminding me. Not that Maddox would guilt-trip me, but he would tease me for it and it's a pretty sensitive spot for me. I just want to avoid it, that's all.

Studying me, Maddox lets his smirk turn into a full out grin on his face. "That good, huh?" I barely even told him anything and he can just tell that it was great. And it was better than great, it was perfect.

Maddox knows me better than anyone in the world and he doesn't even need me to tell him all about the date and about Rowan. All he needs to do is look at me and he can pretty much read my mind. And that's exactly what he does.

"It's about fucking time, man. I was starting to think you were asexual or something. Not into *anyone*," he laughs.

"Why?" I ask, my eyebrows knitting together. That is such a random thought, coming straight out of left field. He must've known I've slept with a few girls. Right?

"You've haven't dated a single girl for as long as I've known you! I know you had sex with some, but you never seemed all that interested in girls whenever we were out. It's not normal—no offense." He exclaims, holding his hands up in defense.

"And you didn't think I was gay?" I question because, if the roles were reversed, the thought probably would've crossed *my* mind.

"Nah, if you were gay, you definitely would've hit on me. Everybody loves me," he jokes and I laugh, shaking my head. Only Maddox would say something like that and actually believe it, too. Like I said, one-of-a-kind guy.

"Honestly, I'm just relieved I don't have to pick on Rowan anymore. And Kennedy too, she scares me a little." He says, and I don't think he's joking. He has a slight fear in his eyes just mentioning Kennedy's name. I laugh, hitting him over the head, and we return back to our game.

Now that I have Maddox's full support, it feels like a slight weight has been lifted off my shoulders. It sounds ridiculous, but Maddox is like a brother to me and I would feel like shit having to hide something this important from him.

"She makes you happy, I can already see it. And you deserve nothing less," he adds right before we start a new game. I can't help but smile a little bit.

For the first time in a long time, I think everything might just be okay. Maybe better than okay. As long as I don't fuck it up.

TWENTY-THREE
Rowan

It's been a week since my first date with Asher and he has been nothing but amazing since.

On Monday at school, after our date, he was waiting for me in first period, sitting in Kennedy's desk instead of his. Kennedy was annoyed, but I was over the moon. He was really making the effort to change. He could've easily sat at his desk and ignored me, but he didn't.

He sat beside me the entire period, and I caught him a few times looking over at me and stealing glances throughout the entire lesson. He even rested his arm on the back of my chair to get close to me, since he knows I don't like PDA. We got a few looks because people must've been wondering how we went from pretty much enemies to this, but he didn't seem bothered by it. So neither was I.

Then, at lunch, he walked into the cafeteria, searched the entire room, and when his eyes landed on me, he walked straight over to me. He sat beside me the whole time and we ate our lunches while we talked about random stuff. It was kind of perfect.

And he has been like that every day this week at school. Perfect.

For the first time in my life, I wake up smiling because I'm excited to see him during the day. And I go to bed with a smile on my face because he makes my day so much better, every day.

We haven't gone on another date yet, but we've been together at school every day and, after school, we've been hanging out and doing homework together at the café across from school. It's been so nice and I really like this new Asher. He's sweet and kind and considerate. All characteristics I didn't even know he possessed, until now.

Yesterday, Asher asked me out on another date for tonight, this time to the movies, and I obviously said yes. After school today, we went to the café, since it has become part of our routine, and then I went home for dinner and to get ready.

After an excruciatingly long dinner with my parents, since they were both sober for a change tonight and insisted we have a family dinner at the table, I'm now sitting in Asher's passenger seat in front of the movie theater.

"Ready?" He asks me and I nod my head, waiting for him to cross his car and open my door. It's something he insists on doing every time I'm in a car, even if I'm getting into *my own* car. He always has to open my door for me. I think it's cute.

We walk into the theater and Asher buys us two tickets for Age of Summer. It's some coming-of-age movie and I thought it would be cute. Buying a large popcorn and two drinks, Asher pays for the food and we walk into the theater just as the commercials at the start come to an end. Quickly, we rush to the top row and slip in at the edge. Luckily, this movie isn't very popular tonight, probably since it's a Thursday night, so there's not many people in this theater.

We watch the first twenty minutes of the movie and it's not too bad, but I can't focus. I can feel Asher's eyes on me and his stare is burning into the side of my face. There are goosebumps rising on my arms and my stomach is warming with heat. Somehow, he has the power to make me feel all kinds of things with just his eyes on me, and we're not even making eye contact.

Instead of turning my head, I pretend I don't notice his eyes watching me, even though it feels impossible. Just when I think he's stared at me enough and memorized my whole face, he leans in and brings his lips right to my ear. I can feel his hot breath from his mouth and he inhales a sharp breath.

"You have goosebumps all over your arms and your breathing is uneven. And it's too dark in here to see, but if I had to guess, I'd say your face is bright red right now." He breathes into my ear and I think my heart momentarily stops beating. He really knows how to make me squirm inside.

Grabbing my cheek, he turns my head toward him and looks into my eyes. In the dark theater, his eyes look like the deep sea—still blue, but so dark it's almost black. I've only ever seen his eyes look like this once before. It was at Maddox's party when I confronted him and I noticed a fire igniting in his eyes and coursing through his body, from his eyes all the way to down to his toes.

Asher holds eye contact with me, not moving an inch and waiting for me to make a move. I've never done any sort of affectionate or sexual stuff in public, even kissing, and definitely not in a movie theater, although I hear that *is* pretty common. Is he expecting something more than kissing to happen in here? Because I'm not sure if I'm really comfortable with that.

Feeling like Asher's expecting something more, I grow anxious that I won't be satisfying enough for him. Especially since PDA is not something I've ever really done and it makes me a little nervous, even if it is in a dark theater.

He leans in just an inch closer and now our lips are touching, but he's not kissing me. He's watching me, so close he can see every pore on my face, and holding my chin so I can't pull away from him. Not that I want to.

"I'm a virgin," I blurt out in a low whisper against his lips and he lets out a low laugh, but he doesn't move away. "In case you were expecting something." The words tumble out of me and part of me feels bad for implying that he's just a guy who wants sex. I don't really know what his intentions are, though.

Asher places his other hand on my other cheek to cup my face and he pulls my head back a little bit so I can see his face clearly. "I *never* expect anything. Just being with you, like this, will always be enough for me." He tells me and I believe him. I know he's not a virgin, just based off of how comfortable and in his element he was at Maddox's party it was definitely apparent. But, it warms my heart that he doesn't care about doing sexual things and he is totally content just hanging out.

My heart warms and I want to kiss him on the lips for that. Leaning in, I softly place my lips on his and open my mouth just the slightest amount. He flicks my bottom lip with his tongue, asking for permission, and I separate my lips more for him to slide his tongue in.

Reaching my hands up from my armrests, I can't help but run my fingers through his hair. It's soft and fluffy and perfect. Asher moves his hands down my neck and my back, resting them on my waist and pulling my body closer to him. Without thinking, I push up the armrest between us and scoot closer to him, so that I'm nearly sitting on his lap but not quite.

We continue making out for ten minutes until I pull my lips away, completely breathless. "This movie's boring," I whisper and a small smile appears on my face. Getting the hint, Asher agrees and we get up to leave. Abandoning our food and drinks, Asher and I walk out of the theater mid-movie and we hurriedly climb into his car.

The second I close my door and we're in the privacy of his dark car, I'm on Asher like a hound dog. My lips find his and I pull him by his neck close to me. He frantically grabs me and suddenly the middle console between us feels like the Berlin wall.

The first thought that comes to mind is to climb over it, so I swing my legs over and find a seat on Asher's lap. My mouth never leaves his and I feel a smile tug on his lips when I'm comfortably straddling him.

We quickly find our rhythm that we had going on back in the theater, but this time I can physically *feel* the effect it's having on Asher. I'm sitting right on his hard-on and I feel it growing every second, which causes all kinds of feelings to start circulating in my body. Anticipation, pleasure, want, *need*, they all boil up in my chest and settle in my lower stomach.

I start slowly rocking my hips back and forth, my center

rubbing directly against Asher, causing friction and frustration. A low groan comes from deep in his throat and I know I'm driving him crazy. Moving lower down my body, his hands connect with my ass and he starts moving my hips back and forth at a faster pace.

A moan escapes my lips and the need in my lower body grows uncontrollable. I separate my lips from his to take a breath and he starts working his way down my neck, nibbling and licking parts of my skin all the way down to my chest.

When he reaches right above my breasts, he pulls away and he leans his head back against the headrest, looking up at me with lazy eyes and a sexy smirk as he takes a breath. All of a sudden, I desperately need his mouth on my skin.

I pull my hands from the back of his neck and I yank my shirt off in one fell swoop, exposing my bra. Tossing it to the passenger seat, I unhook my bra and slide it off my body, throwing it over to where my shirt is. When I do this, I watch as Asher's eyes double in size. He shoots me a questioning look, and when I nod, his mouth immediately finds my left nipple.

Asher spends time sucking, licking, and nibbling each nipple while I continue rocking my hips on his lap. Another moan escapes my mouth and I know I'm growing extremely frustrated, and *very* wet.

As if reading my mind, Asher pulls away from my chest and connects his mouth back with my lips. His fingers trail lower down my body until they find my hips. With one hand resting on my hip, the other dips below my skirt and his fingers push my underwear to the side, exposing my wet heat.

A gasp releases from my throat as Asher swirls two fingers

around my clit. He slides his fingers up and down my heat, and then pushes both of them in my entrance. I gasp again as his rough fingers curl their way into me, and it quickly turns into a moan as he pumps them in and out.

My breathing grows heavy and I can feel the climax building in my body. I rock my hips against his fingers, causing more friction and making his movements rougher. Pulling my mouth away from Asher's, I lean my head back and he latches his mouth onto my breast.

The feeling of his fingers inside me, pumping in and out at a fast, rough pace, and his mouth on my boob, swirling my nipple and sucking, sends me over the edge. I grip his shoulders for support and lean my back against his steering wheel, letting the orgasm bubble to the surface. Within seconds, I hit my climax and it takes over my body completely. I don't hold back, continuing to grind my hips against his fingers and ride out the high.

As I start to come down, Asher's mouth is on mine again, swallowing my moans. I start to slow my movements, stilling completely when he pulls his fingers out of my entrance and his hand emerges from beneath my skirt. Watching me intently, he pulls his face just slightly away from mine and slides the fingers that were just inside of me in his mouth. He licks them clean and holds eye contact with me the entire time.

Panting and breathless, I can't help but smile so wide. That was almost better than at Maddox's party. The effect Asher has over me is absolutely mind-blowing. Whenever I look at him long enough, I get horny. If we keep seeing each other, I don't think I'll be a virgin for much longer.

After pulling my eyes away from him, I start to climb back

over, but he grips my hips firmly, as if telling me I'm not going anywhere. I realize that this is the second time he's given me an orgasm and gotten nothing in return, which means he probably wants something.

"Oh, uh, did you want me to..." I say, looking down at his groin and back up to meet his eyes. I'm honestly not really sure how to go about this. I've never given a hand-job or a blowjob before, but I'm sure he would guide me through.

Instead of answering me, Asher chuckles to himself and his eyes are sparkling with something humorous and daring. "I mean, if you really want to," he laughs. He's joking, I think.

Now, I'm confused.

"Well, I didn't do anything for you..." I respond, letting him know I'm slightly confused. From what I've heard, guys always need something and both times it was only me who came.

Asher slides his hands up to my waist and a smirk plays on his lips. "Oh, baby, you did more to me than you even know."

My jaw drops and I realize I really have no idea what I'm doing. I thought I would be prepared enough when the time came that I got with a boy, considering I've done some research here and there, but I am way more clueless than I thought.

Realizing I definitely have no idea what he means, Asher clears his throat, the smirk remaining on his face. "Watching you orgasm with my fingers inside of you is very satisfying for me. I don't need anything in return," he clarifies.

"Ever?"

He laughs and I see a glimmer in his eyes that tells me he's finding this conversation very amusing. Glad I could be of use,

I guess. "Well, I mean, no. But I don't *always* need something. That's what sex in a relationship is, give and take."

Wait, did he just say relationship?

"I think at least, I don't actually know. I've never had a girlfriend."

Girlfriend?!

My eyes grow wide and my heart starts beating a little faster. Relationship? Girlfriend! Does he think... oh my god, are we having the "are we *dating*, dating" talk? I've never needed clarification more in my life, and I think Asher realizes that when he sees my reaction.

"Not that you're my girlfriend or we're in a relationship," he blurts out and I watch him wince at his own words. "Unless, you want to be." The open-endedness of his sentence—like it's a proposition and not a question, but the ball is very much in my court to respond—is very apparent to me. Except, I don't know what to say.

I can see his finger twitching and I watch as he pops his jaw, releasing the pressure in it as he waits for me to say something. *Anything.*

I need to think.

What do I want? Do I want a boyfriend? Do I want Asher to fill that role? Do I want to be a girlfriend? The longer I take, the more pain I see on his face. Not anger, not frustration. Pain. Because he cares about me, and he wants me to be his girlfriend.

That realization hits me—Asher wants to be in a relationship with *me*—and the answer becomes crystal clear to me.

"I do want to be. In a relationship. With you," I say. I

watch relief wash over his face and he breaks out into a smile, causing me to smile just as big. He leans into my body as I stay sitting in his lap and he takes my face in his hands.

"Me too. I really, *really*, want to, too." He whispers against my mouth right before his lips envelope mine.

In this moment, I know everything I've done was for this very moment right here. Asher makes me feel more alive and more cared for than any other person ever has before. Now I know, I definitely made the right decision.

Asher Madigan is my boyfriend. If someone told me a month ago that this would be my life, I would've laughed in their face. And yet, as he kisses me and runs his hands down my body, nothing has ever felt more right.

Asher and I. Me and Asher. Us.

TWENTY-FOUR
Asher

I got to school early this morning, as I always do, to train on the track, but I was too distracted to put my all into my workout. I could've gone back home and skipped this morning, but instead I just decided to skip the strength training and instead run an extra few miles to kill time.

My brain can't focus on anything right now. All I can think about is Rowan and her body pressed up against me in my car last night. Her body shuddering as she came on my fingers and her deep breaths when she came down from her high.

Watching her, *feeling* her, come all because of my fingers was better than any sex I've ever had. And she didn't even do anything to me. It was the best feeling I've ever had.

If fingering Rowan was that good, I wonder what sex with her would be like. Not that I'm going to pressure her to do anything she doesn't want to.

Last night, when she thought I expected her to give me a blowjob or something, a part of me felt guilty that she thought guys were like that. I know some are, but I'm definitely not. Never with her.

These thoughts have been racing through my head all morning and, when I hit the fifth mile of my run, I decide it's enough for today. As I walk to my car, feeling defeated from my failed morning workout attempt and sweaty from my five mile run, I check my phone for the time. My phone reads *6:58a.m.* and I know pretty soon the parking lot will explode with kids and faculty since school starts at 7:15a.m.

There's already quite a few teachers' cars parked in the faculty lot, but the student lot is nearly empty. So, I decide to sit in my car and wait for the bell, and I watch as several buses pull in, drop off kids, and drive away.

Twenty minutes pass and nearly the entire student lot is full of cars. I'm parked at the back, so I watch all the commotion of kids pulling in, parking, and finding their friends to talk before class in front of their cars.

My usual crew of guys are parked closer to the doors and I know they see my car and are wondering why I'm not getting out. Before I can get out and greet them, I see Maddox pull into the lot and he parks on my left just as I see a flash of red drive in behind him. Parking on my right, the little red car's engine is cut and I get out of my car, circling the front of mine to pull open the red car's driver door.

Rowan steps out of her car with a big smile on her face and I grab her chin, pulling her lips to mine. I know she hates PDA, and I usually do too, but I just can't help it with her. Whenever she's near me, I need to kiss her, touch her, hold her in some way.

The smile on Rowan's face deepens and I feel her lips

curving into the kiss. When I pull away, I see her bright green eyes staring back at me in wonder. I've been trying so hard, putting in so much effort, to show her that I'm changing and I think this moment is another one where I'm proving that to her. Because here I am, kissing her in front of the whole school, the day after I ask her to be my girlfriend. No bullshit, no lies, no teasing. Just me, showing her I care about her. And I want to be with her.

I want Rowan to have confidence in me and to know I'm being one hundred percent genuine and honest with her, and I think I'm doing okay.

"Mmm, good morning to you, too." She mumbles against my lips, a happy tone in her voice. Pulling away from her, I look at her face and take everything in.

The smooth pull of her skin, her low cheekbones, flushed rosy cheeks, striking dark blonde eyebrows, and perfect little button nose. She's perfect in every way, and she's all mine. *Finally.*

Offering a small smile, I reach down for Rowan's hand and pull her out from behind her car door so I can close it. She locks her doors and slings her backpack over her shoulder, never pulling her hand out of mine.

Behind us, Maddox walks over and gives me a disgusted look. "I didn't know getting a girlfriend would make you a whipped motherfucker," he teases me. I shoot him an unimpressed glare and he puts his hands up in defense. "But, I'm all for it."

"Hey, Maddox. Don't hate on us because you're jealous. I'm sure someone will come around one day and cure your loneliness," Rowan teases back. I turn my head back to face her and I flash her a proud smile to match her triumphant one.

We make a great couple; two peas in a pod, or whatever.

Out of the corner of my eye, I watch Maddox roll his eyes and stomp off toward school. I place a quick peck on Rowan's lips and then walk with her, hand-in-hand, toward the school.

We walk through the front doors and I brace myself for the stares and confused looks we're bound to get. Everyone knew Rowan and I didn't get along, it was the highlight of the school day whenever we would get into it. So, of course, people will be confused. But I would prefer if they kept that shit to themselves, since I know it will bother Rowan.

It's definitely a change of events that no one probably expected, seeing us together and happy, so they just need to get their surprise and confusion out of the way. But as we walk down the hall, toward first period, and everyone's eyes follow us, my frustration hits the end of its leash.

I feel like a fucking zoo animal with all this staring. My whole life, I've had an issue with controlling my anger, especially in the last few years, but this is ridiculous. It would send anyone into a fiery rage.

Unable to stop myself, I bark out to everyone in the hallway, "What?!"

Releasing Rowan's hand, I spin around with my arms spread out wide, questioning everyone around us. "Have you never seen two people holding hands before? We're not fucking circus animals! Stare at something else!"

Grabbing Rowan's hand again, I pull her forward toward the classroom. I look down at her, afraid I've scared her with my outburst, but what I see surprises me. Rowan has a childish grin on her face and she's trying to stifle her laughter.

She finds this amusing. Good, honestly. I'd rather her laugh at me than be scared of me or mad at me. Or, worse, be seriously bothered by everyone staring at us.

"They deserved it," I whisper as I bend my head low to brush my lips against her ear. She nods her head and agrees with me, just as we reach the classroom door.

Walking in, Rowan pulls my arm behind her, so we can walk to our desks single-filed but still holding hands. She shuffles down the aisle and sits down in her regular desk, beside a wide-eyed Kennedy. I guess she didn't know we made it official yet.

I take the empty seat on Rowan's left as Maddox walks through the door and assesses the scene. He shakes his head and walks over to us, sitting in the desk on my left. The four of us are sitting in a row, but no one's speaking and the tension between Maddox and Kennedy is palpable.

Slinging my arm over the back of Rowan's chair, I keep my mouth shut because I don't really know what to say to break this awkward silence.

But of course, being his usual self, Maddox speaks up and breaks the silence by stating the obvious. "Well, this is awkward."

"Would you shut up, Sherlock Homes?" Kennedy spits out, rolling her eyes to show how bored and annoyed she is by Maddox's presence.

"Would you ask nicely, Debby Downer?" Maddox teases and I shake my head, predicting how this will play out.

"No," she says firmly and a smile plays on Maddox's lips. Before he can stop himself, he's leaning forward on his elbows and resting his chin in his hand.

"You know what I think, Ken-Ken? I think this is the start to a beautiful friend group between the four of us." Maddox states, a seriousness in his voice, but pure amusement in his eyes. She sends him a warning glare, probably for calling her Ken-Ken.

I'm not too confident we'll become a proper friend group—you know, where we're all *actually* friends—but at least Maddox and Kennedy aren't completely screaming at each other.

I shoot a smirk to Rowan and she returns with a smile. I think this is going better than either of us expected. Who knows, maybe Maddox is right and eventually we will become a "beautiful friend group," or whatever.

Just as that thought crosses my mind, Kennedy shoots Maddox an angry glare and disgust overtakes her entire face. She crosses her arms over her chest and turns toward the front of the classroom, ignoring us.

Yeah, I wouldn't bet on it.

TWENTY-FIVE
Rowan

This past week has been quite interesting, to say the least.

It's officially been one week and one day that Asher and I have been dating and it's definitely taken a lot of kids at school some time to get used to the sight of Asher and I together, instead of at each other's throats.

Last week, after everyone made us feel like zoo animals while we were walking hand-in-hand, I hoped they would get over it and not really pay us any attention. Apparently, though, Asher's reputation as the guy who runs the school brings a lot of attention his way, and by default, my way.

Before, when we couldn't stand each other, I got a bit of attention whenever Asher's wrath came my way, but this past week has been ten times worse. It was like he was the President and I was his First Lady with all the stares and focus we were getting. Every time we would walk past a group of kids, all I would hear are their whispers talking about us.

Luckily, as the week has gone on, everyone seemed to calm

down and their attention shifted to something new and shocking. Probably something having to do with Maddox, since he's always stirring up something. Today was the most calm of the whole week, and thankfully it's Friday so I get a two-day break from the chaos.

School ended ten minutes ago and, as we've been doing for the past week, Asher and I are now walking to the café. It's the cutest little coffee shop that sits across the street from our school where a bunch of kids sit and study before they go home for the night.

On the outside, it's a very chic, rustic look that reminds me of bohemian cafés that are in movies all the time. Inside, there are fake green vines wrapping around the ceiling and it's a very cozy vibe with brown wall paint and even a red brick accent wall. There are several tables and chairs all throughout the café, and there are even comfy couches at the front near the window. The whole place reminds me of a typical California café and it's one of my favorite places to go.

Coming here every day after school has become part of Asher and I's routine because we want to hang out, but I don't really want him back at my house in case he has another run-in with my mom. And for whatever reason, he's been very guarded about us going to his house. Maybe if I were someone else, his guardedness would be suspicious to me, but I can't really question it since I'm doing the same thing.

Sometimes, though, I wish I knew more about him. I don't necessarily need to go to his house or meet his family, but I wonder what they're like. Does he live with both his parents? Does he have any siblings? Cousins, other family? I feel like someone's family and their home life can tell you a lot about them, and sometimes I grow curious about Asher's.

But I feel like I can't ask him about it unless I tell him about mine. And I'm not ready yet. Kennedy's the only one who knows my family dynamic, and even then, she doesn't know everything and I never let her see the whole picture. It's just too personal.

Oh, well. I'm sure I'll learn more about Asher as time goes on. We've only been together officially for a week.

As we approach the doors of the café, the lights are off and it's pitch dark inside. Asher gives the door handle a small tug anyways and, as expected, it's locked. The owner must have had to close for some reason because normally they're open every day after school until 6p.m.

Asher gives me a conflicted look, as if to say, *Now what?*, and I shrug my shoulders. I really don't want him to come back to my house. More and more lately, my mom has been skipping work and spending all day drunk on the couch. I don't need her to see Asher and ask questions. Or worse, start yelling at me in front of him.

I also don't want my dad to come home and see Asher. My dad has never really showed any interest in my life, especially after Rory's passing, but if he sees a boy with me, and in my room no less, I would think his interest would be peaked. And that's the last thing I need, honestly.

All this to say, I would rather jump into a dumpster fire than bring Asher back to my house.

"Want to go to your house?" I ask him, hoping he says yes. Otherwise, we'll probably have to cut our time together short.

Asher's sapphire blue eyes slowly turn a dark blue and I watch as a cold iciness appears in them. His jaw tightens and he reaches a hand up to relieve some of the pressure. It's clear that my question unnerves him.

I've seen Asher mad before, but I've never seen his body react to something like this. He's gone rigid and a slow anger washes over his entire body. Unable to control it, my hand starts to shake in his and I'm afraid I've done something wrong.

I feel my face fall slightly and I immediately regret my reaction because awareness and remorse wash over Asher's features. Slowly, his scary eyes melt around the edges, his tense shoulders and stiff jaw soften slightly. He probably thinks he scared me with his reaction. I mean, I was a little scared, but not really because of him.

"I'm sorry," he whispers and squeezes my hand twice.

Now, regret washes through me and I feel the guilt creeping up my body and settling in my shoulders. "No, *I'm* sorry. It's not you, I promise." I assure him, hoping he believes me. By the wary look on his face, he thinks I'm just being polite.

I sigh and decide maybe it's time that I open up to him a bit. "I'm serious. Your demeanor… it just reminded me of stuff I would rather forget. I guess my reaction is just my go-to response. I promise," I add.

Pain crosses his face, and I think I see the slightest hint of pity underneath it. Or maybe it's empathy. But he doesn't ask about it. After a few seconds, the cold darkness has cleared from his eyes and the tension in his body nearly disappears.

There was clearly something else going on when I asked about going to his house, but I don't push the subject. After all, since he's met my mom, he's never asked any questions. He respects my space and I should respect his.

Although, it's not hard to recognize the likeness between us. I have familial trauma, and as a result I struggle mentally every day, so it doesn't go over my head that Asher may fight similar demons. We're both just two kids who are fighting battles every day and struggling to appear normal to the rest of the world.

I hope one day I can open up to Asher and him to me. I truly think it will bring us closer together, knowing we can find solace in one another. Soon.

"Why don't we go to your house?" He offers and now it's my turn to become guarded. A chill of anxiety shoots up my spine and I try to fight the shake that is being released in my shoulders. Asher's eyes are on me very intently and I can feel the strength of his stare. He's watching me for my reaction, to know if we're more alike than either of us know.

"I would rather not..." I respond, trying to hide my anxiety. His eyes relax slightly, either because he's figured it out or because I convinced him enough to drop the subject.

But Asher's not stupid. He definitely knows and I watch his eyes soften even more when he catches on to my guardedness about my family and my home life.

Asher tilts his head the slightest amount and lifts my chin to force me to look at him. "You are incredible, you know that?" He says, completely out of nowhere. I'm caught off guard at his unprompted words and I can feel tears burn the back of my eyes. No one's ever told me that before and meant it as much as I know Asher does.

"Where did that come from?" I ask him, fighting the tears from falling. I don't want him to think I'm so pathetic that those simple words cause me to cry.

He gives me a small smile and his eyes briefly fall to my lips, then come back to my eyes just as quickly. "I had a feeling you needed to hear that."

Confusion flashes through my eyes until I realize what he's referring to. He definitely knows. Maybe not the details, but he knows I struggle and he knows we aren't so different. A sense of comfort envelops me and a feeling of understanding settles in my chest.

Do you ever think someone was made for you? Like they were specifically put on this earth for you? To love you and care for you and make you feel understood? Because, in this moment, I feel it.

It's definitely way too early to be thinking this way, but I've never felt like this before, and I feel it so strongly. Asher is my person. I've never opened up to him or told him anything about my struggles, yet he sees my reaction and he can understand what I'm feeling. He knows exactly what I need in that moment and he gives it to me.

Coming to this realization, I make a haste decision that, ten minutes ago, I was vehemently against.

Before I can change my mind, I'm opening my mouth to speak. "Let's go to my house," I say and start pulling Asher towards the school parking lot.

Even so much as five minutes ago, I wanted Asher to avoid my house at all costs. But something changed in me when he told me I'm incredible. Something woke up. I don't want to continue living my life in fear of my family.

In the past little bit, Asher has quickly become the most important person to me and something tells me if he were to learn about my family, or be thrown into the mess if he meets my parents, that he wouldn't judge me. Not one bit.

"Are you sure?" Asher asks as I drag him to our cars. "I don't want to force you to do something you're not comfortable with." Even though his sentiment is sweet, I've never been more sure of anything than right now.

The smile on my face tells him all he needs to know and we both get in our cars so he can follow me to my house.

The entire short drive to my house, I'm wracked in anxiety and excitement. Anxiety because the closer we get, the more the reality that my mom may actually talk to Asher sets in. But also, I'm feeling excited because things with Asher couldn't be better. And I'm loving everything about our relationship.

I get out of my car on my driveway and watch from my lawn as Asher parks on the street. He gets out of his car and slowly makes his way up to me, a hesitant look on his face. Instead of going through my door, he picks me up by my waist and spins me around in a circle. I place my hands on his shoulders and throw my head back, laughing.

I hate when people pick me up, but only Asher could make all the concern and fear about being picked up disappear. He releases some of his strong hold from my waist and I slide down his body, connecting our lips on the way down.

This man in front of me continues to amaze me. Two weeks ago, I thought he hated me. Now, I'm falling in love with him.

My whole body tenses as that thought passes through my mind and Asher can feel it because he pulls away. He searches my face with concern, trying to understand my sudden change in demeanor. But all I can think about is the very last thought I had.

Holy shit, I'm falling in love with him. This is too fast. *Way* too fast. Right? But it doesn't feel too fast. It feels just *right*.

I don't even know anymore, if it's too fast or not. All I know is whatever this is that I'm feeling, it's all I need right now. Maybe, it's all I'll ever need.

"Let's go inside," I say. I give Asher an honest smile and he relaxes slightly in my arms, seeing that I'm fine and my rigidness has nothing to do with him.

We walk up to my porch and I try to get my keys out of my pocket to open the front door, but my hands are shaking way too much and I can't get the key through the lock. Seeing my frustration, Asher places his hands on mine and slips the keys out from my fingers. I feel my cheeks flush with embarrassment and I shuffle to the side to get out of his way as he opens the door for me.

As we walk through my front door, my whole body is shaking. Asher slings his arm over my shoulders, proving to me once again how well he understands me. Only he would be able to sense my unease and be able to calm me down by simply putting his arm on me.

My eyes scan the family room and kitchen as we walk further into my house, and I see that it's empty. I release a breath of relief and the tension in my shoulders subsides the slightest amount. I think Asher can feel my relaxation because he lets his arm fall and he grabs my hand instead.

I guide us toward my bedroom and open the door, sticking my arms out to showcase my room. Taking a curious step in, Asher's eyes wander around my room and I take a seat on my bed as I watch him take everything in.

My room is quite simple and generic, but it's mine and I like it how it is. There are small knick-knacks here and there that make it clear someone actually *lives* here, but other than a few trophies and medals from academic tournaments and a few pictures on the wall, there's not much else here.

Asher's eyes catch on a picture hanging on my wall and his body drifts towards it. "Is this you?" I nod my head as he points to an eleven-year-old blonde version of me in a picture with a four-year-old Rory. We're playing in the sand, building a sand castle. It's just the two of us and it's perfect. The picture was taken of us on one of our many beach days when Rory and I would spend the whole day playing in the sand and the water.

A smile touches my lips at the memory, but I can feel my face falling and a frown replaces the happiness on my face. This always happens when I have happy memories of my sister and I. They always bring a smile to my face, but then the reality sets in that I'm still here and she's not, and grief and sadness overwhelm me.

"Who's this with you?" He asks the inevitable question. When I don't answer right away, he pulls his eyes from the picture and looks over to me. There are tears in my eyes and his face falls when he sees I'm upset.

Without saying another word, Asher walks over to me and crouches in front of me, taking my face in his hand. He looks at me for a few seconds and my bottom lip starts to tremble.

He stands back up and sits beside me on my bed. He turns his body to face toward me and he wraps his arms around my shoulders without a word. Asher wraps one hand on the back of my head and brings my face to his chest as he rests his chin on my head.

He doesn't need me to say anything to know I don't want to talk about it. I silently thank him for not asking any more questions and just being exactly what I need right now. Someone to hug me.

Asher is only the second person to hug me when the memories of Rory rush back in my mind. The first was Kennedy, and it only happened once. My parents never hugged me after her death, which is why I usually keep these moments when I break down to myself.

"I'm always here for you. Always." He whispers, his lips in my hair, mumbling the words against my head.

He will never realize how much I need to hear those words. He doesn't even know about Rory and, yet, he knows exactly how to comfort me when the grief of her death overwhelms me.

"Thank you, Asher. Just, thank you," I say into his chest. He squeezes me tightly and kisses the top of my head.

"You never need to thank me." His words send a warm feeling through my body and I squeeze him tighter.

I'm definitely falling in love with him.

TWENTY-SIX
Rowan

After my realization last week, it's been on my mind every second of every day.

It's terrifying because it means either I'll be heartbroken because he won't reciprocate the feelings or I'll have to be completely vulnerable with him about all of my struggles. And I'm not even sure he will be able to be vulnerable with me too. Which only brings me back to heartbreak. So either way, my heart might be in pain.

I think Asher noticed the change with me because he's been more hesitant with his words and cautious every time he touched me this past week. And instead of reassuring him that nothing is wrong and continue on with him as I have the past two weeks, I've just keep him in the dark, questioning my sudden shift in behavior.

Part of me believes I'm subconsciously pushing him away because I don't want to be vulnerable and I'm scared of my feelings about Asher that are growing every minute.

I've always been extremely private with other people and the thought of having to open up completely and let Asher in, with the huge risk of him breaking my heart, is overwhelming. It's too much, honestly.

But, the more I think about it, the more I realize Asher has completely changed himself for *me*. He's working on controlling his anger, he doesn't take out his frustrations on other people anymore—like he did with me—and he's been showing this soft, sweet side of himself. It's honestly like he's a completely different person, but I know that this is who he truly is. The other guy he was, wasn't him at all.

So, maybe he won't break my heart if I open up to him. Although, whenever I start to think this way, my mind is immediately redirected to the tiny voice in my head that tells me he could get up and leave at any point. I might grow too clingy and overwhelm him, and he'll drop me faster than a burning hot plate.

It's a vicious cycle in my mind and I don't know what to do about it. And because of that, I'm pushing Asher away.

This is what I spent all night thinking about last night, and as a consequence, I got almost no sleep. The conclusion I came to, and have come to every time my mind repeats this thought cycle, is that I don't want my fear of abandonment and my trust issues to ruin this great thing that I have with Asher.

Since we got together, he hasn't given me any reason not to trust him yet and there's no reason not to trust that he won't leave me high and dry when I reveal my feelings for him. So, I shouldn't leave him questioning where I stand. And I shouldn't push him away. He doesn't deserve it.

This morning, I decided I needed to put all my issues aside and show him that I'm all in. At this point, I've gone off the deep-end—I'm beyond saving—and I want him to know that. I'm falling in love and there's no way I can walk away, or push Asher away, and just let my feelings fade away.

There's no fading anymore, there's only falling deeper or my heart completely breaking. And above the little voice in my head telling me not to trust Asher, there's an even louder voice screaming at me to let myself be happy. For once in my life.

At school this morning, I asked Asher if he wanted to go to the movies tonight and the smile on his face when *I* asked *him* on a date was the cutest thing I've ever seen. And even though technically I asked, he still paid like the gentleman he is. That only solidified my decision that I shouldn't push him away.

Now, the movie just finished and we're leaving the theater, but I'm not really sure what's next for tonight. Last week, when Asher came to my house, it was a huge step for me. That, combined with the decision to allow myself to be vulnerable and fall in love with Asher, has made for quite the emotional rollercoaster this week. I'm not sure I'm ready for another hang-out at my house, especially when I know for a fact that both of my parents are home tonight.

Luckily, Asher doesn't suggest we go back to my house and, instead, he suggests something that surprises me. "Want to go back to my house?"

I let the shock wash over my face and my lips part a little, my jaw dropping open the slightest bit. He quietly laughs to himself at my reaction and I see a glimmer in his eyes. He must've been reading my mind because this is a very big step toward complete vulnerability for him.

Nodding my head, Asher opens the passenger car door for me and we drive over to his house.

We pull into the neighborhood and I instantly recognize it since it's the same street as Maddox's. It's dark out now, just like it was that night, and all the memories rush back to me. The party nearly a month ago when Asher and I hooked up; me running down this very street as Asher chased me and carried me back to his car.

It's crazy all that has happened since that party. Looking back, that party was the turning point for Asher and me. It feels like an eternity ago, the night that started everything. That party led me to this moment right here, sitting beside Asher, his hand holding mine, as he drives us to his house.

Tonight, the palm trees lining the streets have an orange glow on them from the street lights and the lawns of grass in front of all the houses are browning. It's clear the landscaping around these houses are not looked after.

From what I remember about Maddox's house, his is easily the nicest on the street. And, as we pull into Asher's, I can't help but compare his to Maddox's. There are definitely worse houses on this street than Asher's, but there's also better ones.

The yellow siding on Asher's house is falling apart a little bit and, from what I can tell, it's more yellow than it should be, probably from years of dirt and decay building up. Maddox's house, though, was a light blue that was definitely looked after and kept in pristine condition.

There is a palm tree on Asher's front lawn, which is browned and pretty dead, and I can see another tree in the back of the property arching over the whole backyard and part of the house. The house overall looks pretty beat up, but I do notice that it's definitely better than some of the other houses on this street. My guess is Asher takes care of some of the house, but of course he can't do it all by himself. Maddox's, though, is definitely well-looked after and it's easily the nicest, especially since it sits at the very end of the cul-de-sac.

As I'm analyzing Asher's house, and comparing it to the castle at the end of the street, I realize he's watching me. He's probably trying to read what I think of his house, since he's seen mine. We both know I live in a nicer neighborhood and a bigger house than him. But that doesn't really matter, and I don't think Asher should let it matter either.

Before I can stop myself, I blurt out, "Your house is nice." Amusement crosses his eyes and a small smile touches his lips.

"No, it's not. You don't have to lie." Guilt immediately pangs my chest because now he definitely thinks I was judging his house. He probably thinks I'm disgusted by it.

I don't ever want him to think I think less of him because of his family's financial situation and their home life. Nor do I want him to think that I think I'm better than him because of it.

Knitting my eyebrows together, I turn completely to face him. "You know I don't care, right? About what kind of house you live in? And about your family's financial situation?"

He looks at me inquisitively and stays silent for a moment. As he watches me, I grow more and more anxious that I've sabotaged the night. Maybe it was a bad idea to come here.

That thought quickly fades, though, when Asher's words touch my ears. "I know. And you know I don't care that your family has money, right? Because my house is better, if I'm being honest." He jokes and I can see the teasing smile playing on his lips.

Relief floods my veins and I let myself laugh it off. Giving me a small peck on my lips, Asher gets out of the car and jogs across to open my door for me, as he always does. When I get out, he leads me inside with his hand on the small of my back and he pushes open his front door, which gives me the opportunity to take everything in.

The front door leads straight into a family room, which has a small doorless opening on the other end that I assume leads to the kitchen. Right beside the entryway, there's a staircase that leads upstairs likely to some bedrooms and bathrooms. There's a small door on the wall beneath the staircase, which I assume is a powder room.

The walls are a light gray throughout the entire floor and there's no trim or accent color anywhere. There's not much furniture or decor either, which leads me to believe either no one in Asher's family cares much for interior design or they can't afford it. Maybe both.

Asher leads me to the couch on the far wall in the family room and I can see there's a window with blinds on the one side that, when open, gives a view of the whole street. On the other side of the couch, I can see through the wall opening and confirm my suspicions that it leads to the kitchen. It's pretty small, with only one small section of counter space, a few appliances, and a small table. Behind the table, there's a sliding door, which I assume leads to the backyard.

For the most part, the floor layout is similar to Maddox's house, but his is much bigger with a full dining room, a bigger kitchen, and more space overall on the main floor.

Either way, Asher's house is quaint and quite small—

smaller, at least, than I would have expected—but it doesn't seem like it's too small for him. This makes me question the size of Asher's family because this house seems pretty empty and I don't think it would even fit more than two or three people to live here.

I decide to ask the question, even though I know he probably won't answer it. "Do you live here with your parents?" Asher's jaw tightens at my question, but there isn't necessarily anger in his eyes or his expression. More so, pain and sadness.

"Just my mom," he responds and there's an edge in his voice. I take the hint that he doesn't want to talk about it. I don't really blame him. If his family life is anything like mine, it's definitely not easy thinking about it, let alone talking about it.

"You hungry?" He asks me, abruptly standing up and heading to the kitchen. Thrown off guard by his sudden change, I stand up too and follow him.

Asher starts rummaging through the kitchen, collecting a pan and various ingredients. The slightest rush of anxiety spreads throughout my body, starting in my chest and extending into my limbs. My hands start to tremble the smallest bit and I quickly clasp them together to try and stop them from noticeably shaking.

I've been improving my eating habits lately and trying hard to recover, but sometimes it gets the better of me. Mostly when I'm caught off guard. I thought I didn't need my therapist anymore, but my intense reaction in this moment is proof that I probably still need help from a professional with my recovery.

My mind starts screaming at myself for stopping therapy and a sudden feeling of embarrassment washes over me. I can't believe I'm on the verge of a panic attack because the idea of eating a fucking grilled cheese right now with Asher terrifies me.

I start to internally beg my body to stop shaking and just relax, but alas, my body has a mind of its own—one that isn't even remotely connected to my actual brain.

Asher's eyes slide over to me where I'm standing awkwardly in his kitchen with a paralyzed look on my face, and his eyes go wide. "*Shit*," he mumbles and the feeling of embarrassment grows. I feel like a complete idiot.

A burning feeling pricks the back of my eyes and I can't hold it back. The hot tears glide down my face and I feel like I just took ten steps backward. Not only in my recovery, but in my attempt to be more vulnerable with Asher.

As if he knows exactly what to do, Asher wraps his arms around my shoulders and pulls me to his chest. And, like it's second nature, my arms slide around his waist and I let him hold me. Slowly, the embarrassment fades and my debilitating panic starts to subside. The comfort he brings me by just holding me is enough to calm me down.

Feeling myself start to relax in his arms, I loosen my grip on his waist. Asher notices and he whispers into my hair, "Do you want to talk about it?"

I close my eyes and debate whether I want to or not. I've been wanting to open up to him and maybe this is my moment. From the softness in his voice and the sense of comfort he brings me, I know he won't judge me. I know there's nothing I can say that would push him away. I hope, at least.

The question is, do I take the plunge? Do I tell the only person in this world that could shatter my heart into a million pieces about all the demons that haunt me every day?

Taking a seat in one of the kitchen chairs, I pull my feet up onto the seat and tuck my knees into my chest, waiting for him to sit in front of me. I give myself a few seconds to savor this moment because, after this, everything could change. For worse, or for better. But I won't find out until I open my mouth.

I continue to stare into Asher's eyes for as long as I can before the anticipation eats me alive. Closing my eyes, I take a deep breath and then look back at him.

I brace myself for what I'm about to tell Asher and I keep my eyes steadily on him. He's sitting in front of me, leaning forward with his hands on my knees, and he looks at me with concern.

"My parents always wanted a bunch of kids. Unfortunately, for whatever reason, after they had me, they really struggled to have more. Because of that, they had all these expectations for me to live up to, since I was the only kid they were able to have. I had to take on the responsibility of making them proud and being their perfect child since I was all they had. They didn't have another kid that could step up to the plate when I faltered. I was it. Their only shot.

"When I was almost seven years old, my sister Rory was born. She was their miracle child and she was the best thing to ever happen to me. Finally, I felt some of the pressure come off me. I was only seven years old, but the weight that lifted off my shoulders when they brought Rory home was the most euphoric feeling."

I pause and watch Asher take in everything I'm saying. I see the understanding cross his eyes, probably as he remembers the picture in my room. I take a minute for the thought to sink in for him before I continue.

The hardest sentence to say out loud burns on my tongue and I can feel the acid rising in my throat. "Five years ago, when I was twelve and Rory was six, she passed away from cancer." I feel the hot tears stream down my face, and I try to suppress the sob in my throat.

Asher places his hand on my cheek and wipes my tears with his thumb. The look on his face is so painful and raw and heartbreaking, more so than someone who is simply sympathetic to my situation. In this moment, I know he can relate. I can feel it in my bones; he's been through something similar. Knowing this, it encourages me to go on.

"Ever since she was born, I knew she was my parents' favorite child, and it never really bothered me. But after she passed, feeling the weight of my parents' grief, along with the reemergence of their expectations back on my shoulders, it made everything become too much. That's when I started having panic attacks. My first one happened on my thirteenth birthday, just after Rory died.

"For a while, they happened nearly every morning when I woke up. Sometimes, I would have them throughout the day, too. They've gotten better over the years, as I've learned how to manage them, but I still get the rising feeling of one nearly once a week.

"Around that time, I also started to skip breakfast and dinner in an effort to avoid my parents. It was also because I felt inadequate about how I looked. I wanted to be smaller, skinnier. I thought if I looked different, prettier, I would be happier.

"Things started to spiral and it got to a point where I would sometimes go days without eating anything substantial. Mostly, small salads and water would be all I consumed. The lower my weight got, and the more my bones started to poke out, the prouder I felt. I thought that if I got to a certain weight, looked a certain way, I would be prettier. And maybe then, my mom would remember that even though she lost one kid, she still had another.

"As horrible as it sounds, I thought if I looked more like Rory did, then my mother would love me more. And it kills me to say that because Rory was six years old and a cancer patient when she died. Here I was, in my late teens, striving to look like the body of a deathly ill child." I pause, letting those words sink in. Not for Asher, but for myself.

It's the first time I've ever fortified that thought and admitted that to anyone. Deep down, I always knew that, but I've never consciously formed that thought and processed it. And not only did I do that now, but I also shared it with Asher.

I brace myself for the rest of my story, knowing it's not over yet and willing myself to continue.

"My parents sent me to therapy for a while because I think they noticed my issues and they just didn't want to deal with it themselves. Especially since they, too, were slowly becoming alcoholics. They couldn't be bothered to worry about me more than sending me to therapy. And I don't necessarily blame them. Rory was their miracle, she was their golden child, and she was ripped from them far too soon.

"I stopped going to therapy because it just became depressing at some point. I would go there, talk about my feelings, and then come home to my mom saying some of the most vile things to me while she was drunk. It seemed pointless." I stop and notice that my head has fallen and my eyes have drifted to my fingers, where I'm picking at my nail beds.

"Anyways, that's why I am the way I am, I guess," I finish. I sigh, knowing I've done all I could've. I told him everything. All I'm left with now is an irrational fear that what I just said will make him walk away from me.

Fearing the worst, I look back up and connect my eyes with Asher's. But instead of seeing a horrified look staring back at me, there's an anger in his eyes and I know he's not angry at me, but *for* me. My heart warms at that thought. I know I did the right thing telling him and his reaction only proves this more. His reaction is because he's protective of me and everything I'm telling him makes him physically sick.

Asher's jaw is tight and he opens his mouth, and then closes it, a few times. He's conflicted on what to say and I think he's not sure how to respond to something like that.

"It's okay. You don't have to say anything," I tell him. I didn't tell him so he can feel sorry for me. I don't want his pity, I just want him to understand me better. I want him to feel closer to me, not for him to walk on eggshells around me because he's afraid of how I'll react.

"I want to say something. I'm just not sure what." He responds and brushes his thumb across my cheek. "I am so sorry any of that happened to you, Rowan. I hate that you had to go through all of it. Knowing you've experienced so much pain hurts me. I know what that kind of pain feels like and it kills me that you know it, too."

A bittersweet feeling washes over me and I know I have a sad, heartbreaking expression on my face right now. Because as happy as I am that he's listening to me and comforting me, and that he's not running for the hills right now, my mind can't focus on anything other than the fact that he admitted he knows what this kind of pain feels like.

Sliding his hand to the back of my neck, Asher pulls me to his face. "Thank you for sharing that with me," he mumbles against my lips. I sigh into his mouth as he lightly touches his lips to mine.

It's not a deep, needy kiss, but a comforting one that tells me he's here for me and he's not leaving. It's a very surface-level kiss, just our lips pressed against each other's, but it's powerful and perfect for this moment. This kiss is Asher's way of saying he's sorry I had to go through this and that he's grateful I shared this with him. And it's everything I need right now, in this moment.

He's everything I'll ever need.

TWENTY-SEVEN
Asher

My heart fucking broke hearing Rowan tell me about her past. About her parents and the trauma they gave her. Her eating disorder and anxiety. It kills me, knowing everything she's been through, everything she's had to fight.

I've felt it for a long time that Rowan and I were more similar, more connected, than I ever could have imagined. But the moment Rowan told me, my heart plummeted into my stomach.

My past has haunted me and affected my life every single day since it all came crashing down. Knowing Rowan's experienced similar things only makes everything hit too fucking close to home. It brings up unwanted feelings in me and stirs uninvited thoughts.

After I kissed her, Rowan suggested we do something fun and lighthearted, to make up for the damper she thinks she put on the night. If only she knew, tonight made me fall completely in love with her. Her vulnerability, her trust in me, and the way her eyes glimmered when she realized I wasn't going to leave her side after she bared her soul to me.

Before tonight, I knew I was falling in love. The way my skin burned when she looked my way; the way my body tingled wherever she touched me. How my heart squeezes and tightens whenever she looks sad, and when she's happy, how elation soars through my veins.

I have been falling so hard, so deeply, for the past month. But tonight sealed the deal for me. I'm beyond the point of return, I'm either going down alone or flying high with Rowan by my side. There's no recovering from Rowan.

Most people would think this is happening too fast. After all, it was just a month ago when I thought I despised her. But Rowan is a fucking force to be reckoned with and there's no denying my feelings for her anymore. I think it helped that a part of me—the part I've hidden and pushed down for so long—has loved Rowan since my eyes first found hers in sophomore year.

The only hesitation I have is that I know one day she's going to ask about my past. She's going to want to know about my parents, about where I grew up, and *how* I grew up. I tried to push it down, force it out of my mind, for so fucking long, I'm not sure I'll ever allow those memories to resurface. The pain will be too much. I just hope my present and future will be enough for Rowan.

"Your turn," Rowan tells me, bring my mind back to the game. Moving my Monopoly car token three spaces on the board, I announce I'm going to buy Boardwalk. Rowan has a look of defeat on her face because I now own three quarters of the board.

"Hey, it's not my fault you landed in jail three times already!" I defend myself, holding my hands up in the air. Rowan pouts and gives me puppy dog eyes, and my heart squeezes a little bit.

Giving in, I sigh and make her an offer. "If you give me $100, I'll give you Boardwalk." She could ask me to kill someone for her and I would.

A smile breaks out on her face and she pulls her Monopoly cash from her stack. Sticking out the money, she quickly pulls it away when I reach for it, her eyes narrow and a devious smirk on her face. "I want Park Place, too."

My mouth falls open a little and she tries to suppress her giggle by pulling her bottom lip between her teeth. "Don't push your luck, sweetheart." Her eyes falter for a second at the pet name and I can't tell if she likes it or not.

"You've never called me sweetheart before," she says, more to herself than to me.

I think about her comment and shrug my shoulders. "I've never called anyone sweetheart before. Only you."

Curiosity sparks in her eyes and the corners of her mouth upturn. She likes the nickname, I can tell, but I can also tell there are questions clouding her mind right now.

"What have you called your other girlfriends?" The question slips from her lips and smashes me with a pang to the chest. Hearing those words from her hits me with the realization that she really doesn't know *anything* about my past, not the dark stuff or the normal stuff.

A sigh releases from my lungs and I decide this is a small part of my past that I *can* give her. "I've never had a girlfriend. I've only slept with a few girls, and they were just late night, mostly intoxicated, hook-ups." I pause, not sure how much I want to tell her about the extent of my feelings just yet. "I've never had anything serious before. Nothing even close to this," I add.

The curiosity washes away from her eyes and a surprising look takes over her face. The corners of her eyes are crinkled with the smile she's still biting down on and her green eyes look at me with a love and adoration I've never felt before. No one has ever looked at me like that, which only reaffirms my feelings for Rowan.

"I've never had anything like this before, either. You're my first," she responds. Her admission sends my head spinning with thoughts. She's completely and utterly all *mine*. I'm her *first*. And hopefully, I'll be her last, too.

As I open my mouth to respond, someone bursts through the front door and I hear something drop with a loud *thud* to the ground. My head whips over to the door and I see my drunk mother stumbling through the hallway, the contents of her purse spilled all over the floor, and an annoyed look on her face.

I can immediately tell by the way her eyes are red and angry in our direction, she's not annoyed that she dropped her purse. She's annoyed that Rowan is here. I've never let anyone, friends or more, around my mother for this very reason. She hates people in her space, especially when she's drunk.

Stepping over the disaster she made on the floor and not bothering to clean it up, my mother heads straight for the kitchen. And I know she's not going to get food to sober her up.

Rowan and I both silently watch as my mom grabs a bottle

of tequila from the cabinet above the fridge and takes a swig straight from the bottle, no glass.

I wince at the fucking scene in front of me because this is the last thing I want Rowan to witness. Not only is it fucking humiliating, but it will only prompt more questions from Rowan. Questions I don't want to answer. Ever.

Her eyes slide to my face and the intensity of her gaze burns my cheek. But I can't look at her right now. Not after what she told me tonight. She's realizing in this moment that both of our mothers are miserable, train wreck alcoholics who are plagued by severe grief. I don't need Rowan to start poking around and learn that that's not the extent of our similar, tragic pasts.

Grabbing all the game pieces in front of me, I start to clean up the board game on the table, still avoiding Rowan's eyes. I need her to get out of here, now. Before something happens that I'll regret. Something that will change everything.

I spoke too soon. My mother is already looking curiously at Rowan, ready to spew her worst. Panic buzzes in my chest and I'm already standing, trying to pull Rowan out of my house before all hell breaks loose.

"What's your name, honey?" My mother slurs and stumbles over to Rowan. We're both standing now and I try to push Rowan out the door, but she stays in her position, her feet refusing to move. She probably wants to be polite, but she doesn't realize staying here is possibly the worst thing she could do.

"Rowan Easton. It's nice to meet you, Ms. Madigan." Rowan stretches out her hand and my mother laughs, ignoring Rowan's politeness.

"Oh please, don't pretend to be all sweet and innocent. I know you're just hear to get a quick fuck from my son." Rowan's eyes go wide and an embarrassed blush crawls up her neck, settling on her cheeks. I know exactly what thoughts are circulating through her mind right now and it's killing me.

The look on Rowan's face is horrifying and I can't do anything but keep one hand on the small of her back and the other on her upper arm, ready to guide her out of here when she lets up.

I silently plead with Rowan to get the fuck out of here, but she's frozen in place now. My mother takes this as her opportunity and I nearly lose my shit.

"Just make sure you're on the pill, hon. Girard men aren't ones you want to have babies with. I should fucking know," she slurs and falls onto the couch with a thump.

That's my last fucking straw. All I see is red and I'm about to fucking hit something. Or some*one*. I don't give myself another second before I'm storming out of my house and pacing my driveway. I'm seething so much, I'm almost sure there's smoke coming out of my nose and ears.

I don't realize how it happened, but all of a sudden Rowan's at my side, grabbing at my arms and trying to get me to calm down. Ripping my arms from her grasp, I walk a few steps away from her and leave her frozen in place on my driveway. I don't want to accidentally hurt her in my blind rage. I need to control myself first before I can be anywhere near her.

Screaming at myself to calm the *fuck* down before I scare Rowan even more, I slam my fist into the side of my house where there's brick. There's a bloody patch on some of the bricks now, but I don't give a fuck. I need to get my anger out of my body and this is the only way to do it.

Taking several deep breaths, I feel myself starting to calm down. My mother's in there and we're out here. There's not much else she can do. Now, I just have to clean up her mess. I need to explain.

Placing my hands on my house, I try to steady my balance and control my anger. The tension is still in my shoulders and there's still an extremely heavy weight on my chest, but at least I can fucking breathe. That's all I need to do: breathe.

Rowan walks up to my side again and she places a hand on my shoulder, causing me to flinch at her touch. I quickly recover and start to relax into her hand, turning my body toward her while one of my hands still rests on the side of the house. My head is hanging low because I can't look at Rowan right now. I know I scared her and I fucking hate myself for it.

But when she lifts my head, her hands on both of my cheeks, I connect my eyes with hers and I can see the concern in them. She's not scared of me, she's scared *for* me. Realizing this only causes the ache in my chest to intensify.

I should've never brought her to my house. I thought since it was a Friday, it was a good bet that my mom would be out all night. Almost every single night, she stays out until two or three in the morning and, half the time, especially on Friday nights, she doesn't even come home until the next morning. But of course, I should've known, the one night I bring Rowan over will be the night she comes home early.

"I'm sorry," I whisper. If I raise my voice any louder, it will definitely crack and send a whirl of emotions through my body that I don't need right now. I can see the questions taking up

211

her mind, ready to spill out at any moment, but she holds them back.

Taking my bloody, bruised, and scratched knuckles in her hand, she inspects the damage. I know it's not broken, but I let her look at it to come to that conclusion herself. Looking satisfied that it's nothing but some bruising and serious skin abrasions, I watch as Rowan lets go of my hand for a moment and pulls her arms to the inside her hoodie.

She shuffles her body around, and then sticks her arms back through the sleeves and pulls a t-shirt from inside her hoodie and over her head. Folding and ripping the t-shirt to create long strips, she takes my hand back and carefully wraps it up tightly so that the bleeding can stop.

"What did she mean by Girard men?" Rowan asks, letting the one question slip out as she focuses on finishing the last tie of her t-shirt on my hand. That question pains me because I don't want to get into it, but I know it's the only question she'll ask and she deserves her one answer.

"I was born Asher Girard. I changed my last name to my mom's maiden name, Madigan, when I was 16." I don't explain to her why I changed my name and I don't mention my father. But she accepts the explanation and she doesn't say another word as I lead her to my car and drive her home.

When I pull into her driveway, our silent car ride rests heavily on my chest. As if sensing my unease, Rowan turns toward me and places a soft peck on my lips. The simple action is all I need to calm the storm in my head and the pain in my heart.

She must be so confused by what happened tonight, yet she doesn't push me for any answers. Instead, she kisses me and brushes the hair out of my eyes, comforting me with the simplest of actions.

"Just so you know, I don't care about what your mom says. I care about *you*." She says, looking directly into my eyes with a charged intensity that tells me she's being honest and sincere. She doesn't even know how bad tonight truly was for me, but she understands enough that she knows I need her words and I need them to be true more than anything.

Wrapping my uninjured hand around the back of her neck, I pull her mouth to mine and kiss her with everything in me. I need her to know that I love her—that I'm *in love* with her—without necessarily saying the words, and this is the only way I can do that. I'm not sure why I can't say the words in this moment, but this is all I can give her right now. From the way she kisses me back, with everything in *her*, I can tell she understands.

Breathless, I pull away and mumble against her mouth, "Thank you, angel. You don't know how much I needed to hear that." I peck her lips once more and then pull away, letting her go back into her house before her mom ventures outside and sees us.

She doesn't move though, and instead she asks me another question, one that fills my body with a soft warmth. "Will you be okay tonight?"

She's always looking after me, always making sure I'm okay. Even though tonight was probably hard on her too, her first instinct is to make sure I'm okay. And it takes everything in me not to go inside with her and show her how much that means to me.

Letting that idea pass, I nod my head and run my thumb

across her cheek. I don't immediately respond and instead watch her, my girl, sitting in front of me with awe. Slowly, I pull my hand away and offer her the smallest smile because it's the only one I can give right now.

"Yeah. I'll be fine," I let the lie fall from my lips.

TWENTY-EIGHT
Asher

Two nights ago, when I was leaving Rowan's, it was the first time I've ever consciously lied right to her face.

I felt so guilty I avoided her all day yesterday. But I didn't want her worrying about me because then she might do something stupid. Like show back up at my house.

The truth is that I haven't been fine for a long time. Since I was twelve years old, and my life was destroyed, I've been struggling to find peace.

It wasn't until Rowan came along that I finally saw the possibility of getting out of this six year depression. Although, at first it was because she was the first thing I could focus on that wasn't centered around my family or my issues—even if it was to tease her. Later, though, when I finally admitted to myself it was more than that, being with Rowan felt like I actually could be okay after all.

But when my mom barged through the door last night, she stormed through that illusion and fucking destroyed it. In that moment, the reality of my life hit me. As long as I'm still living with my mother, as long as she's still in my life, I won't ever be fine.

My mother was my hero growing up, and if someone would have told me at ten years old that this would be my relationship with her at eighteen, I would've never believed them. The current state of our lives is not her fault, but her refusal to take care of herself, to acknowledge she has a problem, and to get help for her addiction is what deteriorated our relationship.

Last year, I begged my mother, on my fucking knees at her feet, tears streaming down my face and sobs crawling up my throat, to get help. But she looked at me like I was pathetic. She yanked me off the floor and told me to get out of her sight. That night, I gave up on her. I decided she wasn't my mother, not anymore.

Yet, even harboring all this animosity toward her, I still love her. I always will. And the day she chooses to get better, I will be by her side through it all. But until then, she's not my mother. She can't be. And I won't be okay again until she's either out of my life completely or she recovers.

Truthfully, my whole life the past few years have been a fucking disaster, but it truly feels like Rowan is the small light at the end of this everlasting tunnel. She is funny, kind, and patient. Her laughter plays on a loop in my mind and echoes in my ears whenever she's not around me.

Her empathy inspires me to be more considerate of other people's feelings and situations that I may not see at first glance. She is resilient and one of the strongest people I know. She has gone through some of the worst things a person can experience—and at such a young age—yet she doesn't show it. She works every day to not let it affect her or change how she treats others, something I can't say for myself.

And her heart is my favorite of all. It's so big and open and loving. She doesn't treat me like a broken toy on a mission to fix me, but she listens to me and understands what I need when I need it. And whenever I speak, she looks at me with her sincere green eyes and holds onto my every word like I'm fucking Socrates, or some shit.

It's one of the best feelings in the world. To have Rowan Easton care about you.

As I let that last thought sink in, someone barging through my front door brings me back to the present. Knowing it's my mom, I pay no attention to it and take it as my sign to head to Maddox's until they're done. I get up off the couch and head to the back door, but when I hear a musky, deep voice holler out "Boy!" I'm stopped in my tracks.

I turn to hear the source of the voice and watch as a guy in his forties, about five inches shorter than me with a beer belly, stumbles his way into my house. My mother is in front of him, leading him to the couch.

"You're going to ruin the fucking couch. Can't you do that shit in your room?" I sneer to my mother. Her eyes glare at me, warning me to keep my mouth shut, but I won't back down. She already pissed me off with Rowan yesterday, I'm not going to back down tonight.

The man behind her decides it's his place to chime in, like a fucking idiot. "Don't talk to your mama that way, boy. Show her some respect," he drunkenly slurs. He walks into my space and tries to size me up, but I tower over his 5'9 ass.

"Speak to me again and you'll be knocked out on the ground." I don't back down and this pisses him off. He waits for my mother to say something, but her spineless, drunk self is ignoring the confrontation.

The guy takes this as approval to hit me, but I easily dodge his lame attempt at a drunken punch. I push my hands against his chest, not even that hard, and he goes stumbling back, yelling on his way down to the floor. He looks up at me with a red, hot anger in his eyes, but my mother interferes before I can do anything else.

"What the fuck do you think you're doing?" She screams at me and pushes against my stomach to get me to back up. That may have worked when I was younger, but now I'm older, taller, and *much* stronger.

I don't move from my spot in the hallway and my mother slaps a hard, open-palmed hand against my cheek. Astonishment, surprise, and rage course through my veins and it takes everything in me not to do something in retaliation. But as much as I feel furious and angry right now, I would never physically hurt any woman, especially my mother, no matter how much they may deserve it.

"Just get the fuck out, Asher." She sighs and walks to the man on our floor, who is sitting up with a smirk on his face after watching the encounter.

Never in my life, no matter how drunk and angry my mother has been, has my mother ever told me to get out. Resentment burns in my chest first, but then it turns into fear when I realize she's serious. I'm sure she won't remember it tomorrow, but what the hell am I supposed to do for tonight? For *right now?*

"Leave!" She screams, turning back to me and pointing to the front door. I have enough pride left in me to walk out the door instead of trying to fight her on it and, most likely, getting even more humiliated.

I rush through the door and get in my car, slamming the driver side door shut. I have no clue where I can go and my rage starts to subside as the realization hits. Sadness overpowers my mind and a strong ache squeezes in my chest. I contemplate going to Maddox's, but his parents don't really like it when I spend the night. Besides, the only place I want to be right now is in Rowan's arms.

Without another thought, I crank my engine and drive all the way to Rowan's house. I have no idea how I'll slip into her house without her parents noticing, but my need for her in this moment is stronger than any appeal I could make to logic.

I park down the street and make my way to her window on the main floor. Lightly, I tap the window three times and pray she's not asleep and that she'll hear me.

My anticipation and anxiety only grow the longer I wait here, and I start to lose hope. Maybe she's asleep. Or maybe I scared the shit out of her by tapping on her window at two in the morning on a Sunday night.

Just as I give up and turn away from her house, I hear the slow slide of a window opening. I whip my head back to her window and see her with her head sticking out, confusion and concern written all over her face.

The first words out of her mouth come in a quieted, hushed hurry. "Are you okay?" She breathes, panic in her voice. As horrible as this moment is, I can't help but notice how beautiful she looks. She looks like a real-life angel in her pajama shirt, no pants, and messy blonde hair. It only makes my heart ache even more, knowing she's heaven on earth and I'm the fucking devil wreaking havoc in her life.

Afraid my voice will crack and the sobs will escape my throat, I just shake my head. I hold back the tears burning my eyes and crawl my way through her window, assuming she would've invited me in anyway.

"What's wrong? What happened?" She bombards me with her concern, but all I can do is wrap my arms around her waist and nuzzle my face in her neck. I can feel her heart going a thousand beats per second, and I feel guilty for scaring her, but I just really need to hold her right now.

As goosebumps imprint themselves on my arms, I let myself relax in this moment. Rowan is my comfort, my home. Whenever I'm with her, I feel at home. I haven't had a home for a long time, and my mother and her house are certainly not a home anymore—she proved that tonight. But here, with Rowan in my arms, holding on to me for dear life in silence. *This* is my home.

"Is it okay if we just sleep?" I ask her, finally pulling her out of my arms so I can look into her eyes. She's still close enough that I can easily kiss her, but I just want to look at her right now.

She looks hesitant, but she nods her head and guides me over to her bed. I watch her crawl back into her spot under the sheets as I slip off my shoes, but I decide to leave my clothes on. I slide into bed beside her and she pulls me close to her, taking me in her arms so my face is against her chest.

Without warning, I'm unable to stop it when the sobs break out of my chest and the tears stream down my face. I'm so fucking tired of holding everything in, pretending I'm okay to everyone and even believing the lie myself, but knowing deep down, I'm not even close.

I break down in Rowan's arms, letting out every pent up emotion that I've held in for the past eighteen years of my life. As much as I wish I could, I can't stop it from happening. I sob, for what feels like an eternity, into Rowan's arms and she runs her hands through my hair, pressing kisses on my head to soothe me.

The more I think about it, the more I realize I really don't deserve this girl. She takes me in like a stray puppy, no questions asked. Instead of pushing me away, she holds me and lets me cry into her chest. Her mom would probably kill her if she found me in here, but that worry doesn't seem to take hold in her mind. All she's focused on is making sure I'm okay.

After a while, I feel Rowan's breaths even out and her body goes rigid, so I know she's asleep. I'm not sure I'll be able to get much sleep tonight, but just being here makes everything feel a little better.

The tunnel may have gotten darker tonight, but the light at the end has also gotten slightly bigger.

TWENTY-NINE
Rowan

The sleeping angel beside me is a sight to see in the morning.
That is, if an angel is heavily tattooed and harboring the
traumatic weight of a thousand wars.

Despite all of that though, he's still an angel. And he's *my*
angel.

Last night was the first time I'd ever seen Asher vulnerable
and emotional. The defeat and hopelessness in his eyes ripped
my heart in two. I don't know what happened or why he
decided to come to me in his moment of absolute devastation,
but the thought that he wanted me by his side while he broke
down made my heart swell in size.

Guiltily, I feel selfish that I'm finding comfort in Asher's
moment of weakness. So, instead of dwelling on these
thoughts, I focus on the man beside me. He looks surprisingly
peaceful—a far cry from his appearance last night at my
window—and I'm silently thankful that he was able to get
some rest.

From how distraught he was, I was worried that the lack of sleep would only intensify everything. I knew when I was falling asleep that he was wide awake, but I'm glad to see the comfort of being in my arms soothed him enough to get some sleep, even if it was just the slightest amount.

Absentmindedly, my fingers start running through Asher's hair as he lies on his side, his face mere inches from mine. His arm is tightly secured on my waist and there's no moving, even if I wanted to. Luckily for me, I don't want to get up or move anyways.

I turn my head the slightest amount to glance at the alarm clock by my bedside and I cringe when I see that it's about to go off in three minutes. The last thing I want is for something so trivial to jolt him out of his peaceful sleep, after the night he's had, but I can't move from under his weight to shut it off.

There's nothing I can do to prevent him from being woken up in three minutes, so I take the short time to watch Asher sleep. He truly looks like an angel right now with his fluffy hair and soft skin. I wouldn't be surprised if he had small wings sticking out of his shoulder blades.

I think back to my first impression of Asher and compare it to this moment right here. Back in sophomore year, I thought he was so cute and nice, but very quiet. Then, the first day of junior year when he started picking on me, I thought he was a jackass. As time went on, at one point, I thought he was the devil incarnate.

But now, he's an angel. My angel. And I will do everything I can to protect him from any more pain and hurt. I don't know the extent of his trauma, but I know it's heavy. There's a likeness between us, one I recognized when I told him my past, and I don't need him to tell me anything to know we're similar in that way.

Although, I do hope he opens up to me. I was vulnerable with him, and I shared my story. If I want to be able to protect him, I need to know what it is that haunts him. I need to know more than the little facts about him to be able to understand him on a deeper level.

It terrifies me that I want to push him to share something he doesn't want to, so I just hope he's willing and ready to give me some insight.

BEEP! BEEP! BEEP!

My alarm goes off, right at 5:55a.m. and I feel Asher stir beside me. I watch as he pulls back the arm that was weighing me down and, slowly, his eyes open up and find mine. His face is slightly puffy and I immediately know it's from the tears he shed last night.

My heart cracks when my mind is taken back to the picture of him sobbing last night, clinging to my body. I push away the thought, wanting to be a place of comfort, and not pity, for him.

"Hey, angel." He croaks out and—goddamn—his morning voice is sexy. He doesn't smile, but I know he's glad that he's here, in my bed, with me beside him.

I offer him a small smile, making sure to not let any of my concern peak through. It would kill me if he thought I was just here for him because I felt bad for him.

I'm here because I'm falling in love with him. Simple as that.

Asher puts his arm back on my waist and pulls my body close to him, kissing me softly on the lips. I inhale his scent and, somehow, it's even more powerful than it was last night. Smokey wood and cinnamon, with a slight hint of cigarette smoke—which I assume is not actually from *him* smoking.

"What happened last night, Asher?" I can't help but ask the question. I wanted to ease into it more, but it was on the tip of my tongue and I couldn't stop it from slipping out.

The tortured look from last night returns on his face and I instantly regret demanding for an explanation right when he wakes up.

"Leave it alone, Rowan," he warns. His voice is hard and void of any emotion. He doesn't even try to soften his tone or be more careful with me, like he usually does.

Irritation itches my skin, but I don't want to get into a fight with him. I know he's been through a lot, even if I don't know the details, and I should be more sensitive around the topic.

"I'm sorry. We can talk about it when you're ready." I apologize, thinking that's what Asher wants to hear. But when he pushes me away and swings his legs over the side of my bed, sitting upright on the edge, I'm confused. What did I do wrong?

His back is to me and he's taking deep breaths, which tells me that he's pissed and he's trying to control his anger. "We're not talking about it, period. Let it go."

My confusion and irritation quickly turn to frustration and I can't help the next words that escape my mouth. "I can't just let it go, Asher. Not when you knock on my window at two in the morning, completely distraught, and stay the night because you can't be alone."

The second the last syllable leaves my lips, regret fills my lungs. I want to slap myself across the face. *So much for being sensitive to the situation.*

I sit up in my bed and reach out for Asher, to hold him and apologize, but he's up off my bed faster than light speed.

I open my mouth to apologize, but Asher beats me to the punch. "Well, I'm sorry my lack of an explanation doesn't work for you, Rowan, but this is all I can give you. If it's not enough for you, then *I'm* not enough."

His words hit me like a ton of bricks in the chest and I'm stunned speechless. I have no idea how this escalated so quickly, but I want to take it all back. I search for the words to assure him he's enough for me—he has *always* been enough—but nothing comes out.

Asher stands near my window, staring at me, waiting for me to say something. When it becomes clear to him that no words are coming out of my mouth, he decides he's had enough and he shoves himself through my window, storming off.

I remain stunned for a few minutes before I pick my jaw back up off the floor and realize what the fuck just happened. Scrambling, I reach for my phone and frantically text Asher.

Me: *I'm sorry. I'm so sorry. Please come back. Please.*

After I send the text, I stay in bed for half an hour, staring at my phone nervously. I nearly chew off half my fingers as I bite down on my cuticles, anxiously waiting for him to text me back. He doesn't. When my clock hits 6:39a.m., I decide it's pointless to stay here and wait for his response. The best plan of action is to go to school because he might just be there.

I jump out of bed and get ready faster than humanly possible, hoping he'll be there. *Praying* he will.

Rushing to school, I make it there half an hour before school starts, and I wait. I wait for Asher to show up. I wait and watch as every student gets off the bus or out of their car, every teacher pulls into the parking lot and starts their work day, and every staff member walks into the school to begin the day.

When the warning bell rings for first period, I run to the classroom. Bursting through the door, I see Maddox sitting beside an empty chair. I head right up to him and slide in my seat in front of him, keeping my face toward Maddox.

"Have you seen Asher?" I ask. He looks at me weirdly and then shakes his head, popping his headphones in and ignoring me.

Panic is flowing faster than blood through my veins and worry starts to cloud my brain. Asher was so distraught last night and, after our fight, I saw so much of it return to his eyes. Not knowing where he is, or what's going on with him, terrifies me.

The logical part of me is trying to calm myself down, but the terror wins. I spam Asher's phone with texts, just hoping for one back. Even if it's a 'K' or a thumbs up emoji.

I sit in my chair, in a foggy daze, throughout the rest of first period. Ms. Jacobs drones on and on, but my mind remains steadfast on Asher.

As the fear of what could be happening rises to the surface, I do something I haven't done since I was a little girl: I pray.

I pray to God or whatever higher power is out there that

Asher is okay and that he's just in a mood. I pray that he comes to school later or at least answers my fucking texts. I just pray that he's okay. He has to be okay. I *need* him to be. I will never forgive myself if he isn't.

Please be okay, Asher. Please.

THIRTY
Rowan

One week ago, I was lying in bed with Asher, on top of the
world that this angel of a human being was my boyfriend. I
had never felt closer to him because I shared my traumatic past
and my struggles with him and he accepted me, soothed me,
and loved me.

Now, I've never felt more distant from him. More so than
when he would pick on me or when I didn't even know him.
Right now, in this moment, it's the furthest I've ever felt from
Asher. Because I bared my soul to him, told him things I've
never told anybody else, and he left.

In the past week, I've processed and reprocessed
everything. I turned it over in my head a million times, trying
to figure out what went wrong—what the hell I did to make
him disappear for a week.

The second he woke up, I knew I shouldn't have pushed
the topic. Just because I shared stuff with him doesn't mean he
would want to share similar things with me. But I couldn't help

my irritation at that fact.

If you love someone, and you want to be with them, you should feel comfortable enough with that person and trusting enough of them to share personal things about yourself. *Especially* after that person shared those same things with you.

Asher went on about how he's not enough for me, but maybe I'm not enough for *him*. Love is about being vulnerable and intimate; it's about being completely open with someone in a way that's different from everyone else. It's about letting someone into your mind, body, and soul.

At least, that's what I think love is about. I suppose Asher doesn't think that, and if that's the case, then *my* love is not enough for him. Because I can't be 100% open and vulnerable and intimate with someone if I won't get the same in return.

That's the conclusion I came to this morning. After texting Asher multiple times every day and begging him to come back to me, and hearing nothing but radio silence, I realized that I'm not enough for Asher. If I was, he would've responded to my texts. He would've opened up to me that morning. And he wouldn't have left.

Maybe that's not true, but Asher's not here to prove me wrong. All I have right now are my thoughts and they are running crazy with the possibilities. Ones that always lead back to my insufficiency as a partner.

The worst part is that I'm already too far past the point of just loving Asher. I'm in love with him. But he's clearly not in love with me, which means I need to get over it. He broke my heart one week ago and now it's time for my heart to heal.

That's easy to say in the daytime, when I have Kennedy by my side to hold me up and I don't have to be alone—or worse, be with my parents. But in the nighttime, when I'm all alone and there's no one here to distract me, that's when it's the hardest.

A deep sigh escapes my lips and I sit up in my bed. This is the seventh night in a row that this has happened. I tell myself during the day that I'm healing my broken heart, I'm getting over him. And then the moment I try to fall asleep, all the thoughts swirl in my head and sleep is in a faraway place that will never reach me.

Because I miss him. I miss him so fucking much.

From a young age, I promised myself I would never become dependent on anyone again. Not after what happened with Rory. But Asher took the glass encasing that I curated around my heart and pierced it with his icy blue eyes, shattering it forever to make room for him.

Asher has become part of me. He crawled deep beneath my skin and settled in my bones. Not having him here with me anymore, losing him like this, it feels like my bones have been crushed, my lungs were smashed, and my heart was ripped clean right out of my chest.

The way I love Asher is beyond what I ever thought a human was capable of feeling. I thought this kind of love only existed in books or movies. And losing him has hurt me more than ever. Almost as much as losing Rory, but in a completely different way.

With Rory, I had a year to accept the fact that one day I would lose her to cancer. It didn't ease the pain at all when she did eventually pass, but I had time to process it and I could spend every day before her unfortunate fate making up for the years we'd eventually lose.

But with Asher, it was so sudden I think I may have gotten whiplash. Just when I thought everything might finally be okay, when I came to terms with my feelings, when I accepted that I'm in love with him, it all blew up in my face. There was no time to process, no time to make up for the future where I wouldn't have him anymore.

There wasn't even time for me to tell him I love him. Now, he may never know.

I have no idea where he went or if he'll ever come back. Considering what little I know about his family life, I wouldn't be surprised if he disappeared forever and I never saw him again.

The thought of that makes my chest tighten and my breathing halt. Never seeing those beautiful blue eyes, never kissing those perfect full lips, never having his strong arms wrapped around me ever again—I'm not sure I could survive that.

During the day, I'm strong and say I'm getting over him. But in the darkness of the night, when I'm all alone and desperately in need of his touch, his smell, *him*, I know that I need him.

And it's because of this need that, even though I know I should move on and I shouldn't continue to see the best in Asher when he continues to prove me wrong every day that passes, I still wait for him.

Lying back down in my bed, I stare up at the ceiling with anticipation and despair. My alarm clock reads 1:03a.m. and I know I should give up. It's been a week now. But, the tiny voice in the back of my head reminds me that I can't. For all the reasons I just said and for this: because I love him. It's as simple as that.

Asher—like me—has only ever had people give up on him. This much I know. And I won't be one of them. So, I stay awake into the late hours of the night, for as long as my body can stand it before it slips into a light sleep.

I stay awake for him, for the possibility that he might come back. For the hope that he does.

For the past seven nights, these exact thoughts cross my mind and I continue to wait for him to come back. I wait for him to tap on my window, climb in, and wrap his arms around me.

I wait because, if that's what he needs, I will give it to him. I wait because, if he doesn't need it, then at least he'll know how I feel about him. I wait because, if I don't, my heart might just permanently shatter.

As I start to drift off to sleep, my body giving in and my mind settling on the idea that he's not coming back tonight—if he ever comes back at all—I hear a rustling noise outside of my window.

My eyes fly open and my body shoots back up into its upright position. I hold my breath as the hairs on my skin rise, goosebumps filling the open space. I'm not sure if it's just the wind, possibly an animal outside in the bushes, an intruder, or Asher. But out of all of these options, that last possibility is the one that has me feeling the most panic and peace at the same time.

My heart wants—*needs*—nothing more than for it to be Asher. But my head is swirling with all the other possibilities that the noise could be, not wanting to get my hopes up.

The sound outside quiets and my chest deflates as my back

slouches against my head board. Just as I lose all hope, I hear the windowsill start to shuffle up—since I left it unlocked all week in hopes that Asher would come back—and the goosebumps are back. I watch, in a frozen position from my bed, as the darkness in my room fills with the shine of the moonlight and a gust of wind blows through the room.

This is it. No animal or wind would be able to open my window like this. A chill is sent up my back as I see the outline of a person's body climbing through my window and appearing at full height just inside my room. Before I can let the panic set in that I might be getting murdered right now, I catch sight of black script ink on the person's neck, lit up by the bright white moonlight.

Asher.

He came back to me.

Without another thought, my legs are swinging over my bed and I'm running straight to the window. He must've seen me the whole time because I throw myself at Asher and he catches me.

He catches me. He doesn't let me fall.

My arms squeeze around his neck and I bury my face in his chest. His strong arms match mine as they sling around my waist and hold my body flush against his. I feel his face fall to my neck and he kisses my skin. This little act—reciprocating my embrace and kissing the skin in the small crevice between my neck and collarbone—tells me all I need to know.

Wherever he went, whatever he did, it wasn't because of me. And he wasn't ignoring me. He needed space and he needed time. Space to heal from whatever trauma he experienced and time to come to terms with his past so he can overcome it.

I know this because I needed it, too, once. And now it was his turn to need it. He may have left, but he didn't leave *me*. And that's all I need to know.

We stay in this position for a while, just holding each other and placing small kisses on each other's skin. Finally, he lifts me up and, without a word, Asher carries me to my bed. He carefully places me down on my side and crawls over to his side.

His side. Because he has a side of the bed. My bed. It belongs to him, just like my heart.

I watch Asher slide under the sheets and lay on his side, facing me. His eyes are puffy and his lips are cracked. Whatever he did this past week, wherever he was, it was hard on him. I can see it in the way his face is more hollow and his body is more tense.

"I'm sorry," I whisper. I need him to know that I shouldn't have pushed him. I need him to know that I won't, ever again. And I need him to know that I'm sorry I made him go through whatever he did this past week.

I can barely speak as I feel the sadness rising in my throat and relief washing over my whole body. Sadness that he may still think he's not enough for me, and relief that he's here. "I'm so sorry for everything."

As those final words leave my lips, Asher is shushing me. "Shh," he coos. He tucks a strand of my hair behind my ear and the sparkle in his eyes is back. The one that appears when he looks at me, with awe and wonder and *love*.

"You have absolutely nothing to apologize for. I'm the one who's sorry. I should've *never* left you. And I shouldn't have ignored you for a week. I'm so fucking sorry, angel." He pauses and places a hand on my cheek, wiping away a single tear that fell down my face.

"I want to open up to you and tell you everything. I just have a hard time letting people in. Always have," he explains. "But not anymore. I'm done letting my past haunt me. And I want you to know everything. I *need* you to."

The desperation in his voice braces me for what I'm about to hear. I'm nervous, but I know I need to hear it. And, even more so, I know Asher needs me to hear it even more than I do.

I nod my head and pull Asher close to me, silently listening as he opens a hole into his mind and heart for me to see through.

THIRTY-ONE
Asher

My life wasn't always like this. I wasn't always a cracked soul with a fucked up family. Don't get me wrong, my family was always fucked up. But *I* wasn't always fucked up. I wasn't always so... broken.

For as long as I could remember, my dad was a drunk. The earliest memory I have of my father was at the playground down the street from our house when I was five. My brother, Bentley, and I begged my dad all morning to take us to the swings so we could reach the sky in our seats. He kept telling us to 'shut the fuck up,' but we were relentless.

Finally, after wearing him down long enough, he gave in and took us to the playground. Looking back, he probably was hungover and didn't want to hear two kids irritating him. But, how could two kids understand that?

When we got to the swings, Bent and I ran to two seats beside each other and we started kicking at the ground to get us higher and higher. After a while, we were just moving sideways instead of back and forth because we couldn't figure it out.

We called our dad over, but he was slumped on a bench with a bottle in his hand. I ran over to him and I realized he was asleep. The old bastard fell asleep on a park bench with a bottle of whiskey clutched in his hands while his two little kids played on the playground.

What kind of fucker leaves his five and eight year old sons to play by themselves while he drinks himself to sleep? On an open playground, in a shitty neighborhood, where some predator would love to come and snatch up two kids?

At the time, I remember it didn't faze me. Not even a little, because I was probably used to this shit. When I came into this world, on June 8th, 2000, I was born into a family with an alcoholic, abusive father and a helpless mother who used drugs and alcohol to escape.

The first time my dad ever hit Bentley was about a year after the playground incident, when he was nine.

Bentley asked if he could watch some cartoons on the TV while our dad was watching a baseball game. This pissed him off because he thought Bentley was acting like an entitled brat. Instead of telling Bentley no, our father got up out of his chair and threw his beer bottle at Bentley's head.

Bent ducked and tried to get out of the way when he saw the bottle coming at him. I remember that most of the bottle hit the wall behind him, but a small piece of glass ended up grazing his cheek and cutting him open. He started crying and gripped his cheek in pain. This only upset our drunk father more, and he stomped over to Bentley and slapped him.

The slap echoed throughout the entire house and Bentley

went flying to the ground. He started wailing in tears and our father yelled at him to shut the fuck up before he actually gave him something to cry about. That was the first, last, and only time Bentley cried when our father hit him.

About a month later, my dad started hitting me too. At first, it was in retaliation to Bentley and I asking for something or bothering him. But after a while, we started to get hit because we didn't set the dinner table properly or we forgot to get him a napkin.

It became normal when I had bruises all over my body and my cheeks were always red from being slapped. Then, towards the end, we started getting hit because our father ran out of liquor or just because we happened to be in the room when something else pissed him off, like a player missing a swing in baseball or a dog barking next door.

But even in these circumstances, even with all the abuse and neglect and trauma, my soul never broke. I didn't let it dwindle my spirit. I was adamant to remain a happy kid outside of that house. Happy enough, at least.

Until July 26th, 2012. That was the day my soul completely shattered, my heart was crushed, and my life all-but ended.

The day started normally. It was a Thursday, so Bent and I had school at 8:10a.m. He woke me up at 7:15a.m, we brushed our teeth, got dressed, and ate our cereal at the kitchen table together. Our routine was the same and we always did it together. Then, Bent packed both of our lunches, zipped up our backpacks, and we left for school.

We didn't go to the same school anymore since he was in high school and I was in junior high still. But our schools were across the street from each other and they had the same start and end times, so Bent always walked me in the mornings and walked home with me in the afternoons.

We got there ten minutes early as always and I watched him cross the street to his school. The school day was uneventful and before I knew it, Bent was waiting for me outside the front doors at 3p.m. We walked through our front door shortly after and we sat down at the kitchen table to do our homework, just like we always did.

Everything was normal, the same as any other day. Until it wasn't.

Around 4p.m., our father came home drunk. He yelled at us, something about not making him dinner. Bent tried to tell him it was too early for dinner, but it was no use. I was trying to pay attention to my homework when Bent received the first slap. But it wasn't a slap. It was a punch. A closed fist, full force punch to a fifteen year old's jaw.

I heard Bent scream and that was what caused me to look up. Bent never screamed when our father hit him, not after the first time. But when I raised my eyes, Bent wasn't standing. He was on the floor. Cradling his face in the fetal position, a small pool of blood under his cheek.

I got up, scared that I would be next, and I left him there. I left my brother, hurt on the floor with my father hovering over him. I ran to my bedroom and sat against the closed door, hiding from my father. It went on for half an hour. Bent's screams. I heard thuds and grunts and my brother's cries for help. And I just sat there with my head in my hands, listening behind my door.

When I finally heard my father's heavy footsteps walk away and the slam of the front door, I jumped up and ran for my brother. When I saw the scene in front of me, I started panicking.

His body lay in a pool of blood on the kitchen floor. There was blood everywhere. His eyes were closed and he wasn't moving. I fell to my knees and reached out to him, trying to shake him awake. I thought he was sleeping. I *prayed* he was just sleeping. But I couldn't hear him breathe.

He wasn't moving. He wasn't alive. He was gone. My brother was dead.

I started crying, sobbing, screaming, wailing. The noises coming from my mouth sounded like they were coming from somewhere else, some*one* else.

Why my brother? Why did my father kill him? Why did I *leave* him? This was all my fault. I should've stopped my father. But instead I ran away and left my brother to die.

At some point, the cops were called and I was being pulled away from Bentley's body by a paramedic. I ended up at the hospital with nurses, doctors, cops, and CPS workers all surrounding me. They asked me questions and tried to understand what happened, but I couldn't focus on anything.

My brother, my protector, my best friend was dead.

The four years after Bentley's death were hell. I barely remember anything, but I do remember the agonizing pain I was in. Every time I had a second to sit and think, my head hurt, my heart hurt, my soul hurt. So I dissociated as much as I could. I didn't want to feel the pain, the grief, the *guilt*. It was too much. Everything was too fucking much.

I was twelve years old and my life felt like it ended at the exact moment Bentley's did.

Sometime during those few years, my father was arrested

and convicted of aggravated murder in Ohio, where we're from. Because he killed a child, he was sentenced to death and was placed on death row.

He's currently at Chillicothe Correctional Institution in Ohio. My mom told me all this stuff a few years after because I was too out of it to even process anything. At some point, the prosecution actually tried to get me to testify in the trial, but I could barely string five words together—let alone testify on a stand for however long in a murder trial.

After years of sitting in custody and waiting trial, my father was convicted and sent away, two months before my sixteenth birthday. Immediately after, my mom moved us to Jacksonville to "start fresh," or whatever. Like I could just forget my brother, her *son*.

Everything moved so quickly. One day, Bent and I were brushing our teeth together and the next, my father was murdering him on our kitchen floor. Then, my father was sentenced to death and I was living in Jacksonville with my mom. And I lost the most important formative years of my life because I could barely remember a goddamn thing.

I've been broken since that afternoon. I've been a shell of myself just going through each day trying to make it to the end. I haven't been living, I've just been surviving. I miss Bentley more than anything. I feel guilty that I left him. And I hate my father for what he did. I fucking hate him.

That's the emotion that I'm left with every time I think about it. I feel the sadness, the longing, the guilt, but most of all, I feel the anger. The disgust, the hatred towards this man who cared so little about his own child that he killed him in a drunken fit of rage.

I haven't spoken to my father since I was twelve years old, and yet, the bastard still rules my entire fucking life. Everything I've done since the moment I found Bentley has been a result of my anger. My anger towards the situation, my anger towards the universe for taking Bentley from me, and my anger towards myself for leaving him. But most of all, my anger towards my father.

Hating that man isn't enough. I want him dead. He's supposed to be dead, and yet there he is, still sitting on death row, getting to live each day while my brother is buried in the ground.

I've never even had a chance to visit Bentley's grave. When I finally took a minute to catch my fucking breath and realize what the fuck my life's become, I realized I never visited him. I know where he's buried, but I just never went. Every day since our move to Jacksonville, I've thought about taking a drive back to Ohio to visit his grave, but I never have. Until now.

When I got into a fight with Rowan—because I didn't want to open up about my past—I realized everything I had to lose. Rowan was the first person to make me *feel* again after Bent's death.

Granted, in the beginning when I was picking on her, what I felt was disdain, but at least I was feeling *something*. And now, she makes me feel alive and love and happiness.

She makes me *want* to be alive, want to be *happy*. She makes me want to live, instead of just survive. And I realized in that fight that if I didn't share my past with her, I could lose her.

And it wasn't that I didn't *want* to open up. It was that I couldn't. Not until I finally came to terms with it myself. And to do that I needed to visit Bentley's grave. And I needed to visit my father. I needed to see my brother to apologize and I needed to see my father to finally let his hold over me go.

I can't harbor this anger and hatred anymore. I needed to let my father *go*. So I did exactly that.

I left Rowan's house and I got in my car and drove straight up to Ohio. I went to visit Bentley's grave and I apologized for leaving him there that night. I apologized for playing a part in his death and I forgave myself for it because I knew he forgave me, too.

Then, I went to the prison and I visited my father. He told me I was the only visitor he had had since he got locked up and he was happy to see me. I didn't give him enough time to speak before I told him to go fuck himself.

That day at the prison, I finally rid myself of him once and for all. I let him and all my anger go. He wasn't my father anymore, he was the man who killed my brother. And justice will come to him. Justice will be served the day his sentence is carried out and that man will die alone. Just like Bentley had to.

I found peace in that.

THIRTY-TWO
Rowan

My heart is broken. Absolutely shattered.

Hearing Asher's story and where he went last week is absolutely gut-wrenching. I can't even imagine what it felt like for him, going through all that.

While we both lost siblings—and simultaneously, our parents—he lost his in a much more violent, horrific way. The pain that must have come with that, it's earth-shattering.

Our family issues are incomparable, but I understand the likeness I initially felt with Asher, now. For both of us, we only have ourselves. No more siblings, no more parents—no more family.

"Asher…" I start, but I'm at a loss for words. This is probably how he felt when I opened up to him, but he had the amazing ability to say exactly what I needed to hear in that moment. Now, I'm sitting here in the same position he was in and I'm speechless; I want to tell him what he needs to hear, but I have no idea what that is.

"You don't have to say anything. Just being here, listening—it's exactly what I need." He whispers, reading my mind.

I watch Asher for a moment in awe. This man has been through more than any one person should ever have to go through in five lifetimes, let alone one. And yet, he's here, opening up.

He's healing himself from his traumatic past and showing that he truly can overcome the hardest of battles, as long as he is supported and cared for. Both of which he showed me, and I'm now showing him.

"You amaze me," the words slip out and a light blush crawls onto my cheeks when I realize my admission. A sad smile appears on Asher's lips and my embarrassment quickly fades.

"*You* amaze *me*, Rowan. Every day, since the moment I saw you."

The only thought that comes to my mind appears in a quick rush of adrenaline. I'm so overwhelmed by it that I need Asher to hear it, right here in this moment.

"I love you," I whisper, breathless. The spark in Asher's eyes intensifies and takes over his entire pupils, to the point where I think his eyes are brighter than the sun. But his eyebrows furrow and a pained look crosses his face.

"Before I can say it back—and I *really* want to say it back— I need you to hear this. The reason I had to go back to Ohio, and for as long as I did, was because I needed time to process everything. I stayed in a motel and I just needed some time to finally come to terms with it all. I had to work it through in my head. It wasn't because I needed to be away from you. I just needed to be there, alone.

"But I got all your texts. Every single one. You have no idea how badly I needed them, to help me get through it and remind myself why I was doing it in the first place." Asher pauses and takes a breath.

His thumb slowly rubs my cheek and my heart nearly bursts at his next words. "To remind myself of the kind of man you deserve—the kind of man I want to be for you."

"You are that man, Asher. I promise you," I whisper as I pull him closer to me so that he's as close as humanly possible.

"Thank you for saying that, angel," he whispers back. I brush my mouth against his and I start to separate my lips when Asher pulls away slightly.

"I promise I will kiss you. But first," he pauses. His eyes look directly into mine and I feel like he can see straight into my soul. "I love you, Rowan Lila Easton. I love you more than life, more than Barack Obama loves Michelle, more than a kid loves ice cream. I love you more than I've ever loved any*one* or any*thing*. You, my love, have my entire heart. I am yours, wholly and completely. So, when I say that I love you, I want you to know that I mean it. More than I've ever meant any other words that have ever left my lips."

There are no words that I could possible say that could top that. So, doing the only thing I can think even slightly measures up, I let my fingers find the back of Asher's head and I pull his lips to mine.

Our mouths connect and I swear someone set fireworks off in my room. I slide my tongue across his bottom lip and he opens his mouth so that our tongues can dance together.

The longer we kiss, the more I feel our bodies fusing

together, starting with our mouths and moving all the way down as our limbs intertwine to become one.

I am no longer Rowan without Asher. And Asher isn't Asher without me anymore. We are the same body, heart, and soul. Because that's how much I love him, and how much he loves me.

Our love is all-encompassing and I wouldn't have it any other way. We're perfect for each other and it amazes me we had gone so long being apart from each other.

"I love you, Asher Madigan. More than the sun and moon and Saturn." I mumble against his lips and he breaks away from my lips, a big grin on his face as his quiet laughs fill the space between us.

"Why Saturn? What about the other planets?" He asks between soft chuckles. My lips break into a grin and I can't help but laugh, too.

"I don't know. It was the first planet I could think of," I giggle.

His laughs become even louder and I can't help but break out into a full laugh with him. "For a straight-A student, you don't know much about astronomy, huh?"

"Fine, how about this: I love you more than the whole universe. Every planet, star, and meteor in existence." I offer and his laughs are replaced by the softest smile I've ever seen.

"Perfect. Just like you," he smiles and places a kiss on my forehead. Asher pulls my head to his chest and we fall asleep just like that.

In a perfect position of intertwined limbs and connected hearts.

THIRTY-THREE
Asher

There's something bright shining in my eyes and the sound of an annoying bird chirping outside a nearby window that's ringing in my ears.

I fling my arm over my eyes and squish a pillow over my left ear as I grind my right ear further into the pillow underneath my head. Instead of covering most of my face, the pillow hits something beside me—or rather, some*one*.

"Ow," whispers a soft, feminine voice beside me. I let go of the pillow, letting it slide to the back of my head, and open one of my eyes to find Rowan staring up at me. "Morning," she whispers with a small smile on her face.

Looking into her green eyes, the memories of last night—and the last week—rush back to me. I'm always confused and disorientated when I wake up, but seeing this perfect girl beside me, tangled up in my arms, everything falls back into place.

This is the second time I've ever woke up beside someone

before and, while I could do without the bright sun or outside noises, I never want to wake up any other way.

Slowly, the foggy cloud in my head clears and reality is exactly as it's supposed to be. Waking up next to Rowan, her goofy smile being the first thing I see in the morning, is the life I'm meant to live. I can feel it in my soul—the one I didn't realize I still had left until a few weeks ago.

"Good morning," I respond and the corners of Rowan's mouth upturn as her cheeks warm the slightest shade of pink. I can tell exactly what she's thinking without her saying a word, that's how well I know her.

"I like your voice in the morning," she says anyway. I lightly connect our lips and take in the sweet taste of her mouth. Morning breath was always something that turned me off completely, and frankly just the thought of it was disgusting, but Rowan's is practically non-existent. She tastes as perfect as she does any other time of day—like mint and sweetness and *home*.

She pulls away first and rustles underneath my heavy limbs to crawl out of bed. "We have to get ready for school," she explains as she walks to her door and leans against it.

"Is that so?" I tease, knowing she pulled away because, if she didn't, that kiss would have progressed much further than it should on a school morning. For her, anyways. I'm down for whatever, wherever, whenever.

Rowan groans and pushes herself off her door to walk back over to me. Instead of crawling back into bed, she pulls the sheets off of me and exposes my shirtless body to the cold room.

Goosebumps hit my skin and the hairs on my arms stand

up. It was nice and warm beneath the sheets—and with Rowan close to me—but now, without Rowan or the sheets, I'm completely exposed to the frigidness of her room.

"You have to go before my parents hear or see you." Rowan stands expectantly at the side of her bed, gesturing for me to leave the same way I appeared last night. She obviously didn't take the teasing well, so now I'm being punished.

I flash her my puppy dog eyes and the way her face falls the slightest amount tells me she's torn. I can nearly hear the small crack in her new-icy frontier, but the sound rummaging in the kitchen down the hall sends her into full-on crisis mode.

The reality that her parents can barge into her room right now hits me and I quickly scramble out of bed. Not because I'm afraid of them, but because I know how horribly they treat Rowan and I wouldn't want to be the reason they do something even worse to her.

Rowan hands me my shirt, her hands shaking and a panic evident in her eyes, and quickly pecks my lips. I take an extra second to deepen the kiss and place my hand on her lower back, hopefully calming her down.

"I love you," I whisper against her mouth and feel her exhale on my lips. "I'll pick you up in thirty minutes."

She nods and pecks my lips once more, then watches me climb through her window. Once I'm on the other side, I turn once more and give a small wave to my girl. She smiles and I watch her let out a deep breath.

She's relieved now that her parents can't catch me in her room. On the one hand, I completely understand her panic. Getting caught with a boy in your room usually isn't a good situation for a teenage girl.

But I know it's more than that for Rowan. Her parents wouldn't just freak out, they would scream the most vile, disgusting, wicked things at her. That's why Rowan was freaked out—not because she knew I shouldn't be there, but because of what her parents would say to her if they found me.

I fucking hate her parents for making her live in so much fear and panic. And I hate them for causing her so much pain and mental torture.

Rowan is the kindest, purest, most genuine person in a world full of hatred, jealousy, and anger. It kills me that so much negativity and pain is brought to her life by the two people who should only ever love and support her.

I stand in my place outside Rowan's window for a few minutes longer than I should, but I have to watch her for a bit before I can leave. She turns away, thinking I've left, and she makes her bed, lays out her clothes, and pulls her hair back as she exits her bedroom door—probably to get ready in the bathroom.

As I watch her leave, I decide I shouldn't just stand out here looking like a stalker. Unfortunately, I don't really have anywhere to go. Last week when I left Rowan's, I only went back home to grab the essentials and as much of my clothes as I could while my mom was gone, since she kicked me out of the house.

I lived in a motel in Ohio for the past week, but there's no way I can permanently stay in one, not with the small amount of money I saved up from my part-time job at the grocery store and side jobs working on peoples cars or fixing up things in their houses. My only option is to live out of my car.

Luckily, my mom's work schedule at the bar—and then her

"after-work job" that usually finds her in random men's houses or motels—keeps her out of the house at least from 2p.m. to 2a.m. every day. Sometimes she stays out all night, but during those hours, I know for sure she's not there. So, at least I can slip into the house to do some laundry, swap out any essentials, and grab some food.

I sigh and start to head down the road towards my car, since I have thirty minutes to kill before I can come back to Rowan's. Last night, I parked down the road so Rowan's parents wouldn't be suspicious of a random car in their driveway, but I'm starting to regret parking so far because it's way too early for such a long walk. It's like the crack of fucking dawn.

Finally reaching my car, I slide into the driver's seat and pick out a random pair of jeans, a change of boxers, and a hoodie—since it's getting much chillier in the late October air. I spend ten minutes trying maneuver myself into my fresh clothes while still sitting in my seat, until I finally get everything on.

I toss the old clothes into my designated-laundry garbage bag and get out to put the old and new clothes all in the trunk. I don't want Rowan, or anyone else from school, to see that I'm literally living in my car. They'll only have pity on me, and I don't need that shit. Never have, never will.

There's still ten minutes before I have to pick up Rowan, so I decide to head to the Starbucks drive-through one street over to kill time. Rowan usually gets an iced caramel latte from the coffee shop we go to after school, so I decide to get that for her and an iced black coffee for me.

The barista asks if I want anything else and I internally

debate getting Rowan something to eat. Although, I know she's still struggling and recovering from her eating disorder, so I'm not sure pushing food on her is the right way to go.

I've never been close to someone with anorexia, so I'm always cautious about saying the wrong thing or doing something triggering for her. But I always remind myself to just be there for Rowan and not treat her like a fragile glass that'll easily break. If I do something wrong, she'll tell me and that's all I need to remember.

Deciding to get a croissant in case Rowan wants it, I place the drinks in the cup holders and put the croissant in the middle console. I check the time and it says *6:59a.m.*, which is right when I told Rowan I would pick her up, so I quickly head back.

Pulling into her driveway, Rowan is already standing in front of her garage, waiting for me. She was gorgeous this morning when she was still half asleep, and she's just as gorgeous now that she's all ready to go.

Rowan's dark blue jeans hang loosely on her hips and are baggy down her legs, but she pulls them off better than anyone else ever could. She has a plain black t-shirt on that is the slightly cropped since the bottom hem hits right at the top of her mid-rise jeans. She's wearing plain white sneakers and her outfit is simple, but perfect for her because her beauty outshines anything she could possibly wear.

I can tell she brushed her hair because it's not nearly as disheveled as it was this morning and it's much more tamed now. She has no makeup from what I can tell, not that she needs it anyway. She's perfect exactly how she is.

The sunlight hits the side of her face and the green in her

irises shines bright enough to show their true light emerald color. Her skin is so soft and the sun only enhances the soft glow of her face and the light pink in her cheeks.

She looks like a goddess standing right before me and I can't help but think about how lucky I am. Rowan Easton is my angel sent from heaven and I am the luckiest person in the entire world that I get to love her and be with her.

I only wish I could be a heaven-sent angel for her. Instead, she gets fucked-up, old me.

"You okay?" Rowan asks from my passenger seat, pulling me out of that last thought. I didn't realize Rowan moved from her spot on the driveway to my car already. "You look lost in thought."

"All good, angel. Let's go." I brush off her concern and shift my car in reverse. Rowan starts to play with my radio, finding a station she likes, and I silently thank her for choosing music over talking.

I drive quickly the whole way to school, letting the music on the radio fill the silence between us. Rowan doesn't seem concerned though—and if she is, she doesn't show it—so at least it's not uncomfortable or awkward.

When I pull into a spot in the parking lot, I reach over to Rowan and put my hand on her cheek as she turns to look at me. "I love you," I say as I brush my thumb across her cheek. Rowan smiles to me and returns the words.

"I love you, too."

No matter how many times she tells me, I'm not sure I'll fully believe it. I'm hard to love—impossible, even—and Rowan deserves a million times better than me. But that's my own issue, and she doesn't need to be concerned with it, so I'll keep it to myself.

Hopefully one day, she'll tell me she loves me and I'll finally be able to fully accept it, the way she accepts my love. I'm tired of only accepting the love I think I deserve. And Rowan doesn't deserve that. *One day…*

I get out of the car and open Rowan's door for her, walking hand-in-hand into the school with her. There's no other place I would rather be than by Rowan's side. It's the first time I've ever felt like I found a place where I belong. At Rowan's side.

As we walk through the front hallway, the first thing I hear is a massive wave of whispering hitting my ears. The further we walk, the stronger the whispers become. In a flash, everyone's voices rise even higher and I'm suddenly catching random snippets from various conversations.

"His dad is in prison for child murder…"
"His mom is a whore and a drunk…"
"No wonder he has issues, his family is so fucked-up…"
"Rowan better get out while she still can…before he kills her just like his dad killed his brother."

That last one feels like a blow to the chest and all the air from my lungs disappears into thin air. My whole body freezes and I stop in the middle of the hallway. Rowan's hand pulls me forward, but she comes to an immediate halt when she realizes I'm not following her anymore.

Rowan's hand falls at her side and she turns toward me, her face grim and a red, hot anger in her eyes. She heard that last comment, too. And by her reaction, she is furious.

From the corner of my eye, I catch sight of Maddox

rushing toward me from the other side of the hallway, a school newspaper in his hand. "Dude, did you see this?" He asks when he reaches me and shoves the paper in my chest.

Before I have a chance to look, Rowan grabs the newspaper and quickly scans her eyes over the front-page article. Over her shoulder, I read the headline in big bold letters and all feeling in my body sinks down to my toes.

WHY DID MYSTERIOUS ASHER MADIGAN DISAPPEAR FOR A WEEK?

Tragic past revealed: killer dad, murdered brother, prostitute mother

All the color drains from my face and it takes everything in me not to take all my anger out with my fists. I beg my body to get itself together and brush this off, but instead I'm frozen in the middle of the hallway.

Everything around me starts to move in slow motion and I see everyone's eyes bounce from Maddox to Rowan to me. The yellow-tinted light in the hallway grows brighter and brighter and brighter until I think I'm going to faint. Every inch of my skin begins tingling and it feels like my whole body is buzzing. The loud whispers continue to blare in my ears, but it slowly gets drowned out as a high-pitch yelling replaces all the sound in my ear.

"WHO THE FUCK IS RESPONSIBLE FOR THIS?" Rowan's screams pull me out of my trance. "Who is it?!" She demands, her face redder than I've ever seen it. And I swear I see steam blowing out of her nose and ears.

From what I could tell, the article was anonymously written and published, but seeing how angry Rowan is, I don't think anyone is going to speak up and tell her that right now.

Maddox grabs Rowan's shoulders and pulls her back from where she's standing right in people's faces.

"Rowan, stop." My voice sounds foreign in my ears, and I'm still so out of it I don't know how I even said those words. But I did, and Rowan's frantic eyes find mine. Her entire face softens when she sees the look on my face, probably because all the color is drained from my face and my features are as hard as a metal shield.

I'm just confused and shell-shocked. How did anyone find any of this shit out? I changed my fucking last name for a reason. And why would anyone publish this for the whole school to read? I know I can be a bit of an asshole, but this is just sinister. Airing out my trauma to the whole school is beyond fucked. It's straight-up evil.

The questions are racing through my mind, but I can't be bothered to demand answers in this hallway right now. Anyway, even if these people knew how any of this happened, no one would tell me.

My eyes find Rowan's again and the flames in her eyes return when she sees the tears burning in the corner of my eyes. I fight with everything in me not to let them spill, but Rowan knows me better than anyone, and she can see how hard I'm fighting right now, even if no one else can.

Rowan whips back around and faces the hundreds of kids who have gathered in the hallway since we first walked into the school. "I will lock every one of you fuckers up in this school and burn it to the fucking ground if a single person says one more fucking thing about Asher or his family ever again! Do you understand me? You shouldn't be afraid of Asher. You should be afraid of *me*!"

Pride and love fill my swelling heart and I close my eyes, taking in Rowan's words. Even after everything, she stills defends me and threatens the whole school with arson and murder.

I inhale a sharp breath and open my eyes to see most of the kids have scattered in a hurry. Without thinking another thought, I grab Rowan's waist and lead her outside of the school doors.

Ever since I got together with Rowan, I tried harder to do better in school, since she's a straight-A student. But I can't go another second inside of this school, so I make the executive decision that I'm skipping school today. And hopefully Rowan will stay with me.

She makes no objections as I lead us back to my car. When we both climb in, I finally take a deep breath, the back of my head hitting my headrest, as I let the last ten minutes hit me like a rock.

"I'm so sor—" Rowan starts, but I interrupt her.

"No. Don't say you're sorry, it's not your fault," I insist. Rowan sighs and brings her hands to cup my face. She kisses me tenderly and I've never felt more grateful that she's here.

"You didn't deserve that." She says as she pulls back and slides her hands down my chest. "But, Asher? I need you to know I meant every word I said in there." She pauses and brushes her thumb across my chest.

I study Rowan and wait for her to elaborate, just as her next words settle deep in my chest and crack open my heart. "I swear to God. If anyone ever says anything like that about you again… I'll fucking burn them all to ashes."

J.J. RHODES

THIRTY-FOUR
Asher

I'll fucking burn them all to ashes.

Those words have been echoing in my head from the moment Rowan said them a month ago because they are the only words that could possibly explain just how much I love her, and how much she loves me.

We'll burn the world to ashes for each other.

This past month has been unlike any other. I thought I loved Rowan a month ago, but the love I feel for her right now is nothing compared to back then. And it won't compare to what I'll feel for her in a week, a month, a year.

Every day for the last four weeks, I've woken up with Rowan in my arms. It's easily the best way to start any day. I don't think I'll ever be able to sleep alone again.

If someone had told me a month ago, a year ago, five years ago, that I would be here, I never would've believed them. Every day, I wake up amazed and flabbergasted at how my life ended up this way. But then, the doubt and concern echo in the back of my mind, reminding me that I'm way out of Rowan's league.

That's the last thought that crosses my mind when I climb through Rowan's window and see her already huddled up under her sheets. Usually, she waits for me at her window, ready to help me in at nine o'clock sharp. But, not tonight.

I scramble through the small passage-way, trying not to make any noise, but also not giving a shit. Something's obviously wrong.

"Asher?" Rowan's voice hits my ears and it's thick with tears. She's been crying—*sobbing.*

As if setting off an alarm inside me, Rowan's voice sends me into a sprint over to the side of her bed. I crouch down and take her face in my hands, brushing my thumbs across her cheeks to wipe away the very fresh tears.

"I'm here, angel. I'm here," I soothe. Rowan's chest rises and falls quickly, and tears are still falling from her eyes, telling me that whatever happened was bad.

The only thing I can think of that could help her is to just be close to her, so I tuck my left arm under her waist and use my right to envelope her body in my arms. I lift Rowan up and slide in underneath her sheets, placing her body on top of my mine and resting her head on my chest.

"You don't have to talk about it. But if you want to, I'm here."

I feel Rowan's shoulders shake more strongly against my body and I realize she's now crying harder. Guilt consumes me because I think I may have made it worse by saying that. Shit, I never know the right thing to say.

"She told me I was a waste of space; space that should've

been taken up by my sister." Rowan whispers, the words barely able to leave her mouth. Rage pierces my chest because I instantly know exactly what she's talking about—*who* she's talking about.

"You don't deserve that," I whisper into her hair as I place a kiss on the top of her head.

I don't trust what else would come out of my mouth, so instead I keep it simple and let Rowan cry it out. All I could possibly say would only make her even more upset, and all she needs right now is comfort. So that's what I give her.

"I've thought about suicide in the past, and when my mom said that tonight… it brought back so many of those feelings." Rowan's confession creates a thickness in my throat and twists my heart in an iron grip.

She continues on, so I let her get it all out, instead of interrupting her. "How fucked up is that? A mother making her child want to kill herself. But, of course, I can't do it. It's just like she said, I'm a coward. I can't even go through with ending my own life."

"No, Rowan." I say, my voice strained as I pull her red, swollen face up to look at me. "You are not a coward. Not even fucking close. You're the strongest person I know and you deserve to live, more than your mother or any other person in this world."

Rowan closes her eyes and lets my words sink in. More tears continue to fall from her closed eyelids and I wipe away every single one.

"I don't deserve you," she says as she opens her eyes. Those words pierce my lungs because they're the exact words I've been telling myself about Rowan since the moment I first saw her.

"Wrong, angel. It's me who's undeserving of *you*." I correct her and Rowan starts shaking her head. Before she can protest, I pull her mouth to mine and swallow whatever words she was about to say.

Our lips move in perfect synchronization and the familiar taste of her mouth rushes to my taste buds—mint and sweetness and *home*. I don't want to push this too far, especially considering her cheeks are still tear-stained, so I pull away to stop myself.

A small pout appears on her lips and it takes everything in me not to kiss it away. "Why did you stop?" She asks and I have to bite my lip to keep from laughing at her pouty face.

"It's not really the right time, is it?" I counter her question with my own. A few times we've gotten close to having sex, but I always stopped it before it got too far.

Rowan's a virgin and I don't want to pressure her into doing something she doesn't want. Which is also why, when things got to a certain point, I've always made sure to focus on her. As I tell her every time we get there, I get enough pleasure from watching, touching, and pleasing her.

Without responding, Rowan gets up from her position on top of me and she walks out of her bedroom, carefully opening and closing her door so her parents don't hear. She's gone for a few minutes, and just as I start to wonder if I should check on her, she walks back in.

Now, her hair is pulled up and away from her face in a ponytail and it looks like she splashed her face with water. She looks refreshed, as if the last ten minutes didn't happen.

I watch Rowan close her bedroom door and walk back

over to me. When she reaches me, she finds her previous position in her bed, but keeps her head closer to mine and kisses me deeply. There's a small hint of urgency and hunger in her kiss, and I reciprocate it, even though I know I shouldn't.

A small moan escapes her throat and that makes me pull away from her. "We shouldn't," I say, breathlessly. I want to, more than anything, but it doesn't make it right. She was just having a breakdown, for fuck's sake.

"Asher, I *want* to. And I know you do, too. We love each other," she insists, but I'm still torn. "I want to feel close to you, as close as physically possible," Rowan adds.

I shake my head, trying to clear the horny fog that is clouding the logic in my brain. "You were just sobbing, Rowan."

Her face falls slightly, but she quickly recovers. "You're putting me and my feelings first, and I love you for that. But I promise you, this is exactly what I need right now."

A frustrated sigh leaves my lips and the next words fly out of my mouth. "I can't fuck you five minutes after you told me you thought about killing yourself. You deserve better than that."

"It's not fucking when you're in love, Asher. It's making love. And I want to make love to you, more than anything right now. And I need you to make love to me." My reservations slowly subside as those words leave Rowan's lips.

Making love. It's something I've never done, but somehow it makes the whole atmosphere in this room completely change. Suddenly, the air becomes thick with sex and the pressure in my pants rises.

Sex with Rowan was something I never let myself think

about when we got together because I didn't want my horny mind to ruin what I had with her. But, making love, it changes everything.

"Will you have sex with me, Asher?" Rowan asks for my consent and I chuckle quietly to myself.

"Yes," I whisper and pull her mouth to mine. My brain goes into overdrive and I can't think anymore. Luckily, my hands and body know exactly what to do.

Rowan climbs onto my lap and straddles me, connecting our lips and pushing her hot, wet heat on my dick through my pants. She moans in my mouth as she feels my dick harden underneath her. I swear to God my dick is harder than fucking concrete right now.

The pressure in my pants grows more than I ever imagined it could when Rowan begins to rock her hips against mine. The action causes me to dig my fingers into her hips, but I quickly release when I remember I could hurt her. I need to calm down—*slow* down.

"Don't be fragile with me," she whispers as if reading my mind. Those five words cause me to change course completely. I wanted to go slow and make this special for her, but now, there's no way I can. Rowan has released something deep inside of me. Something needy and rough and hungry.

Even though Rowan and I have never had sex, I've explored her body in more than one way; with my eyes, with my hands, with my *tongue*. They've seen everything. The only thing left is to explore with my dick.

Rowan starts to pull her shirt over her head and my hands instinctively work on her pants. With urgency, Rowan and I work together until we're both naked, our clothes a pile on the floor.

My hands run over her body, touching everywhere. Her thighs, her hips, her stomach, her boobs. My lips continue to suck on hers as our tongues play with each other, causing my hard-on to grow higher and higher.

I wanted my dick to explore her mouth, but I can't wait that long. I need to be inside her. Now.

My left hand settles on her hip and my right hand grips her throat as I separate our mouths and flip her on her back in one swift movement. Rowan gasps at the sudden and rough act; another one escaping when I settle myself between her legs.

I dip my head to connect our foreheads and place my mouth against hers, but I don't kiss her. "You asked for it rough, remember that."

Rowan's eyes go wide and her lips curve into a smirk. I take that as all the confirmation I need before I lean back up on my knees. My eyes quickly graze over Rowan's lower body and the pleasure in the pit of my stomach grows.

I quickly grab the condom from my wallet on her bedside table and rip it open with my teeth, sliding the latex on my dick.

Placing my hands on the back of her thighs, I spread Rowan's legs wide open and take a minute to admire the scene in front of me. Rowan, all spread out, open and ready for me to take her.

Without another second of hesitation, I pull Rowan by her thighs toward me and drop down to my elbows beside her head. I use my left hand to line my tip up perfectly with her entrance and hold her thigh as I push inside of her, slowly.

A sharp gasp escapes Rowan's lips and I groan as half of

my shaft rests inside of her. She doesn't tell me to stop, so I push even deeper inside of her until my full length is inside. She's so tight and she feels *so* good.

"Oh my God," she moans and I connect our lips again, swallowing her words. I pull back out slowly, but Rowan's hands find my lower back as she pulls me back to her.

She wants it again. *Don't have to tell me twice.*

Without warning, I push back into Rowan, harder and faster than the first time. She whimpers in my mouth and I do it again. I keep moving in and out of her entrance as my grip on her thigh tightens.

"Fuck," I moan against her mouth. Her eyes are closed, but the pleasure all over her face tells me all I need to know. She's close. I pull my face away from her so I can watch as she comes from dick inside of her.

I keep the rhythm of my movements steady, hard, rough, and *fast*. I watch as Rowan's lips separate and she arches her body up, so my shaft can hit that perfect spot.

"Jesus," she moans.

"My name's Asher, baby. Jesus has nothing to do with this." My words cause a smirk to play on Rowan's lips, but her eyes stay closed.

"Asher... I'm coming." Rowan moans and her words help get me to the edge, too.

I slam one final, hard thrust into Rowan and I watch as she climaxes just as I explode in the condom. To help us both ride out the high for as long as possible, I continue pushing in and out of her, but my movements slow down as we both come down.

Rowan opens her eyes and looks up at me with such

euphoria in her eyes, it's intoxicating. I pull off my condom and throw it in the trashcan beside her bed, never once breaking eye contact with Rowan.

"I guess I should go clean up," she says. But before she can get up, I pin her down with my hand on her stomach.

"Allow me," I say as I dip my head between her thighs and lick up the mess I made. I hear her whimper under my touch, her heat very sensitive and tender and sore.

I stop myself from making her come again with my tongue, and instead swallow all her juices and climb back up to her.

As I come down from my blissful high, I place one more kiss on Rowan's mouth and tuck her into my body, with her head on my chest. She looks up at me and I watch as the crimson flush on her cheeks turns into a blush pink.

That was by far the best moment of my life. Being so close to Rowan and sharing the most intimate part of myself with her, it was euphoric.

And yet, the only thing on my mind is that I stole something from her. Something that wasn't mine to take. Something that should've been given to someone who actually deserves Rowan, who wouldn't fuck her after she was crying. Someone who isn't *me*.

And those thoughts bring me to the only ending: that, one day, she might grow to hate me for it.

As the saying goes: the highest of highs bring the lowest of lows—what an understatement.

THIRTY-FIVE
Asher

"Bent!" I yell, searching for my brother in the house. *"Do you remember the girl I told you about? In my letter?"*

I continue looking around the house, going in each room and checking to see if my brother is hiding, busy, or asleep.

"Dude, where the hell are you? I have huge news!" I yell again, hoping wherever he is, he hears me. Something in my chest stops me from moving to the next room. The hairs on my neck stand up and I feel the sudden presence of someone behind me.

Quickly, I whip around and come face-to-face with my brother. *"Shit, Bent. You scared the shit out of me!"*

Bentley doesn't say anything, but there's a small grin on his face. He finds this amusing. I glare at him and his left eyebrow raises, non-verbally asking me what it is I wanted to tell him. It's something he's done since we were kids. Always a boy of few words, using body language to speak for him.

"Do you remember the girl I told you about in my letter? From a few years ago?" I pause as Bent doesn't say anything or show any recognition

of what I'm saying. "You read my letter, didn't you?"

Bentley's expression remains cold and steadfast, but of course he would read my letter. He's always been there for me my entire life, he would never purposefully ignore my letter.

"Well, anyway, her name's Rowan. I've been kind of an ass to her for a while. But I turned it around. And now she's my girlfriend," I pause, letting my words sink in. Bentley regards me with a serious expression, as if trying to understand the truth behind my words.

"I love her, Bent. I'm so in love with her—I don't even understand it sometimes. She's my person, you know?" I add, hoping my words can wipe the skeptical look off Bent's face.

Bentley continues to watch me intently and I wait there, hoping he'll say something to break this awkwardness.

After what feels like eternity, Bentley walks close to me and embraces me in a hug. I haven't been this close to him in years. I can't remember the last time I had his arms wrapped around me, my big brother.

Right before I pull away, Bent hugs me a little tighter and whispers something in my ear.

"Don't forget who you were before all this."

"Asher!" I hear a voice whisper with urgency and panic, pulling me out of my dream. I don't have time to process the dream or what's happening because the image in my head is gone and I'm back in reality.

My eyes shoot open, recognizing the angelic voice and realizing something's wrong. "My parents are awake!"

Rowan is scrambling through the pile on her floor for her clothes and she occasionally throws me an item of my clothing. "You have to get dressed and leave. I'm sorry."

I climb out of the oh-so-comfortable bed and pull on my

boxers and pants. "You don't have to apologize, angel. I know that—"

I'm stopped mid-sentence when Rowan's bedroom door is thrown wide open. I'm putting my head through my shirt when a woman's voice echoes through the bedroom.

"Rowan! You're going to be late for school!" The woman screams as she barges into the room. But when she takes in the scene before her—Rowan's messy hair, my half-naked body, the sheets in shambles—her jaw falls open. "What the hell is going on?" I pull my shirt down to cover my torso as I find the wide and frantic eyes of Rowan's mother.

"Mom! I—"

"Shut the hell up, Rowan! Just shut up!" Her mother screams and I open my mouth to stand up for Rowan when she shoves me toward the window. "You! Get the hell out of my house!"

I clamp my mouth shut, stunned at the shift of attention to me. I weigh my options as her mother stands before me, expectantly. The anger in her eyes is definitely there, and I don't want to agitate the situation, so I decide maybe it's best that I leave. I grab my wallet as I walk over to the window and give one last sad look to Rowan. I don't want to leave her alone with her mother, but I'll only make everything worse for her if I stay.

"No! Asher, wait—" Rowan pleads and the sound of a slap sends me into a rapid 180 spin. Rowan's gripping her cheek, tears falling from her eyes, and her mother is exhaling steam.

"You will not see that boy anymore, do you understand?" Her mother speaks to Rowan, pointing a stern finger in her face, as if I'm not even there anymore.

Against my better judgment, I rush to Rowan's side and pull her body to me. I wrap my arms around her neck and kiss the top of her head, ignoring her mother. I'll be fucking damned if I just leave while Rowan's mother physically and verbally abuses her.

"Kid, if you don't leave right now, I'm calling the cops!" Her mother threatens and I close my eyes, knowing that if the cops come, I'm done for. With my family history—my dad being a murderer and my mother being a prostitute—my word means nothing, especially in an argument against a well-respected middle-class woman.

I place one last kiss on Rowan's head and pull away from her, turning to face her mother. I shield Rowan with my body, so she doesn't have to face her mother head-on.

"You know, my dad was abusive to my brother and I when we were younger. You remind me a lot of him. Hitting your kids and getting shitfaced every night." I speak to her in the most condescending tone I can muster without full-on yelling at her. "You know where he is now, my dad? He's in prison. Where you'll end up if you ever place another finger on Rowan again." I threaten, which causes her mother to falter.

But she recovers and does what she does best: slice peoples' hearts in two with her bitter, nasty words.

"If you stay with her, you'll only be ruining her life. You have to know that, right? Bad boy from the wrong side of the tracks with the pretty, smart, innocent girl in the big house." She seethes and I let her words sink in. "You'll break her fragile heart. But she'll recover and she'll find someone who actually deserves her. Someone worthy of being with her. And you? Well, you'll either end up in prison or dead."

I feel Rowan move from behind me, probably ready to protest and insist that that's not true. The problem is… I know it is true. I've known it since the second I saw Rowan. And I've known it every moment we were together.

Which is why I need to let her go. Her mother's right, she'll be heartbroken, but she'll recover. And I won't. But I have to do it. Because I will only ever ruin Rowan's life.

Bentley's words from my dream come back to me.

"Don't forget who you were before all this."

Before my relationship with Rowan, before I decided to be nice, I was an asshole. I was a jerk and a piece of shit before all this. I was fucked up—I still am—and, at the end of the day, I'll only ever drag Rowan down with me, back to hell where I belong.

"Asher—"

"It's fine. I'll go." I interrupt and move away from the ice cold eyes of Rowan's mother. All my body wants—all my soul *needs*—is to turn around and kiss Rowan one last time. But if I do, I won't ever be able to let her go. And no matter what my body, soul, and heart want, I have to do this. I will only ruin Rowan.

The reality of being without her in this cold, angry world hits me and fills me with debilitating fear and dread. She's the only place left where I feel like I have a home. Being at her side is where I feel the most belonging.

But I have to what's best for her. And that's not me. I can't be with her, even if it kills me. Even though I know—it *will* kill me.

So, I keep my back to both Rowan and her mother as I climb through the window. I don't look back as I walk across her lawn to my car. And I don't change my mind and sprint back to Rowan when I reach my car.

Instead, I climb into the driver's seat. I turn on the engine and I drive away from Rowan's street. Away from Rowan's life.

Away from Rowan.

THIRTY-SIX
Asher

I skipped school yesterday and Rowan spammed my phone with messages. They ranged from asking if I was okay, to telling me her mother's stupid and I shouldn't listen to what she said, to begging me to respond.

The last time Rowan sent me these kind of messages, I was in such a dark place and it nearly killed me to read each one. It's crazy how one month later, I'm in the exact same situation, but so completely different.

One month ago, I was doing everything I could to fix myself and start healing after everything I've been through. All to be a better man for Rowan. Now, I'm trying to get over Rowan so she can get over me and go on to be the amazing person I know she's destined to be. The person she can't be with me by her side. Because I'll only hold her back.

The past twenty-four hours have been gut-wrenching. That's the only way to describe it. I actually think I'm growing a stomach ulcer.

One of the worst feelings someone can experience is having to let go of the love of your life because you know you're bad for them. I know it, Bentley knows it, and Rowan's mother knows it. I just wish Rowan knew it, too. It would make it so much easier for her if she just saw how much better off she is without me.

But every time I think about it, I have to remind myself that I'm doing this for Rowan's best interest. She may not know it, but it's the truth. I can't be what she needs.

That's why I had to skip school yesterday. I needed time to figure my shit out, even if it was only one day. I couldn't be in the same cafeteria as Rowan, sit behind her in first period, or pass her in the hallway. She would've tried to convince me of a lie: that nothing matters but us. Everything matters.

Although, I have to go to school today because we have a test in first period. For better or worse, Rowan's rubbed off on me since we've been together and now I take school a bit more seriously. I could easily skip the test, but the hassle that would come as a result is not worth it.

Besides, I think my brain is looking for an excuse to see Rowan. Even if it will end up forcing me to break her heart even more.

I brace myself before the front doors of the school, knowing what's waiting for me on the other side. Her car was already in the parking lot and she's probably waiting at her locker for me to walk through these very doors.

Taking a deep breath, I push through the doors and lift my head in the cocky, confident way I rehearsed for two years. Back when I would tease Rowan and run the whole school.

It's funny how easily I can fall back into this role. For the longest time, it felt like I was wearing a mask, covering up the real me inside as a way to protect myself from the evil in the world. But, over time, I think the mask melted with my real face and replaced the boy I used to be.

I thought being with Rowan brought that old boy back, but maybe it was just a new mask to cover the me I had become. Because walking into this school, my head high, ready to fire at anyone who comes in my way, feels more comforting than it should if it were only a mask.

That is, until I see her. My eyes fall on the 5'8 blonde turned away from me and I feel my heart literally pull me toward her so hard I think it will rip out of my chest if I don't follow it.

My face falters and I try with all my strength not to walk over to her, take her in my arms, and kiss away all my thoughts, all my doubts, and all the truths. I nearly achieve that when Rowan turns around and I'm met with her hopeful green eyes, blush pink cheeks, and plump lips.

Before I know it, I'm walking over to her. My head drops a little and I feel the mask sliding away, down my neck, and to the floor.

"Shit, there you are. Are you okay? What happened? Where were you yesterday? Why didn't you answer my texts?" Rowan bombards me with questions the second I'm close enough for her to whisper to me.

I don't respond because I'm afraid of what will come out of my mouth. It's obvious she still doesn't see it and I know the only words I can possibly say right now will break her.

"Asher? What's wrong?" She asks again and reaches for me, but that's where I draw the line. I do my best to be distant and give her a cold look as I pull away so she can't touch me. "I don't understand…"

"Yeah, obviously." I spit out and wince slightly at the harshness of my voice. Rowan takes a step back with a hurt and sad look on her face. The shock on her face only suffocates my lungs more, but I started this. I need to finish it now.

I take a step back and lift my shoulders back up to resume my high-and-mighty stance; the mask returning with ease. "Look, babe. You were fun for a while, but all your drama just isn't worth it for some mediocre sex." I say, loud enough for people nearby to hear.

I nearly throw up at my words, but if there's one thing I got from my fucked up parents, it's the ability to hit people right where it hurts. I clench my fists, willing this heaviness in my chest to let up so I can walk away and not look back.

Two tears fall down Rowan's cheeks and I almost take it all back right there. *What the fuck am I doing?* I silently beg Rowan to yell at me, hit me, *hate* me. Anything but cry for me.

But then, Rowan wipes her tears and the fire returns to her eyes. Her jaw tightens and she takes a deep breath, a coldness washing over her entire body. I've never seen her like this before, so cold and… broken. Something tells me I've officially pushed her too far.

"Goodbye, Asher."

The second those words leave her lips I know she's gone from me forever. There's no coming back from this. Rowan isn't mine anymore, and she never will be again.

I'm too stunned, too gutted, too *heartbroken*, to respond, so instead I watch as Rowan shuts her locker quietly, walks around me, and out the front doors of the school.

People always try to pinpoint the moment their lives change course, the moment everything changes for them. The moment they go completely off the deep-end, never to return again.

I've only ever had one moment like that in my life: when Bentley died. But, standing here, right now—Rowan walking away from me, her heart at her feet and mine in her hands—this is one of those few moments for me.

The day Bent died, I lost my soul. Being with Rowan, it brought a small piece of it back. But standing here, after I forced Rowan to leave me, I'm not just losing the last piece of my soul. I'm losing my heart, too.

Now, as I stand here, soulless and heartless, I'm wishing for nothing more than a black hole to open up in the floor and swallow me whole.

THIRTY-SEVEN
Rowan

I've never felt pain like this before.

I've felt enormous amounts of pain before, but nothing like this. The type of pain I'm used to is mental—grief, survivor's guilt, anxiety, abuse. This type of pain is emotional and physical.

My heart is in so many pieces, I'm not sure I'll ever be able to collect all the pieces and put it back together. It's like someone dropped a wine glass from a balcony fifty-feet high—and the shattered remains on the concrete is my heart.

There is a weight so heavy on my chest, if I closed my eyes I would think someone was sitting on me. And every time my mind imagines it, that person is Asher. He's crushing my body, my mind, my soul from the inside out.

I'm not sure how I got home. The last thing I remember is saying goodbye to Asher. Those words were some of the hardest ones I've ever had to say, but I had to say something. Something that would hurt him to hear just as much as it hurt me to say.

After that, I was in such a fog of hurt and pain and agony that I don't remember walking home. I just remember wandering. Wandering for however long, with no destination, willing my heart to pick itself up from the ground, put itself back together, and find its way back into my chest.

The second I'm at my front door, my body goes into auto-pilot and I let myself in, lock the door behind me, and head straight for my bed. When my face hits my pillow, the tears start flowing. Faster and harder than they ever have before.

They fall because Asher left me. They fall because I'm not even sure if the last two months of my life were even real with him. And they fall because the only scent filling my nose right now is Asher's shampoo and his cologne from when he slept here, in this very bed, with me two nights ago.

I feel my stomach lurch and I think I'm going to be sick. Running to the bathroom, I cover my mouth with my hand and make it to the toilet before my body is emptying all the contents of my stomach. Not that there's much in there—my stomach's been in knots and I haven't been able to keep anything down since my mother barged in on Asher and I yesterday morning.

Sweat pricks my forehead and I can feel salty tears streaming down cheeks and falling into my mouth. I wipe my mouth with the back of my hand and lean against the wall beside the toilet as I think about how the fuck I got here.

I should've known getting involved with Asher would only end one way. He was an ass, to me and everyone else in that school. But, he changed—or I thought he did, anyway. He was sweet and gentle and thoughtful and *kind*. More and more, every day, he reminded me of the sweet boy from the beginning of sophomore year.

Obviously, I'm a gullible, naïve girl and Asher is a mastermind liar. Now, I can't help but look back at every memory, every moment we spent together and question whether he was being genuine or not. Was it all a game to him? Did he want to see how long it took me to fall in love with him? Was any of it even *real?*

I can't believe I once thought he was made for me. That I was made for him. I may love him, but he obviously doesn't care about me. And I'm definitely not made for him; if I was, he would've never done this to me. Because I could've never done this to him.

It hurts to think this way because a part of me wants to believe him when he shared his past with me, when he was vulnerable with me, when he told me he loved me. But there's no way to tell if it was the truth or not. Because if you really love someone, you wouldn't be able to do what Asher just did to me.

I close my eyes and let that last thought marinate in my head as I make my way back to my bed. In a cloud of anger and haste, I rip off all the sheets on my bed because they're covered in Asher's scent and I want it gone. My whole room smells like him, his presence is everywhere.

Doing the only thing I have any power over right now, I march my sheets to the washer and shove them inside. But then, something snaps in my chest and panic shoots its way up my neck to my head. I quickly pull the sheets out and dig my nose in, making sure his smell is still there.

I'm not ready to get rid of him yet. I know I should, but I

can't. Not yet. So, I quickly bring the sheets back to my room and make my bed again. I tuck myself deep underneath the duvet and his smell wraps itself around my body. It's like a blanket that's on fire, but I'm so cold that I invite the flames to bring me warmth, even if it will kill me.

A strong pain shoots through my side and I'm forced to turn over to alleviate the sore spot. But nothing can stop the pain and hurt coursing through my body.

People say it takes time to get over a broken heart, but I'm afraid time will only make the pain worse. Because every second that has passed since Asher said those words at school, the pain has only increased. It's approaching the point where it's unbearable and it's getting worse the longer I have to live in this cycle of pain.

I thought losing Asher the first time was one of the worst feelings I could ever experience. But then he came back and promised me he would never do it again. Losing him a second time, after his promise, hurts a million times more. Because, now, not only have I lost him, but he lost me too. I can't possibly see a way out of this for us.

I don't trust him anymore and I know I can't love him anymore. His words mean nothing to me and my love means nothing to him, which means we have nothing. All the hope and love and peace I once felt with Asher—for *us*—is gone.

I once said I would burn the world to ashes for him. Little did I know he would burn me before I ever got the chance.

THIRTY-EIGHT
Asher

I've been living in a hazy fog for the past week.

My mind has been existing in a fuzzy cloud and the only clear thought that has passed through my mind is that I love Rowan. And I can't be with her.

I've looked for a thousand ways to get myself out of this depression, but nothing is working. My heart is in so much pain and my mind is so numb. Maddox has tried to cheer me up by bringing me to different parties and finding me other girls to help me forget.

But none of it matters. It's not going to change anything. My life doesn't matter without Rowan, it's not worth living. So instead, I just exist. Like I did before Rowan and like I'll have to after her.

There was only one split second that I felt something, that I awoke from this haze, this past week. I was sitting in first period, waiting for Rowan to show up—which she hasn't all week—and Kennedy walked in.

285

It was the fourth day in a row that Rowan missed school, so a small part of me hoped she was behind Kennedy. But, she wasn't. Instead, a fired-up and angry Kennedy stormed into the classroom and her eyes fell on me. She marched right up to me and slapped me right across the face. The impact was so hard that my head flung to the side and I think I pulled a muscle in my neck.

"You are a disgusting piece of shit. *Fuck* you," she hissed at me and stomped right back out of the classroom. Everyone was shocked and gasps erupted across the classroom, followed closely by intense whispering.

That small moment sparked a flame inside of me, and for a second I thought the numbness would disappear. But it was quickly blown out by the tiny voice in my head that reminded me Rowan was better off. And even if I wanted to, she would never take me back. Not now, not anymore.

So, all I'm left with is this numb feeling. It's not even a feeling, really, because it suppresses anything I could possibly feel, so that I'm left with this hollow nothingness. It reminds me of how I felt dead inside after Bentley's death.

Bentley. Fuck, if there was ever a time I needed him more it would be right now. He always knew exactly what I needed. Sometimes it was words of wisdom, other times it was his comfort. Right now, I would just take a hug, nothing more. Just like in that dream I had, the one right before my life fell apart. Where I reminded him about the letter I wrote.

The letter. If I can't have Bent here with me in the flesh, maybe that letter can bring me some comfort. Deciding I'm done with school today, I rush out of first period before Ms. Jacobs starts her lesson and I run out to my car. Within seconds, I'm starting my car and speeding back to my house.

I'm pretty sure that letter is still in my room somewhere. I completely forgot about it until I had that dream. I just need to remember where the hell I put it.

When I'm back at my house—my mother's house now, since she kicked me out—I run up the stairs to my old room. I head straight to my dresser and move all the clothes aside. I used to hide shit at the back all the time, in case my mother ever decided to come snooping through my stuff, so I check there.

But it's not there. *Where the fuck did I put it?!* Slamming the drawer shut, I lock my hands above my head and think. I would've put it somewhere safe, but not immediately in sight so that I wouldn't stumble on it and feel guilty.

The journal at the back of my closet. Right after Bent died, I would write to him multiple times a day, all in that journal. And I hid it in an old shoe box at the back of my closet. I quickly rush to my closet and, within seconds, the journal is in my hand.

I ruffle through the pages, my chicken-scratch writing taking up most of the pages, and finally I see the last entry. *August 15th, 2016.*

Falling to my knees, I push my back up against the wall for support and I start to read the letter sixteen-year-old me wrote to my dead brother.

It takes me only a few minutes to read it and, the second I read the last word, I immediately start again from the first line. I re-read the letter three times before I finally start to process everything.

What happened to the boy I was when I wrote this letter?

The one who finally had a sliver of hope return to him when he saw Rowan. The boy who thought he deserved Rowan— no, that he was *made* for her. He wanted nothing more than to love Rowan, and he got his dream. And then, I fucked everything up.

I fucked it up because I thought I didn't deserve her, that she deserved so much better than me. But why did the boy back then deserve her and not me?

What changed? I was an ass to Rowan, but the second I had her, that boy came back and everything changed. She said it herself, and I felt it, deep in my heart. That boy resurfaced, the boy who deserved to be with someone as amazing as Rowan.

I became that boy when I was with her, and I let other people's opinions push that boy back down. One of those people being Bentley, in that dream. The dream that reminded me of this very letter.

"Don't forget who you were before all this."

As if a ton of bricks falls on me right there, the air is sucked out of my lungs and I stop breathing. Everything rushes to me at once and I'm paralyzed with my realization.

Bent didn't mean who I was before I got in a relationship with Rowan—when I was an ass. He meant before *everything*. When I was this boy before this letter—the boy before Bentley died. The happy, free-spirited kid.

That little boy, with so much hope and joy, he came back when I was with Rowan. He found his way back into my heart and showed me what true love is. He gave me a glimpse at what a lifetime of loving Rowan could be like.

I've loved Rowan for two years—since I wrote that last letter to Bentley—and when I finally had her, I pushed her away because of my own fears that I wasn't good enough for her. But I was good enough. Rowan told me that herself, and I still ignored her.

My mind is swirling with confusion—sadness and heartbreak. What the fuck do I do now? I've pushed Rowan too far away, there's no way I can get her back now.

But it's that kind of thinking that caused me to push her away in the first place. I'm not sure I can fix this, but I have to try. At the very least, I need her to know exactly how I feel—even if she won't take me back or she really is better off without me. I need to let her make the decision, but I have to fight. Fight for Rowan and fight for *us*.

The clarity I've been searching for—begging for—this past week finally dawns on me and everything falls into place in my head.

Panic and urgency wash over my body as I spring up from the floor. It's been a week and, for all I know, Rowan could be completely over me. Or she could be completely heartbroken. Either way, time is limited and I need to see her. Now.

With the journal still in my hand, I rip out the letter and shove it in my back pocket. Then, I run out the front door and straight into my car. My drive takes me all of five minutes before I'm parked in Rowan's driveway and rushing to her window.

For a split second, I stop and wonder whether I should park down the road in case her parents come home, but the thought quickly vanishes. All that matters right now is Rowan and I couldn't give less of a fuck about her parents.

When I reach her window, it's locked and her curtains are drawn, so I can't see if she's in there. But I know she is. She hasn't been to school for a week, plus when Rowan's not inside, her curtains are always open. I asked her about it once and she told me the sunlight that comes in makes her room warm, so that when she comes home it's all cozy.

I walk back to the front of the house and decide to try my luck with the front door. Low and behold, it's unlocked, so I push my way through and head straight for Rowan's room.

When I burst through the bedroom door, Rowan's body shoots up in her bed and she looks terrified. My chest rises and falls as the panic slowly subsides with one look at her. *My angel.*

But then, her face falls and her eyes are pricked with tears as she goes back down to hide under her sheets.

"Get the fuck out, Asher. I never want to see you again," she spits out, but it's muffled from the duvet that's pulled above her head. I shake my head, even though she can't see it, and I crouch beside her bed.

"I can't do that, angel—"

"*Don't* call me that." She yells as she quickly sits back up in her bed. The pain in her voice only hurts me even more because *I* caused it. My heart twists and it feels like a fist is wringing it dry.

"Rowan, I'm sor—"

Tears start falling down her face rapidly as she interrupts me again. "I don't get you! You tell me you love me and then you push me away. You tell me the sweetest things that you love about me and then you say the meanest shit at school!" She yells and I close my eyes, the impact of her words feeling like physical blows to the chest. "Why?"

"Because—because…" I start, searching for the right words, but there are none. "Because I thought I was ruining your life. Like your mom said."

Rowan scoffs and angrily wipes away the tears on her cheeks, even though fresh ones quickly replace them. "I told you, Asher! How many fucking times do you need to hear it? I love you! You're not ruining my life! You think I'm stupid enough to let that happen? Don't flatter yourself, you don't have that kind of power over me." She huffs, leaning back against her pillows and turning away from me.

"Then what are you doing now? You haven't been to school in a week," the words spill out, and I instantly regret them.

"My heart is *broken*, Asher. I'm in love with you and you shattered my fucking heart into a million pieces." That hits me right in the stomach and I feel like my entire body was crushed underneath a bulldozer. Before I can stop them, tears are falling down my face, but I don't stop them. I need her to see how much this hurts—how much I *love* her.

Taking a deep breath, I sit on the edge of Rowan's bed and I cup her face, turning her to see me. "I'm fucking stupid, okay? I'm fucked up and I do fucked up shit." I wipe her fresh tears with my thumb. "I'm *so* sorry. I should have never said those things to you."

"No, you shouldn't have." She responds, pulling my hands away from her face. "You're not fucked up, Asher, and you need to start believing that. Until you do, you won't be able to see the good things you have. You'll only push them away."

"I know. And I hate myself for pushing you away. But, I'm

trying. I'm trying so hard to see that I'm not fucked up. I'm doing it for you. I promise, I'll try harder. Please," I plead. "I will get on my fucking knees and grovel to you until the end of the world if that's what it will take for you to see that I love you and I'm sorry."

Rowan's face twists into an unrecognizable expression and my heart twists with it. "Don't you get it, Asher? Your words don't hold any weight anymore! You keep saying things like this and I never know if you actually mean them. You say one thing and then your actions show me something completely different." She pauses and her eyebrows furrow. "I don't trust you anymore," she whispers. Those words hit me right in my chest and I nearly fall over from the impact of them.

"Please don't say that." I beg, my voice strained and a sob crawling up my throat. "I know what I did was stupid and it hurt you more than you ever deserve. But, I'm here to fight for you. I will never stop fighting for you, Rowan. And I'll do whatever it takes to earn your trust back."

I completely understand how she feels, but I owe it to her and to myself to keep trying. To keep fighting for her, for both of us, even when she's given up.

Rowan closes her eyes and exhales a deep breath. When she opens her beautiful eyes again, the coldness I saw for the first time last week returns. "That's the thing, Asher. It's too late. What I needed was for you to not leave me, for you to not humiliate me again at school. But you did both of those things anyways. So, I don't know what it will take—I don't know if there's anything you *can* do."

Another tear falls down my cheek and I swear I actually heard something crack inside me. "Please," I croak.

"How do I know you won't break my heart again?" She asks, shaking her head. That question echoes in my head and a light bulb goes off.

Reaching into my back pocket, I pull out my letter to Bentley. "Here's how." I put it in Rowan's hands and confusion washes over her face. She opens the letter, but her eyes stay on me. She's questioning whether I'm being sincere, so I give her a small nod and she starts to read.

I watch the tears fall down her face as she reads it, and I pray they're happy tears. Or, at least, tears of relief.

When I think she's read the last line, I open my mouth. "I wrote that letter after the first day of school, sophomore year. When I saw you for the first time," I tell her and I know she's listening, even though she continues to stare at the paper. "You may deserve better than me, but that's for you to decide. I can't decide that for you. All I can do is be here and show you how much I love you."

"Asher—" She starts, but I cut her off. I need to get this out before she shuts me down again.

"Rowan, I've loved you since I was sixteen. I love you more now than I did when I first told you that I love you more than Barack Obama loves Michelle. My love for you has only grown ten-fold when I told you I love you more than kids love ice cream. And I mean it even more than I did when I said I love you more than life."

Rowan finally lifts her head and watches me, tears in her eyes. She's searching my face for any dishonesty or lies. She won't find any, though. Because these words are the truest words ever spoken by anyone on this earth.

She takes a deep breath and suddenly the tension and

conflict leave her eyes. "I love you, too." Tears fall from her eyes and her voice hardens as she says *too*. "But please don't ever leave me again. I don't think I can handle it," she sighs.

The second those words leave her mouth, I scoop her up and place her in my lap, so I can look in her eyes while she's in my arms. "I swear to you, Rowan. I will never leave you again. You're stuck with me, angel."

Her bottom lip pouts slightly and I can see the hurt in her eyes slowly fade away. "Promise?"

"Yeah, baby, I promise."

"Okay." She nods her head slightly and I don't waste another second before my lips are on hers, breathing her in and letting her heal the pain in my mind.

The longer my lips are on hers and my arms are wrapped around her body, the more I feel my heart and soul slowly find their way back into my body. This one kiss from Rowan has the ability to heal every broken part of me, and it does exactly that.

I was wrong when I said there was nothing special about Rowan Lila Easton. I could think of a million things that are special about Rowan; I could spend the rest of my life going through them. But the most important one is that she loves me, completely, hopelessly, and irrevocably. And I love her just as much—if not more.

Rowan truly is an angel on earth. My angel. And *that's* what makes her the most special person in the entire world.

EPILOGUE
Asher

Six Months Later

The bright blue sky dims into a dark gray as I drive within the Athens county lines. Pathetic fallacy at its finest.

I've been thinking about this trip for six months. Since the moment Rowan took me back. I knew I wanted her to come—to see where I grew up. I wanted to share this part of me with her. And I really wanted her—no, *needed* her—to come with me to Bentley's grave.

When I brought up the idea a month ago, Rowan immediately went into planning mode. She was so excited, I thought she would burst. She wanted to go right away, but we still had a month left of school. So, instead, she booked the hotel for the week between the last day of class and graduation.

Rowan thought it was the perfect way to close this chapter

of our lives and start a new one together. I do, too.

We've been driving since five o'clock this morning and I can feel the exhaustion hitting me. But, as I drive closer and closer to the cemetery, adrenaline starts moving through my body and the exhaustion is dwindling away.

Rowan suggested we stop at the hotel first, but I can't be in this town again and not immediately go see my brother. I have to talk to him before I can even think of doing anything else. Thankfully, Rowan understands.

Although, it looks like it's about to rain and I'm not sure Rowan will want to sit outside in a cemetery while it's pouring. I just hope the sky can hold on for an hour. That's all I need. For now.

The last ten minutes of the drive go by in a flash compared to the previous eleven and a half that it took to get here. As I pull into the parking lot, a small pit grows in my stomach and I can feel the nerves making an appearance. Bentley's not alive, so it's not like he can disapprove of Rowan. But visiting my brother's grave just feels so intimate and personal.

Just as I begin to regret this whole trip, Rowan silently takes my hand and rubs her thumb across the back of my hand. She doesn't even have to say anything to bring me comfort and wash away all my doubts. Fuck, I love her so much.

I take a deep breath and let my stomach settle. This is going to be good, everything will be okay. I turn and give Rowan a smile, then we get out of the car.

She doesn't say a word as I lead her to Bentley's grave, across all the rows of gravestones. Some have flowers—a mix of dried up and fresh—others are bare. There are a few that have other items, like toys and necklaces.

Bentley's grave is at the very back and, as we approach it, I see it's bare—exactly as I left it nearly eight months ago. Guilt pangs my chest that I don't visit more often, and that I never bring anything when I do. Especially since no one else visits him.

I mean, who would? My father's in prison for killing him; my mother's an alcoholic who drowns her sorrows in alcohol; and, we didn't have any other family that we knew of or spoke to. It was me and Bent against the world; now it's just me. And Rowan. I have her now.

When we reach Bentley's grave, I take a deep breath and sit on the grass in front of it. Rowan takes my lead and sits beside me, leaning into my side. Normally, I like to be alone, especially for these type of personal things. But having Rowan here, right by my side, is everything I never knew I needed.

I open my mouth and search my brain for the words, but nothing comes up. Taking a moment, I think about what I want to say to him. What I should say. What I *need* to say.

"Hey Bent. I know it's been a while. I'm sorry for that," I pause. Wherever he is, I hope he hears this and I hope he sees me right now. If there was ever a time I needed Bent to see and hear me, this would be it. "This is Rowan, I told you about her a few times. She's the mystery girl from my letter two years ago. She's also the one I told you about last time I was here."

Out of the corner of my eye, I see some leaves rustle and blow around on the ground. But there's no wind coming from any direction. My stomach lurches slightly as I consider the idea that Bentley may actually be here, listening to me. Rowan lightly squeezes my hand, letting me know she's here, and I take the leaves as a sign to continue.

"I'm sure you know I was in a bad place after you died. Truthfully, I've been in a bad place every day since then." My voice cracks, but I push through because I need to get this out. "Until a few months ago. Rowan helped me get out of that bad place and find my way back. She has brought me so much happiness and she showed me what it's like to enjoy life again. To actually live, instead of just survive. You and her were the only people who never gave up on me."

I inhale a shaky breath and I turn to Rowan, wanting to say these next words to her face. "Rowan is the best thing that's ever happened to me. And I'm so in love with her, I never thought I could feel this way." A tear slides down Rowan's cheek and I wipe it away with my thumb, a small smile on my face. "Anyways. Bent, I want you to meet her because she's the reason I was able to get to this place in my life: happiness."

Turning back to my brother's gravestone, I rub my hand across the top. It's the closest I'll ever get to touching him now and, for the first time in my life, that thought doesn't cause my heart to stop beating for a moment. It still hurts to think about it—I don't think it will ever *not* hurt—but now, I know I'll be okay without him.

Rowan leans forward and places a gentle kiss on my cheek, cupping the other side of my face with her hand. The gesture is so soft and pure, it makes my stomach erupt in butterflies.

"Do you mind if I talk to Bentley alone?" She whispers in my ear and I close my eyes, letting that sink in. The love of my life talking to my brother. I've dreamed of this for as long as I've known Rowan.

I nod my head and stand up. There's a spot behind a tree

that seems far enough that I wouldn't be able to hear Rowan, but I know that I'll be able to catch most of her conversation. I know she asked for privacy, but part of me needs to hear what she's going to say.

Sitting down on the ground out of Rowan's sight-line, I rest my back up against the tree and lean my head against it. Rowan starts talking and I can hear every word, so I close my eyes and take it in.

"Hi Bentley. It's Rowan now," she pauses and I assume she's collecting her thoughts. "I wish I could've met you. Asher doesn't talk about you much, I think it hurts him to think about how your life ended. He blames himself, and I know you and I both know he shouldn't. But he does."

Two heavy tears slip out of my closed eyes and I just let them fall. I'm pretty sure Rowan knows I'm listening, but I decide to stay here and take in her words in solitude.

"Anyways, I'm glad I'm here now. I'm not sure what Asher's told you about me, but he and I aren't all that different. I had a sister and she passed away, too. Not in the same way you did—she died of cancer when she was six. So, even though Asher insists I'm the one who helped him, he helped me a lot, too. I don't think I would be where I am today if I didn't have him by my side, helping me through the hardest times and toughest battles.

"Asher has helped me overcome more than he'll ever know. And you're partly the reason for that. He wouldn't be the man he is today if it weren't for you. I never got to meet you, but I feel like I know you in a way. From what Asher tells me, I see parts of you in him every day. So, thank you, Bentley. Thank you for being the amazing person you were, in your short fifteen years on earth. And thank you for watching over Asher every day since." Her last words slip off her tongue and I exhale a shaky breath. Rowan must've known, more than me, how much I needed to hear those words.

Rubbing my sweaty hands on my jeans, I stand up and walk back over to them. Rowan stands as I approach her and, the moment I reach her, I open up my arms, wrapping them around her waist, and I kiss her. The kiss is tender and sweet. Thankful and loving.

I don't say anything when we pull apart, I just take her face in my hands and look deeply in her eyes. She understands what I'm trying to say—without saying it—immediately. It's the most intimate moment we've ever had and it's perfect.

Rowan slips her hands in mine and we sit back down on the ground. She crosses her legs and leans into my side as I wrap my arm around her shoulders. We sit there, cuddled up together, as I start to catch Bent up on the last few months of my life and Rowan listens.

The rain never comes, so we stay there, at Bent's gravestone, for an hour. Slowly, the clouds start to clear and the sun peaks through, shining down directly on Rowan and I on the ground. At one point, the sunshine hits Bentley's gravestone in a way that lights up the gray rock, reminding me of Bentley—always happy, always cheery, a ray of sunshine among the darkness. The word 'brother' on his gravestone shines especially bright under the direct sunlight and it brings me comfort, as if he's up in the clouds shining down and showing me that he's here and he's listening. And that he loves me, his brother.

Between the sunlight now and the leaf from earlier, I know

Bentley heard everything, wherever he is. I just hope he's happy.

After a while of talking, my sentences run off and I'm not sure what else to say. It's not easy to have a conversation with a gravestone, but the quiet is comfortable. Rowan doesn't interject and, eventually, we just sit there together, quietly letting the moment go on.

The silence doesn't overwhelm us or make things awkward because both Rowan and I are just taking everything in. We're both just processing everything and thinking about the past six months.

Every morning I wake up, it amazes me how I got to this point. How I fell in love with this amazing girl and how she was able to love me, all of me.

After Rowan found out about my family, I thought she would give up on me; most people would. But, instead of running away, she threatened everyone at school that she would lock them up in the school and burn it to the fucking ground if they ever joked about it again.

That was the moment I fell in love with her completely. Because I saw how much she loved me, and because I knew I would do the same for her. In a heartbeat.

I would burn the whole world down to ashes if it ever wronged her again. She's been through hell and back and I'll be damned if I let the world take another stab at her.

You and me against the world, angel. And we'll burn it to ashes.

THE END

ACKNOWLEDGMENTS

First and foremost, I have to thank my parents. For always supporting my writing and encouraging me to pursue it. Also, for allowing me the space and opportunity to spend the summer writing this book and turning it from a dream to a reality. And mostly, for not giving me any inspiration to write Asher and Rowan's parents and forcing me to rely completely on my imagination.

I also want to thank my brother. We may fight and get mad at each other, but at the end of the day, I'll always be in your corner. When I was writing Rowan and Rory's relationship, and Bentley and Asher's, it was easy to write such a strong sibling bond and love because you're my best friend (even if you deny it) and the third person I ever loved (after our parents). Love you, kid.

Thank you to all my friends and family who asked to read this book when I told them I was writing it (you know who you are) because your support and interest made me feel proud of my book. I've always been very shy and embarrassed about my writing, but you all have helped me gain confidence with it.

And a huge thank you to every person who buys this book and reads it. You all have no idea how happy it makes me for people to actually read something I wrote and published. It fills me with so much fulfillment and it encourages me to keep writing. So thank you, always.

Finally, I have to thank myself. For persevering every time I got in my head and convinced myself that this book is terrible and that I should stop writing it. There were so many times where I questioned whether it was even good, if I should scrap the whole thing and start again, and if I should even publish it. But I pushed through and I'm so proud of myself for it. Even if some people don't like it, I can confidently say I love this book and I'm thankful to myself for getting to this point.

ABOUT THE AUTHOR

J.J. Rhodes is a lifelong writer and this is her first fully realized book. She was born and raised in Toronto, Canada, where her passion for writing stories developed at a young age. She hopes to write and publish more books in the future.

Made in the USA
Middletown, DE
27 December 2022

20555332R00187